Rocky love

Kay,
I hope you enjoy this Rocky romance! Thanks for reading.
♡Duaney
wynn

Rocky Love

Copyright © 2021 by Delaney Lynn, Lady Bookers Press

This is a work of fiction. Names, characters, businesses, places, events, locales, and incidents are either the products of the author's imagination or used in a fictitious manner. Any resemblance to actual persons, living or dead, or actual events is purely coincidental.

All rights reserved. No part of this publication may be reproduced, distributed, or transmitted in any form or by any means, including photocopying, recording, or other electronic or mechanical methods, without the prior written permission of the publisher, except in the case of brief quotations embodied in critical reviews and certain other noncommercial uses permitted by copyright law. Please do not participate in or encourage piracy of copyrighted materials in violation of the author's rights.

Ordering Information:
Quantity sales. Special discounts are available on quantity purchases by corporations, associations, and others. Orders by US trade bookstores and wholesalers. For details, contact the publisher.

Editing by The Pro Book Editor
Cover Design by Murphy Rae
Beta reading by Kirsten Iversen

1. Main category—Fiction/Romance/Contemporary
2. Other category—Fiction/Romance/General

ISBN: 978-1-7378753-1-4

First Edition

*For Bootsy, Tucker, Mama, Tiny, and Kaner.
The best furry friends I could ever ask for.*

Part one

Will love be enough to keep them afloat?

Chapter one

Past

I'm the new girl in school. The one you remember showing up in the middle of the year with no friends, doomed to be a loner, eating meals alone in the cafeteria, and spending Friday nights at home while the rest of the student body takes advantage of fake IDs and open houses. It's my senior year, and my dad's job brought us to the middle-of-nowhere, Indiana. I grew up on the beaches of Orange County, where the sun always shines and everyone knows how to surf. I can't remember the last guy I dated who wasn't a surfer. I spent most of my free time at the beach with my friends, suntanning in our bikinis while the boys showed off their skills inside the barrel of a wave. I guess I can thank them for my nice bronze skin in the dead of winter.

Winter. That's another conversation. White powder snow covers the ground here. The warmest coat I owned until a week ago was a cropped leather moto jacket. That's how I found out we were moving to Indiana. My dad walked into my room and surprised me with a coat so heavy and full of fur I was sure we were going to become Inuit. But I wouldn't be lucky enough to live among the indigenous circumpolar people in Alaska, Canada, or even Greenland. No. I get to live in Indiana!

My dad's job allowed us to live the expensive lifestyle California had to offer. He couldn't refuse the opportunity to take over a law firm that would nearly double his salary. But what good does all that money do in Portlet, Indiana? Sure, it has bought us a house five times the size of our old one back in California. But is a big house really worth it when I had to leave all my friends and my entire life behind?

No, it's not. Especially when it's my senior year. I guess you could say that I'm bitter. There's only one semester left in the school year. Six months until I'm a high school graduate and can move back to California for college. College was the only way my parents justified the move to me.

"But, Harlow, it doesn't need to be permanent for you. You'll be able to attend whatever college you want with my new income," my dad had said when I threw a temper tantrum the second the word *Indiana* left his mouth.

I'm a daddy's girl. Because I'm an only child, my dad has spoiled me rotten. My mom is a stay-at-home mom who does anything but stay home. She frequents the shopping malls, but only the ones with valet parking. How dare anyone make her walk all the way to her car in a parking lot when she is holding heavy shopping bags full of the newest Versace trends and red-bottomed stilettos? When my dad said that his salary would double, her eyes nearly fell out of their sockets. My mom was all for the move, but for all the wrong reasons.

My dad keeps me grounded. I don't have the expensive tastes my mom has. I don't care to follow trends or be that basic bitch who orders Starbucks for an Instagram picture. I may be a bitch, but I set my own trends and avoid Starbucks at all costs. I would describe my style as rocker chic. Most of the clothes that I own are black. Black makes you stand out in a world of pastels and patterns. Everyone in California dresses the same. There are no unique styles—everyone and their mom wears floral printed skirts and flowy crop tops that hardly cover the skin beneath their breasts.

"Harlow Brooks," the teacher calls out in first period.

I raise my hand, acknowledging my presence.

"Class, we have a new student joining us for the rest of the school year. Harlow, can you come join me in the front of the classroom for a moment?"

I roll my eyes. The classic first day of school introductions. I've been watching the new kids do this since first grade, though I've never moved and have never been the new girl, until now. My friends used to joke at the inelegance of the situation. Who wants to introduce themselves in front of a group of people they've never met? It's always made me uncomfortable. I hate awkward situations, and here I am being put into one. I already hate Indiana.

I walk to the front of the classroom. It's cold outside today, so I chose to wear my classic black jeans with rips in both knees and black booties. It's my go-to Harlow look. I didn't want people thinking I was gothic, not that I even care what these people think, but I chose an edgy mustard-yellow sweater with puffed sleeves for a pop of color.

I always line my lips with ruby red lipstick, my signature back in California. Girls always knew which man I had my eyes on because there would be remnants of my lipstick on their lips. Guys swoon over my lips. They're full and plump. My mom doesn't go a day without complaining about her need for filler. How had I gotten the perfect lips when I came out of her? Jealousy doesn't look pretty on Erica Brooks.

Every eye in the classroom is on me. I see girls gossiping in the back corner. I'm used to that. It wouldn't be high school without some cattiness. Pretty girls love to hate pretty girls. My dirty blonde hair falls just below my chest. Born with my mom's white-blonde hair, I made it a point to add lowlights to give it some edge. It's another point of contention between my mother and me. I had no desire to look like every other girl in California with blonde hair. I work hard to keep my blonde dirty. No one in this classroom has hair like mine. I already like that I stand out.

"Why don't you tell us a little bit about yourself?" the teacher says.

I keep my gaze straight ahead until I speak. When I'm about to open my mouth, my eyes fall on the person sitting in the second-to-last row. His hair is dark. I love dark hair. It was so hard to find a boy in California with dark hair who was normal. Most of the guys I hung around had shaggy blond hair; they sported the typical beach boy surfer look. It got boring. I mostly settled for light brown hair as a last resort. But his hair is so dark it is almost black. He styles it differently than I've ever seen. It's long but doesn't fall over his eyes. It's practically in a perfect mess on top of his head. His eyes are as blue as the Pacific Ocean. The one thing I loved most about California, the ocean. I love it even more in his eyes. His lips curl in a slight grin.

When I realize I've been staring at him for far too long without speaking, I look back up to the class but not before we make eye contact. He's looking directly at me, almost through me. I know he caught me staring. I need to play it cool.

"Hi. I'm Harlow. I just moved from California to the wonderful state of Indiana," I say sarcastically.

The class laughs.

My eyes move to the boy in the back. His smile when he laughs is mesmerizing. His teeth look perfectly imperfect, and I love them.

I'm done with my introduction, so I take my seat. He's sitting directly behind me, and I can feel the heat of his gaze on my neck. He smells of fresh pine. I'm distracted for the entire rest of the class.

I quickly walk out of the classroom when the bell rings, having no desire to make friends in this state. I want no ties to Indiana, nothing that can hold me back. It's only six months. Six months and I can be free of this stupid state, with its stupid snow, and the stupid hot boy in my class.

I find my locker for the first time after first period, the piece of paper the school office gave me with the number and combo in hand. I twist the lock, entering the number sequence. When I attempt to open my locker, it doesn't budge. I try again, and it still won't open.

"Shit," I mumble.

"Need some help?" I hear from behind me.

When I turn, I'm immediately taken aback. It's him. Cute boy from first period is standing next to my locker, asking if I need help. Did he follow me here? Are the boys in Indiana that clingy?

"It's stuck," I say.

"Wrong locker."

"What? How would you know?" I look at the piece of paper in my hand and look back at the locker number. *Shit.*

"This is my locker," he says smugly.

Of course. His locker would be next to mine.

"Sorry," I say as I move over one locker.

I enter in the combination, and it opens without difficulty. As I'm shoving things into my locker, I can feel his eyes on me. I pretend not to notice, shut my locker, and walk away. I don't look back, even though I know he's watching me walk away. His presence does something to me, makes me nervous. And it doesn't help that he is the definition of hot in my book. It might be harder than I thought to make it through the school year without a fling. If I had to break my rules for anyone, it would be him.

I manage to make it through the rest of the day, only introducing myself in three other classes. Cute boy from first period isn't in any of them. I don't go to my locker again in an attempt to avoid him, deciding somewhere between lunch and sixth period that it will be best to not break my rules. I can make it the next six months without any sort of fling. The beautiful state of California is waiting for me. I'm sure whatever college I attend will have plenty of dark-haired boys to choose from. I don't need to drop my panties at the first one that makes my mouth water, especially if he's from Indiana.

When I get home and pull into the driveway of my new giant house, I sigh. There's at least a foot of snow on the ground. My mother didn't shovel, my dad's been at work all day, and they probably haven't hired any help yet. I open my car door and put my feet in the snow, feeling it seep over the top of my booties and down to my ankle. It's cold, really cold. I grab my backpack from the passenger seat and make my way to the front door.

Mom's sitting at the counter, online shopping. "There's no Chanel at this mall, Har! Can you believe that?"

"What a shame," I say sarcastically.

"The neighbors invited us over for dinner tonight."

"I think I'll stay home. I have a lot of homework already." I don't care to make nice with our neighbors. I want to get this school year over with and get back to the beach.

"Harlow, it's not until seven. Get started on it now. Your dad will want us to go as a family."

I roll my eyes. "Fine."

I spend the next several hours finishing assignments before it's time to get ready for dinner with our new neighbors. My mom makes me change for dinner, so I wear a short black dress that accentuates my curves and displays my long legs. It's one of the few expensive pieces my mom has bought me that I wear. I appreciated her finally buying me something in black. She often buys bright colored dresses to make me look more girly. I keep those in the back of my closet.

My dad gets home from work shortly before it's time to leave. "How was your first day of school, sweetheart?" he asks me as he kisses my forehead.

I shrug. "It was okay. People are already talking about me."

He laughs. "Never fails."

We step outside to walk toward the house next door. I silently praise whoever shoveled our driveway and sidewalk. Our next-door neighbor's home slightly resembles ours but is noticeably smaller. It would be unlike my parents to not have chosen the biggest house on the block.

My dad knocks on the front door, and a petite older woman greets us wearing an apron. She must be their housekeeper.

"Come in," she says. "They are waiting for you in the dining area."

We step into the foyer. The house is exquisite, decorated with beautiful modern furniture and with floor-to-ceiling windows throughout. We're led into the dining room, and the homeowners meet us. My parents introduce themselves before they step aside to introduce their only child. I step forward.

"This is Harlow," my dad says. "Harlow, this is Mr. and Mrs. Walton."

"It's very nice to meet you both," I say as I take their hands one by one to shake them.

"Jeff, your daughter is lovely," Mr. Walton says.

I smile politely, learning quickly that Mr. and Mrs. Walton go by David and Monica. As we are about to take our seats, I hear footsteps coming down the stairs toward us.

Monica's face lights up. "Aiden, our guests are here," she says.

I turn my head in the direction of the newcomer. My mouth falls open. I can't hide my shock.

"Sorry I'm late. I was just finishing up one of my assignments," Aiden says as he kisses his mom on the cheek. He turns to face my father. "Hello, sir, I'm Aiden."

My dad takes his hand and shakes it firmly. "It's nice to meet you, Aiden. I'm Jeff. This is my wife, Erica." Then he turns to face me. "And this is our daughter, Harlow."

Aiden smiles. "Harlow."

"Hello," I say as I take my seat.

Aiden walks around the table to the only empty seat, one directly across from me. His eyes don't leave mine.

"Aiden is a senior at Liberty," Monica says.

"Harlow just began her last semester there today," my mother responds.

My dad turns to look at me. "Did you have any classes together?" he asks.

I shake my head. "I don't think so. But I wasn't paying much attention," I lie.

David turns his attention toward Aiden. "Son, you should introduce Harlow to your friends. Make her feel welcome."

Aiden smiles. "I intend to."

I can't take my eyes off Aiden. He intrigues me. The boys back home acted nervous around me, but not him. He's almost arrogant, maybe even a little cocky, and that makes me uneasy. He's so different. I want to know more, but I've already told myself no dating in Indiana. Nothing serious. I have no desire to meet his friends or spend any more time with him than I have to. His locker is next to mine, we have first period together, and apparently, he's my next-door neighbor, so I have a feeling we will run into one another quite often over the next six months.

I take my gaze off him and bring it to my plate, which had been served a decadent lamb chop with roasted potatoes and asparagus. Rich people food. I'm used to this by now, but I would be lying if I said I wasn't more of a 'burger and fries' kind of girl.

I make it through dinner without glancing at Aiden again, then to the front door where my parents say goodbye.

"Dinner was marvelous," my mom coos. "You must join us for dinner at our home once we are settled."

Aiden's parents smile and agree.

Aiden walks over to me and places his hand on my shoulder.

My eyes are instantly brought back to his as a result of his unexpected touch.

"I'll be seeing you around, Harlow," he says.

"I suppose you will, Aiden."

Chapter Two

Past

The next day at school, I can't avoid my locker quite as much. Whoever thought senior year would be easy was so very wrong. It's the second day of the semester, and I've already been assigned two papers and a capstone project. Aiden sits behind me again in first period. We don't talk in class, which comes as a relief to me, but I can still feel his presence behind me.

As I walk toward our lockers after the bell has rung, I notice him standing there waiting for me.

"So, we're neighbors at school and at home," he says.

He has one shoulder leaning against his locker. He's watching me as I open mine so I can shove my books inside. After I've grabbed the books I need next, I slam my locker shut.

"Apparently," I say before I begin walking to my next class.

Aiden quickly follows. "You're a bit of a black sheep, huh?" he says.

I stop abruptly and turn to face him. "What is that supposed to mean?"

"You don't fit in," he says matter-of-factly.

"I don't want to fit in." I turn and walk again down the hall. Aiden is still following me.

"Did you fit in in California?" he asks.

"No, I made it a point not to."

"Did you have friends?"

I reach the classroom but stop outside the door. "You're nosy," I say.

"You're intriguing."

I roll my eyes. "Yes, I had friends. *Have* friends," I correct myself.

"Want to make new friends?"

"No." I move to walk into the class but am pulled in the opposite direction when he grabs my arm. I turn around, bewildered. "What are you doing, Aiden?"

"We have another minute before the bell rings."

"So?"

"I'm having a party Friday night."

"Good for you."

"You should come."

"I'm not interested."

"Harlow."

The way my name rolls off his tongue is riveting. It causes me to lose my breath for a moment. I'm snapped back to reality when the bell finally rings.

"Please come!" he yells as he runs off in the opposite direction.

I stand motionless outside of my classroom. What the hell just happened?

I pass Aiden in the hall a few times during the day but avoid eye contact at all costs. I walk to my car with my mounds of books after the last bell, ready to finally get home. I'm caught off guard when someone yells my name from across the parking lot. When I turn to see who it is, I immediately tense. It's Aiden. He's running in my direction and slows as he reaches me.

"Which one is yours?" he asks.

I point to the white Range Rover ahead.

"Nice. Mind if I catch a ride home with you?"

"You don't have a car?"

"I have a car."

"Then why do you need a ride home?"

"It's not here."

"Fine."

We get into the car without saying another word. I don't bother to ask how he got to school in the first place. The drive home is about twenty minutes, give or take a few if I get stopped at the light in the one major intersection near the Portlet Mall. The first five minutes are spent in silence, then Aiden turns on the radio and clicks Bluetooth, where my phone is automatically connected.

"What do you think you're doing?" I ask.

He smiles, grabbing my phone out of the cup holder. "It's too quiet. Let's see what kind of music you listen to."

"Aiden!" I yell. I reach to grab my phone, but he pulls it away.

"Hands on the wheel, Harlow."

"Give me my phone back!"

"I want to know what kind of music you listen to. What's your password?" he asks.

"I am not giving a stranger my password."

"We're hardly strangers, Harlow."

I roll my eyes and start muttering my password, not quite sure why I'm giving into him so quickly. "3-8-2-5."

He lets out a deep-bellied laugh. He has a nice laugh, and I instantly realize that I like listening to it.

"What?" I ask.

"You spelled out 'fuck' with numbers? *That's* your password?"

I glare at him before setting my eyes back on the road. Honestly, I'm surprised he figured it out that quickly.

I can see him smiling to himself as he's scrolling through my music. A song plays through the speakers. I instantly recognize it because it's one of my favorites. *Ophelia.*

"Good choice," I say.

"I'm surprised you're into the Lumineers."

"Why are you surprised?"

"Most girls our age only listen to Justin Bieber or Harry Styles. But with the way you dress, I wouldn't have been surprised if you were into heavy metal."

I give him a dirty look. I don't want to be categorized with girls who listen to that teeny-bopper music, but heavy metal also isn't my style.

"You've got good taste in music, Black Sheep."

"Doesn't that make me a normal sheep, then?" I ask.

"Nope."

I turn onto our block, and Aiden quiets the music. "We should carpool to school," he says.

"Why?"

"Because we're neighbors. And we go to the same school. And we drive the same route. And we come home the same—"

"Okay, okay," I cut him off. "I get it."

"Good. I'll drive tomorrow. Be ready at 7:30," he says as I pull into his driveway, and he steps out of the car. "See you in the morning, Black Sheep." He shuts the door.

I stay parked in his driveway for longer than I should. I lean my head back and sigh. Aiden is not making it easy to avoid him.

We decide to switch off driving to and from school each day that week. Aiden drives a silver Porsche with less room in it than my Range Rover. I am surprised when he pulls into my driveway the next morning sitting behind the wheel of a sports car.

"Are you compensating for something with this car?" I ask as I get in.

He grins. "Excuse me?"

I don't answer. We have a contemptuous relationship at best.

I find out several things about Aiden during our short car rides to and from school. He absolutely hates the color red because it reminds him of blood and the time he broke his arm in the third grade. I notice the lightly scattered freckles under his left eye. You'd never notice them unless you were looking, which I catch myself doing too often. He has this way about him that makes me want to be around him more, as though twenty minutes in a car isn't nearly enough time. I find myself looking for him in the hallways, trying to talk to him during class, anything to squeeze in a few extra moments with him daily. My favorite thing about him is the way he smirks when he tells a joke, then immediately searches my eyes for approval. I can't help but smile around him, though I still try to hide it. But there are always moments when he catches me laughing at his joke or grinning at something he says, and that's when I see his face light up. It's contagious, seeing him happy. It makes me want to be the reason he smiles.

When he drops me off at home that Friday, he reminds me of the party. "I'd better see you tonight, Harlow."

"Why do you care if I go to your party?" I ask.

He shakes his head in dismay. "Just come have a good time," he says. "There are some people I want you to meet."

"I already told you I don't want to make friends."

"They don't have to be friends. Think of them as acquaintances. Acquaintances who are fun to underage drink with."

Much to my dismay, I go to Aiden's party. And I get drunk. But not because the people there are fun to underage drink with. Nope. I get drunk because of a pretty little thing named Amanda.

When I walk into Aiden's house, there are people everywhere. I see someone doing a keg stand in the kitchen, beer pong set up on the dining room table where we ate dinner the other night, and topless girls in the indoor pool. Apparently, Indiana knows how to party.

"You made it!" I hear Aiden say. He's walking down the stairs with a beer in each hand. "Let me get you something to drink. Let me guess, you hate beer and want a vodka soda."

I shake my head. "I hate vodka. I'll take a beer."

He looks surprised. "My kind of girl," he says as he hands me one of the two beers in his hands. "Come on, I want you to meet my friends."

He takes me to the back of the house, toward the naked girls and the giant indoor swimming pool. There's a group of people sitting in lounge chairs, and I am instantly drawn to a petite brunette who eyes me like I'm Eve tempting Adam to eat the poisonous fruit. That must make her Satan.

"Harlow, these are my friends." He points to them one by one. "Max, Jess, Nick, Matt, and…" His voice trails off.

Satan gets up and stands next to Aiden.

He hesitantly puts his arm around her. "This is…uh, my girlfriend, Amanda."

Girlfriend? What the fuck? He never brought up having a girlfriend. Why would he not tell me he has a girlfriend? We've been alone enough this week that I feel that this is something I should know by now, something you would think should come up in conversation. Does she know that we carpool? Does she know that I live right next door?

Then I internally scold myself. Why do I even care? I said no relationships, and that includes Aiden. This is a good thing.

Amanda holds him tightly. "Harlow?" she says, her nose scrunched. "What kind of name is that?"

I roll my eyes and walk to the bar, fighting the urge to say something bitchy back.

Aiden follows. "Sorry, she's kind of a bitch."

"You don't say," I snap back. "I told you, I wasn't interested in making friends."

He nods in understanding. "You're not leaving, are you?"

"Why, Aiden? Why does it matter? And when were you going to tell me you have a girlfriend?" My tone is harsh, but I can't help it. His having a girlfriend is a good thing, but I'm still pissed about it for some reason.

He looks at me sheepishly, but then he shrugs it off like it's nothing, and his normal smug presence takes over. He looks cocky, like he did the first day we met. "I'm telling you now."

I nod, turning to face the guy who designated himself as the bartender. "I'll have two shots of vodka."

"I thought you hated vodka," Aiden says from behind me.

"I do." I turn back to face him. "I also hate that you have a girlfriend, but sometimes you just have to deal with the shitty things in life." And I can't believe I just admitted that.

I down the shots back-to-back and ask for two more. Aiden stands watching, baffled. I can see Amanda sitting across the pool eyeing us. I've never seen her at school and never even heard of her. Then again, I haven't seen any of Aiden's friends at school. Not that

I pay attention. Aiden is pretty much the only human I notice in the halls. Luckily, my plan to have no friends and no boyfriend just got a whole lot easier. This last week carpooling with Aiden has been nice, but now that I know he has a girlfriend, I can go back to my miserable life in Indiana. I'm counting down the days until I'm free.

Chapter Three

Past

I refuse to pick up Aiden for school the following Monday. Why doesn't he carpool with his girlfriend? I'm sure she would love that. I also avoid him at school, just like I avoid everyone else.

He shows up at my house the next morning, but I act as if he isn't there. While his car sits in my driveway, I get into my Range Rover and drive away. He follows behind a few seconds later.

He tries talking to me every time we're both at our lockers. I pretend I don't hear him and walk away. I've successfully kept my distance from him for three weeks before my mom and dad invite him and his parents over for dinner. They've since hired a housekeeper. God forbid my mother has to cook while my dad's at work.

My Aiden avoidance streak: over.

They come by on a Friday night. Our housekeeper, Rosa, prepares crab cakes with risotto and peppers. We all sit in the living room while the adults enjoy a cocktail before dinner. Aiden and I sit in silence. He participates in some of the conversations, mostly when it's appropriate, but for the most part remains silent like me. I'm hoping this dinner will go by quickly. The last place I want to be is in the same room as Aiden Walton.

My dad insists on showing Aiden's parents our wine cellar in the basement. They let us know they'll return shortly, and before I know it, I'm stuck alone with the boy himself. I don't look his way. In fact, I make it a point to keep my gaze everywhere but in his direction. But he's not trying to avoid eye contact. He's intentionally staring directly at me. I can feel his eyes itching my body like poison ivy.

"I'm sorry I didn't tell you sooner," he says, breaking the quiet.

I play dumb. "Tell me what?"

He sighs. "You know what."

We sit in an uncomfortable silence for a few moments before he speaks again. "I didn't think it would matter that I had a girlfriend, Harlow."

"It shouldn't matter. I don't want it to matter," I surprise myself by saying. "But it does. It matters."

He stands and walks toward me, taking a seat on the couch beside me. "It doesn't have to."

I don't know what that means. Regardless, I'm not sure why I care so much. I don't want a boyfriend, even though I feel this unusual pull toward Aiden. I don't even want to be friends, to have friends. But for whatever reason, the fact that he has a girlfriend has been the hardest pill to swallow since finding out I was moving to Indiana.

Our parents return a few seconds later, interrupting us before I can speak. We gather in the dining room and eat a delicious meal. Rosa really is a great cook. Admittedly, she's a huge step up from our housekeeper in California who insisted on juice breakfasts and fake meat for dinner.

The Waltons walk out after thanking us for the hospitality. Aiden doesn't look my way again. He follows his parents out our front door without a single word. It annoys me how much I hate that.

Another week goes by, and I've come to accept the fact that Aiden has a girlfriend. Time continues to pass until I'm five months from graduation. Only five more months until I'm free from this torturous place. I don't use the word torturous lightly, because being in a room alone with Aiden is exactly that, torture. Despite my acceptance of his girlfriend, Aiden's mere existence is enough to make me feel weak. I can't get him out of my head. And as a result, I convince myself that there would be no harm in a little social media snooping. I find Aiden's Instagram profile right away and come to a few conclusions about his past relationships: I think he and Amanda have been dating for about a year. Before Amanda was Rachel, and before Rachel was Annabel. Apparently, I'm not the only girl who has fallen victim to Aiden's spell because even before Annabel, there's a slew of girls that he's taken pictures with in that *more than friends* kind of way.

I notice Aiden doesn't have a type. Every girl looks completely different, but they're all undoubtedly beautiful. It makes sense for a guy like Aiden to only date the most attractive girls, so this doesn't surprise me. What does come as a shock is how insistent he has become on trying to spend time with me. It feels like a small victory at first, especially after the cold shoulder he gave me at the end of dinner. But still, I made it clear I wasn't interested in meeting people and that I wanted nothing to do with him after finding out he had a girlfriend. It's a lie, something I'm still trying to convince myself is true. But still, the more I push him away, the more it doesn't seem to faze him. Aiden does what he wants. He still pulls into my driveway every other day. I continue to ignore his existence as I get into my car. He follows me to school. He tries to talk to me at our lockers. I ignore him and walk away. He's even resorted to passing me notes in first period. Despite my best efforts, I know if I read them, I'll give in. So I don't. They end up in the trash once the bell rings.

It's the weekend again, and my parents have left for a fundraising event. They used to attend them frequently in California, but they haven't been to one since moving. I didn't think they'd exist in such a small town. They've been gone about an hour when the doorbell rings.

I'm wearing a loose T-shirt with pajama shorts, cuddled on the couch alone and watching a movie. At first, I wonder who could possibly be ringing my doorbell. I have no friends and everyone who knows my parents in this town is probably at the fundraiser with them. But a sudden thrill takes over when I think about the possibility of it being Aiden.

I nearly run to the foyer, eager to see if I'm right. As I open the door, I'm pleased to see Aiden standing in front of me with his hands in his pockets. He looks smug when he asks if he can come in.

"No," I say as I try to shut the door, but his hand stops me, and he walks in anyway. In all honesty, I didn't fight very hard.

"What are you doing?" I ask. "I said you can't come in."

"Harlow."

Damn. My insides turn, and I feel an unwelcome fluttering in my core. Why does he say my name like that?

"What?"

"Do you have plans tonight?" he asks casually, as if we've been hanging out and speaking to each other the last few weeks.

"No."

He smiles. "Great. Let's hang out. Show me around." He walks through the foyer into the living room he's already familiar with.

"You've already seen my house."

"Not all of it. Show me your room."

I raise one eyebrow, and the expression on my face must show my concern because he laughs and shakes his head. "You're not as tough as you act, Black Sheep."

Both of my eyebrows quickly drop, and I scrunch my nose to show him my frustration. He walks up the stairs like he already knows where my bedroom is.

"Where are you going?" I ask.

"I want to see your room. I'm assuming the bedrooms are upstairs, yeah?"

"Yeah." I walk past him and lead him into my room. It's mostly empty. We've only lived here a little over a month, so I haven't unpacked much.

He walks in behind me and looks around. "This doesn't look like the bedroom of a girl who intends to stay in one place."

I sit on the bed. "I don't plan to stay."

He sits next to me. "Are you going back to California?"

"Yes. After graduation."

"Are you going to college there?"

"Yes."

It's silent for a few minutes before I decide to ask him something. "How about you? Where do you want to go for college?"

He glances around the room. "I never had any intentions of leaving Portlet. I grew up here. After high school, I could just start working for my dad's company and make a pretty good living right off the bat. No one has ever pushed for me to go to college. They don't see a point."

"Is that what you want to do? Work for your dad's company?"

He shakes his head. "No."

"What do you want to do, then?"

He looks at me and shrugs. "I think I might have to check out the West Coast."

I blush and turn away, but not before he notices. I stand and walk to the other side of the room. The emotions take over again, and I need to push them away, hide them, but it's so hard when he's right here next to me. There's no reason I should feel anything toward Aiden. I hardly know him. I'm convinced it's those damn blue eyes that remind me of home and that dark head of hair that makes me weak. Also, he doesn't take my shit. In fact, he mostly ignores it like I ignore him. He won't leave me alone. He's consistent in his fight to spend time with me, I'll give him that. This whole thing would be so much easier if he'd just leave me alone.

I stand and face him again, this time with my irritation evident. "What are you doing here, Aiden?"

"You've been avoiding me. Ignoring me."

"Yes, I have been."

"Why?" he asks, like he doesn't already know the answer.

I throw my arms up in annoyance and humor him. "You have a girlfriend!"

He stands and walks to me. "What does that matter, Harlow? Do you like me or something?"

"No," I lie.

He's standing so close I can smell the pine scent of his bodywash. He's taller than me, and I have to look up to see his eyes. From this angle, I can make out the delicate formation of his jawline. It looks tense right now, like he's clenching his teeth. Do I make him as nervous as he makes me? Or is he just as frustrated with me as I am with him?

"Then what's the problem?" he asks.

My heart beats rapidly inside my chest. He's so close to me I could kiss him. I see him moving his gaze from my eyes to my lips. I don't have any lipstick on right now, but that hasn't stopped him from staring.

"Where's your girlfriend?" I whisper.

"Don't know."

I take a step back. This can go very wrong, very quickly. I see him suck in a breath like he's been holding it all this time. Our distance allows him to breathe again. Hell, *I* can finally breathe again.

"So, you're the cheating type?" I ask pragmatically.

His eyebrows raise. "Excuse me? What the hell would make you say that?"

"You were going to kiss me."

He laughs. "I can assure you I was not going to kiss you."

"Can you just leave already?" I ask, annoyed.

"Harlow."

Jesus. There he goes again. The way he says my name, I can't handle it.

"What?" I ask, my voice weak.

"I would never cheat on my girlfriend. I have never cheated on any of my girlfriends. That's not me."

"Then what are you doing here, Aiden?"

He sighs. "I don't know. You interest me. You're different."

I roll my eyes. "Gee, thanks."

"I don't mean that in a negative way."

"Yes, you do. You call me Black Sheep, for crying out loud! A name to literally describe an odd member of a group. Talk about making a girl feel insecure."

"You don't strike me as the type to feel insecure."

I grin. "You're right. I'm not. I don't give a shit what people think about me."

He smiles. "I like that."

He walks back to my king-size bed and takes a seat, acting like there's nothing wrong with what he's doing, what he's making me feel. "Tell me about California. And your friends. I'm especially interested to hear about your friends."

Against my better judgment, I follow him to my bed and lie on my stomach, resting my hands under my chin. He lies on his side so that he is watching me.

"California is the most amazing place on this earth, and I've been a lot of places," I start, instantly feeling my mood lift as I talk about home. "The beaches give you a sense of freedom. The sand feels like warm silk lathering your feet. The blue of the ocean is ever-changing depending on the mood of the day." I look away from Aiden. "Your eyes remind me of the Pacific Ocean."

"How so?" I can't see him, but I can picture the smirk on his face.

"When you're acting like an arrogant ass, which is most of the time, they're a deep blue, like the deepest parts of the ocean. The biggest waves crash there. The strength of them can withstand almost anything. When you're lost in a moment, like you were a few minutes ago, they're more crystal blue." I blush, thinking about his eyes fixated on my lips. "They remind me of the shoreline. The waves are simpler there, not so strong, actually weak. It's the only fragile moment the ocean has. It's vulnerable to the shore and gets pulled and pushed with the current."

I use the silence to glance his way, noticing his eyes resemble the crystal blue I'd spoken of. He's focused on my lips again, but his gaze quickly finds its way back to my eyes. "Did you date in California?"

"Yes, plenty."

He looks intrigued. "Tell me more."

"Well, my last boyfriend was a surfer. His name is Collin."

"What happened to Collin?"

I shrug. "I grew tired of him. He was good at surfing, but I think that's about the only thing his brain could fully comprehend. After a while, it becomes mind-numbing trying to hold a conversation with someone who has no intelligence and the attention span of a four-year-old."

Aiden laughs, his deep bellowing laugh that warms my skin. "Harsh!"

"It's true."

"Were all the guys you dated unintelligent surfers?" he asks.

"Most of them, yes."

"Have you ever gotten your heart broken?"

I think for a moment. "No."

Aiden looks surprised.

"What?" I ask.

"Never?" he asks again.

"Never. Have you?"

"I guess so."

My eyebrows lift. "Really? Are you a hopeless romantic?"

"I don't know about that."

"You must be," I say. "You seem like the kind of guy that's always in a relationship." I leave out the part where I *know* he's the kind of guy that's always in a relationship, thanks to his Instagram.

"I suppose I am then," he says. "And you seem like the kind of girl who only dates guys she knows would never hurt her."

My face falls blank, and Aiden sits up. "Is that why you're avoiding me, Harlow? Are you afraid I'm going to hurt you?"

"How could you hurt me? I'm not even yours to hurt."

"But you could be."

That's enough. Aiden might not be a cheater, but something tells me if I tried to kiss him right now, he wouldn't stop me.

I jump off the bed and walk to my door. "My parents are going to be home soon."

Aiden slowly stands and nods in understanding, though I can tell by the way he moves that he doesn't want to leave. He walks out of my room and out of my house, the growing tension in his wake at an all-time high.

When I hear the front door shut, I fall to the ground. I protect myself. I protect my feelings. I don't let people in who can hurt me. Even with most of my friends back home, the relationships were all surface level. I've never let people in. How has he figured that out already? Aiden is the only person who has ever figured that out. He already knows me better than my own parents do.

Chapter four

Past

The next week at school is never-ending. The days slow down, the bell takes longer to ring, and Aiden isn't easy to ignore anymore, and neither is his girlfriend. I went from hardly noticing her to seeing them around every corner. When I stop at my locker between fifth and sixth period, they are standing there playing tonsil hockey. I gag to myself and slam my locker shut extra hard to make a point. I notice them walking in the hallways together hand in hand and her constantly laughing at something he says.

Have they always been this touchy-feely at school? Was I really that blind to it before? I can't get his words out of my head. What did he mean by, *I could be*? Was he really willing to end things with his girlfriend for me? I shake the thought out of my head and remember that I'm not interested in a relationship. Even if Aiden is unlike any guy I've ever met, he is off limits.

The days since he showed up at my house unannounced turn into weeks. David and Monica must go out of town a lot because Aiden throws a party almost every weekend. He doesn't personally ask me to come over again, not for a single one of his parties. It's not like I need an invitation, Aiden's parties are open to everyone at school. But still, I can't get myself to show up. Not because Aiden might not want me there, but rather, I don't *want* to be there. Can't be there. Can't see him and Amanda together any more than I have to.

It's been exactly twenty-nine days since I've spoken to Aiden, not that I'm counting. I'm pathetic.

It's Sunday morning. My mom spends Sundays at the spa most of the time, while my dad devotes his time to his at-home office. It's a typical day in the Brooks' household until it isn't anymore. The doorbell rings, and I stay in my room and think nothing of it, because why would I? I hear Rosa answer the door, followed by her hurried footsteps up the stairs, stopping at my bedroom door. She gently knocks.

"Harlow?" I hear her say.

"Yeah?"

Rosa opens the door slowly, poking her head inside. "Aiden Walton is here for you."

The sound of his name causes me to break out in a cold sweat. I nod to Rosa and follow her downstairs. I feel like I'm on autopilot, not really remembering ever getting off the bed or walking down the stairs, but the second I see him standing in the foyer, eyes pleading, I feel that unwanted fluttering in my core. He smirks when he sees me, though it takes every muscle in my face to keep my expression flat. I don't want him to know that I'm happy to see him, that I'm happy he's finally gone out of his way again to see me. I missed his incessant hounding.

"Hi," he says.

"Hi."

"Are you busy?" he asks.

"No," I say because I want to know why he's here.

"Come with me," he utters as he walks outside.

I don't hesitate. I fall into step with him toward his Porsche.

"Are we going somewhere?" I ask.

He nods.

"Where?"

"You'll see."

I don't know what's come over me, but I don't question him again. I've missed being around him, feeling his attention on me. I hate seeing him and Amanda in the hallways. I can't help but think that could have been him and me. Maybe it still can be. I try to imagine what it would be like to date Aiden, but then I remember that he has the power to break my heart. It's better that we only interact every few weeks. I'm convinced that taking him in small doses will be enough. I protect my heart, he stays with Amanda, and I still get to enjoy him sometimes. I should be keeping my mind set on finishing school and getting the hell out of Dodge anyway, but this internal battle in my head over Aiden seems never-ending.

He opens the passenger side door for me, and I get in. I watch as he walks around the front of his car before he sits in the driver's seat.

He turns on the radio a few minutes into our drive, but it's only quiet background noise. I can't make out the song that's playing.

"Where's Amanda?" I can't help but ask.

Aiden keeps his eyes on the road. "Let's not talk about her today."

I don't argue. She's not exactly my favorite topic of conversation. "Okay."

A few minutes pass before he brings us onto the freeway. I have no idea where he's taking me, but the thrill I feel at his impulsiveness is one of my new favorite things about him.

"You've been on my mind, girl. Like a drug," Aiden says out of nowhere.

Air escapes my lungs, and I can't seem to get it back. I try to stay calm. I know he's quoting the Lumineers song he played in my car, but why? Are those words true? Has he been thinking about me as much as I've been thinking about him?

"Heaven help a fool who falls in love," I mumble under my breath.

He grins from ear to ear.

We drive for several more minutes before Aiden slows, pulling into a parking space. Trees surround us, so my initial thought is that he's brought me to a random forest preserve, but for what reason, I have no idea.

When I step out of the car, I realize how chilly it is outside. I'm in a thin knit sweater, having forgotten to grab a coat on the way out.

It's the middle of March, and the weather still hasn't warmed up like I'd hoped. When does summer even start in the Midwest? I make a mental note to Google that tonight.

Aiden must have known a California girl like me wouldn't take well to the frigid air because he pops open his trunk and pulls out a fleece blanket, wrapping it around me. It warms me instantly, though I'm not sure if it's the blanket or the thoughtfulness behind his gesture.

"Thanks," I say.

Aiden smiles, nodding his head.

"Where are we?" I ask, glancing around the gravel parking lot surrounded by tall spruce trees.

He ignores my question. "Follow me."

I do just that, following him across the gravel parking lot and down a dirt path. The dirt soon turns to sand, and I instantly realize he's brought me to a beach. I didn't even know Indiana had beaches.

"Indiana has beaches?" I ask, unable to hide the excitement in my voice.

Aiden looks amused. "It's no Pacific Ocean, but it's Lake Michigan and nonetheless, a beach. Water, sand, and all."

I must look like a little kid in a candy shop. I'm beside myself that he would think to bring me here. It's probably the most considerate thing anyone has ever done for me. I turn to face Aiden, who's watching my euphoric response to seeing the lakeshore. My feet move in his direction, and before I can stop myself, I find my arms wrapped around his muscular frame.

"Thank you, Aiden," I whisper.

His lips brush against my forehead. "You're welcome."

He holds onto me tightly for a few seconds. When we separate, I'm disappointed to no longer be touching him. We walk closer to the water's edge, and I take my shoes off to feel the smooth yet grainy texture beneath my toes. The water inches toward us and covers my feet in one plunge. My mouth immediately drops open at the sharp sting of the ice-cold water.

"Shit."

Aiden laughs beside me. "It's still winter here, Harlow," he says, still laughing. "The water isn't going to warm up for a few more months."

"Shit," I mumble again, feeling like small, tiny needles are poking and breaking the skin of my feet.

I take a few steps back and sit on the cool sand, wrapping my feet in the fleece blanket while also trying to warm them with my hands. Aiden takes off his jacket and throws it over me, the blanket no longer covering my upper half with the way I wrapped my feet inside it like a burrito.

"Here," he says.

"Thanks."

He sits next to me, and we look out over the lake.

"It's beautiful," I whisper, finally feeling warm again.

"Is Indiana growing on you?"

I grin. "A bit."

We spend a few hours sitting in the sand. We don't talk about Amanda at all. In fact, we discuss just about anything else. It's hard to get the images of them in the hallways at school out of my head, but I try to remember that it's him who showed up at my house. It's him who brought me to the beach. He's thoughtful. He's kind. He cares to get to know me. He somewhat already does know me, and it's more than I can say for any other guy I've ever had a thing with. I try to keep my guard up around him. It's part of how I protect myself, but he's somehow already put a crack in it.

Though we talk for hours, it's still hard for me to ask questions that would allow me to build a deeper connection with him. I don't want to learn more about him because the more I know, the more I think I'll fall for him. I already know that's what is happening here. I'm falling for Aiden Walton. I'll be leaving this place in a few months, and it's already going to be hard enough to leave him. He's weaseled his way into my heart, no matter how hard I've tried to fight him off, no matter how hard I've tried to avoid it happening.

"Harlow," Aiden says, breaking into my thoughts.

I fall back in the sand. "I hate the way you say my name," I admit.

He lies back with me. "How am I supposed to say it?"

"Maybe just don't."

He laughs. "What would you like me to call you then?"

I think for a second. "Black Sheep was okay."

"I thought you said that made you feel insecure?"

"Come on, Aiden. You know that nothing could actually make me feel insecure. I'm like a rock."

"A rock?" he questions.

"Rocks are secure. They're rough around the edges, but the insides are made of grains and minerals that keep it solid. Whatever I'm made up of keeps me tough as shit."

Aiden laughs to himself. "I don't think you're as tough as you act."

I turn on my side. "Yes, I am."

He imitates my movements until we're facing one another. "You're going to miss me when you move back," he says confidently.

"What makes you think that?"

"I don't think, Black Sheep. I know."

I roll my eyes. "Are you ever not full of yourself?"

"What fun would that be?"

The sun sets. We sit and watch until it disappears behind the lake, the air turning more frigid as the heat from the sun fades. Once it's fully set, we walk back to Aiden's car, and he drives me home.

"Thank you for taking me to the beach," I say as we pull back into my driveway.

"We should go again. Soon."

I nod, wondering how soon he'd like to go, and open the door to get out. Aiden quickly opens his door and walks around to the passenger side to help me out. He walks me to my front door.

What a gentleman, I think to myself.

"So, can I drive you to school again tomorrow?" he asks.

"I don't think that's a good idea," I say, careful not to mention why it's not a good idea.

Amanda.

"Yes, it is," he says firmly. "I'll see you in the morning." He turns and walks back to his car, not giving me any explanation.

I stand on my front steps watching as he backs out of my driveway, drives next door, and pulls into his own driveway. I continue to stand in place as he gets out of the car.

"Do you like the view?" he yells.

I shake my head. "Goodnight!"

"Goodnight, Harlow!"

Chapter five

Past

He's back in my driveway at 7:30 a.m. I put more effort into my appearance today than I have the last few weeks. I don't know if that makes me pathetic or clever. When I finish putting on my high-rise distressed denim jeans with my favorite band tee, I line my lips with a tube of ruby red. My hair is in a messy ponytail, making me feel edgy, maybe even a little brave. Only badass chicks can rock a power pony. I walk to the car and see him smiling as I near him. He gets out of the car to open the door for me like the nobleman he is.

"Good morning, Harlow," he says.

"Morning."

After we're both in the car, he waits an instant before starting the engine.

"Does everyone in California dress like you?" he asks, eyeing my jeans and T-shirt before his gaze locks on my red lips.

"Nope."

He laughs, his eyes still fixated on my lips.

"Is there a problem with the way I dress?" I ask.

He shakes his head. "No, not at all. I just wanted to know if all the girls would look like you when I move there."

I raise one eyebrow. "When you *move* there?"

He doesn't say anything.

"I can't tell if you're flirting with me or insulting me," I say after he doesn't acknowledge the question.

He shrugs. "If I admit that I'm flirting, or what I'm thinking, then I'm afraid I'll scare you off. You're a hard egg to crack, Harlow."

"Try me," I challenge.

He smirks. "All right. I think you're insanely beautiful."

I scrunch my face. It's my natural reaction to a compliment like that. I know I'm aesthetically pleasing to the eye; I've been told time and time again. I've even been offered modeling contracts, though I've turned them all down, much to my mom's dismay. But no one has ever actually called me beautiful before. Beautiful describes the girls Aiden has dated in the past. The perfect cookie-cutter image of what a woman should be. Amanda is beautiful. Me? I don't think of myself as beautiful. I dress in mostly black or dark colors and always have bright red lips. My hair is chaotic half the time, and I have an attitude that could put my mother's to shame. How can someone like Aiden find me beautiful?

When I don't respond, he starts the car and drives in the direction of our high school.

"I have to ask," I say after the first few minutes of the drive are spent in silence. "Did you and Amanda break up?"

"It's complicated."

"What's complicated? It's a yes-or-no question."

"We aren't in a yes-or-no relationship."

"So, you're in a relationship still," I say, annoyance evident in my tone.

"It's complicated," he repeats.

"So I've heard."

And that's the end of our conversation. I'm reminded why I was against carpooling in the first place, why I try so hard to avoid Aiden. Why did he take me to the beach yesterday if it's still complicated between him and Amanda? Why has he been trying so damn hard to spend time with me when he already has a girlfriend he could be spending time with?

We arrive at the school ten minutes later. We walk in together, still not talking, and make our way toward our lockers. I can see Amanda waiting at Aiden's locker. She looks upset, worried even.

I don't say anything as we approach. I open my locker and mind my own business, but I can't help but overhear their conversation.

"I haven't heard from you since Saturday," Amanda says.

"I've been busy," Aiden replies.

"Too busy to answer a phone call? Or even send me a text?"

Aiden sighs. "I told you, Amanda, I need some time to think."

"What is there to think about? I don't understand why you're being like this. What did I do?"

"Nothing," Aiden says. "I just need time." After a few beats of silence, he clarifies. "Time apart."

"Aiden, please don't do this. Not right now."

She sounds like she's on the verge of tears, and I can't help but feel bad for her. This is probably my fault. I haven't pursued Aiden in any way, but it seems like he needs time to think about whether he wants to be with her or *me*. He didn't talk with her yesterday because he spent the entire day with me. *Shit*. Am I a home-wrecker? Guys with girlfriends never interested me in the past. I've tried to avoid Aiden since finding out he had a girlfriend, but he isn't letting that happen. He is most definitely not avoiding me.

Amanda walks away, tears finally breaking free.

"Damn," I say. "Who's the heartbreaker now?"

Aiden rolls his eyes. "Come on. Let's get to class."

We walk together to first period. He doesn't seem at all upset about his inevitable breakup with Amanda, and I feel selfishly pleased at that.

I bring up something Aiden said in the car once we take our seats. "Are you really moving to California?" I ask.

He shrugs one shoulder casually. "Maybe."

"For college?" I ask.

"Maybe," he says again.

I sigh. "Now who's being the hard egg to crack?"

"I've recently been inspired to not settle," he says.

"Settle in what way?"

"Taking that job at my dad's company. I told him yesterday that I wanted to go to college instead."

"Really?" I ask, surprised. "What did he say?"

"Honestly, he didn't care either way."

"Most parents would be thrilled their kid wants to go to college."

"My parents aren't most parents."

"Mine either," I say.

Aiden still sits behind me every day, and I'm thankful that I can't see him during class. I would be way too distracted. The teacher assigns us a final project, and once she's done explaining the details, Aiden asks if I'll be his partner. I don't talk to anyone else in this class, or really anyone at school, so I'm relieved when he asks, even if it means spending more time with him while he's in a complicated relationship with Amanda. Our teacher wants us to create a time capsule of high school. We are to find two artifacts each that describe the last four years, and the most creative group doesn't have to take the end of the year final.

"I have a feeling my high school experience is much different than yours," I say to Aiden.

"Let me guess. Surfboards and sex."

My mouth falls open. I push his shoulder. "Sex?"

"Don't tell me you didn't sleep with all your surfer boyfriends?"

I give him my classic bitch face. "I don't kiss and tell."

His eyebrows raise. "Are you a virgin, Black Sheep?"

I smirk. "Wouldn't you like to know?"

I'm not a virgin. I've actually had a lot of sex. A lot of meaningless sex, but that doesn't matter. I have nothing against one-night stands, mostly because that means no feelings are involved. I don't tell him this because, for whatever reason, I don't want him to think differently of me. But girls have needs too.

"If I had to guess your artifacts, I would say beer cans and bras."

"Whoa, whoa, whoa. You think I'm that shallow?"

I shrug. "I don't know much about you."

"Because you don't try."

The bell rings.

"I know," I say as I stand, collecting my books. "And I don't plan to."

I turn and walk out of the classroom. Aiden catches up to me before I can make it ten feet out the door.

"Why don't you try?" he asks.

"For one, you've had a girlfriend the entire time I've known you. I'm not in the business of getting to know guys with girlfriends."

"Okay, well, let's say Amanda and I break up. For good. Would you try to get to know me then?"

I think for a second. Of course, I would. Unfortunately, I *am* in the business of being a bitch and protecting my heart. This guy would most definitely have the capacity to break it. So, I lie.

"No. I wouldn't."

He shakes his head. "I don't believe you."

"You should."

He follows me to my next class.

"Go to class, Aiden," I say.

"No, I'm not leaving until you tell me why you really don't want to get to know me."

"You're going to be standing there all day."

"If that's what it takes."

I exhale dramatically. "Aiden, I'm a shell of a human. I'm a stone-cold bitch. Did you know my name actually means a pile of rocks? I'm a rock down to my core. Literally."

Aiden grabs my hand. I look down when his fingers touch mine. My bitch face drops, and I immediately become vulnerable to him. I look up and see that he's watching me, staring.

"I'm not going to hurt you, Harlow," he whispers.

My eyebrows drop together, and my mouth is slightly parted. I'm speechless. For the first time in my life, I have nothing to say. I'm not staying quiet to prove a point or to be a bitch. I truly don't know what to say to that. He understands this. He gets me. He knows me. Aiden gives my hand a final squeeze as if to confirm my thoughts. He can see that I don't want to get to know him because then I'll have something to lose. What he hasn't realized is that I'm already going to lose him no matter what.

Aiden walks away as the bell rings. I take my seat and hear nothing for the next hour except Aiden's words repeating in my head.

I'm not going to hurt you.

Why do I believe him?

Chapter six

Past

Earlier this week, Aiden drove us home from school. He told me that his parents would be out of town for a couple of days and wanted to know if I would come over.

"Are you throwing another party?" I asked.

"No. I hoped you still might want to come over though."

I smiled. I couldn't say no.

It's now Saturday night, and I'm trying to decide what to wear over to his house. I don't want to dress too nice because it's not a date, just two friends hanging out at home on a Saturday night. I settle on black leggings that make my ass look great with a loose-fitting top. My hair falls just below my breasts.

I'm about to walk over to Aiden's house when I hear the doorbell ring. Rosa is cooking dinner, so I tell her I'll get it. When I open the door, Aiden is standing there.

"I was just about to come over," I say. "Is everything okay?" I instantly worry that maybe he's changed his mind, maybe he found better plans.

But he's beaming, the light in his eyes contagious, and I find myself smiling, the concern fading. "I wanted to pick you up for our date."

I frown. "*Date?*" I question. This isn't supposed to be a date. Dates lead to dating, and dating leads to heartbreak.

"Yes. Date."

"This isn't a date, Aiden."

He shakes his head. "Whatever you say. I still wanted to walk you over to my house. Are you ready?"

I nod hesitantly, following him to his house.

"Hungry?" he asks.

"Yes."

He leads me into the kitchen.

"What's for dinner?" I ask.

"I cooked this myself, so don't judge."

I look at him, surprised. "You cooked for me?"

"Don't flatter yourself. I cook a lot."

"Don't your parents have people for that?"

Aiden pulls out two plates as he sets the table. "When they're out of town, I let Janet, our housekeeper, have the weekend off. I don't need to be waited on hand and foot."

Maybe we're more alike than I originally thought. I've always judged my parents for not lifting a finger for themselves.

I take a seat at the table, and Aiden places the meal in front of me. He's made chicken parmesan, and it smells amazing.

"Finally, not rich people food. Italian is my favorite," I say, my mouth watering.

"Nothing can beat a good pasta dinner."

When we've finished eating, I take the plates and walk them to the sink. Aiden cooked, so I feel obligated to wash the dishes. He stands next to me and dries the ones I've handed him.

He smirks. "Well, this is fun."

"Washing dishes?" I question.

"Playing house. Getting our hands a little dirty."

"My hands are quite clean, actually," I say, showing off the soap spuds between my fingers.

Aiden puts the cup he's drying down on the counter. He's eyeing me in that devilish way I've come to recognize, and I instantly know he's up to something. Before I can react, he grabs the sprayer from the sink and points it at me. I drop the plate I'm holding into the sink full of water, soapy liquid splashing everywhere. I put my hands up in surrender.

"Aiden, don't," I warn.

He looks mischievous. "I've never seen you look so helpless, Harlow."

"Aiden," I say again.

"Harlow."

I close my eyes, trying to hide the way he makes me feel when he says my name like that. I keep my mouth shut and my eyes closed. How does he affect me so easily? Why do I want to pull him closer to me every time my name leaves his lips?

"Harlow," he says again. "Tell me what you're thinking."

"I don't want to get wet," I lie, slowly daring to open my eyes again.

"Are you sure that's what you're thinking?"

"Yes."

He sprays me before I can react. I try to run, but he reaches for me. Soon, he has me pinned against the counter, completely soaking me. I laugh hysterically as I try to get away from him. I wiggle beneath his grasp, finally slipping away. Freeing myself, I run like hell to get away. He drops the sprayer in the sink and chases me, tackling me to the floor and leaving us both soaking wet.

"Look what you did," I say.

Aiden holds himself up by his arms and looks down, eyeing his wet shirt. "Guess I'll have to take it off."

My eyes grow big at the thought of a shirtless Aiden. He sits up, and I can't take my eyes off his chest, his abs. He laughs when he notices me staring.

"Do you like what you see, Black Sheep?"

I don't answer. Sometimes staying quiet is the best thing I can do in situations with him.

"Your turn," he says casually.

My eyes move away from his abs. "My turn?"

"You're soaking wet."

I look at my drenched shirt, realizing he wants me to take it off. "I guess I am."

Aiden stands and stretches his hand toward me. "Come on. You can borrow one of my T-shirts."

I take his hand and stand. He leads me to his bedroom.

The first thing I notice as I walk through the door is his bed. It's big and directly in the center of the room, resembling a floating cloud with the way it hovers above the ground.

I learn a lot more about him from his room than he could learn about me from mine. He has dark blue walls, there's a giant Lumineers world tour poster framed above his bed, a football jersey on another wall above trophies, and tons of framed pictures. I didn't know he played football, though from the number of trophies he has, it would seem that he's pretty good. I'm surprised his playing never came up in conversation before.

Aiden walks into his closet and comes out dressed in dry clothes and holding a T-shirt for me. *Vikings Varsity Football.* "Walton" is written across the back above the number one. He hands me the shirt and turns around, giving me privacy so I can change.

I quickly take off my dripping wet top and replace it with Aiden's football shirt. He turns back around once I've given him the okay.

"That looks good on you," he says.

"I didn't know you played football."

"Look at you, Harlow. You're learning more about me already."

I ignore his sarcasm and sit on his bed.

"What position do you play?" I ask. I ignore the nagging voice in my head telling me I will regret this later, that I'll regret allowing myself to get to know him. It's not like discussing football is deep. It doesn't mean I'll get my heart broken if I know what position he plays in a silly high school sport.

"Quarterback," he answers.

"Figures."

"What's that mean?"

I shrug. "You seem like the quarterback type."

"Please explain."

"Popular, tall, good-looking, ladies' man, athletic, abs of steel."

Aiden joins me on the bed, grinning. "You think I'm good looking? *And* have abs of steel?"

I grab a pillow and hit him. "Shut up."

He grabs the pillow from me and playfully attacks me with it. He falls on top of me again, with only the pillow between us. Our faces are only inches from each other and my heart races, suddenly making me feel as though I'm having a mini-heart attack. I've had dozens of guys on top of me, most of them naked, and they didn't make me feel the way I'm feeling right now.

Aiden's eyes are the color of the shoreline, light blue and full of lust. He's looking at my ruby red lips, and I'm afraid he's going to kiss me. If he kisses me, there will be no turning back. I won't know how to stop, and I'll be in this, officially having something to lose. Aiden isn't the type of guy you can kiss and walk away from. It's exactly why I don't get myself into these types of situations in the first place.

I remind myself that I'm leaving in three months and push him off me before he can take this any further. He rolls onto his back, still clinging to the pillow. I notice he's breathing heavily and not looking at me, his gaze focused on the ceiling.

"Harlow," he whispers between breaths.

I lie on my back beside him and look up. "I told you, I don't like it when you say my name."

"You don't like when I do a lot of things."

"I know. I'm a bitch."

"I don't think you're a bitch. You're just scared."

"Scared of what?" I ask.

"Falling in love with me."

My jaw clenches. "I'm not falling in love with you, Aiden."

"Because you won't let it happen."

"It can't happen," I say sternly.

Aiden sits up on his elbows, finally taking his focus off the ceiling and turning all his attention on me. "Why? Why can't it happen?"

I don't look at him, fixating on a speck of dust I see on the ceiling fan. "I'm leaving soon."

"I'll leave with you," he says as if it's no big deal, as if he's not suggesting he leave everything behind for me.

I pick myself up off the bed, his words like knives to my chest. I want them to be true. I want to think that if Aiden and I started dating, I wouldn't have to say goodbye to him, but that's not the reality of the situation. We hardly know each other. It would be insane for him to pick up and leave to follow me back to California.

He sits up, studying me with the same pleading eyes Amanda had at school the other day.

"Aiden, you hardly know me. You can't say you're going to follow me across the country."

"Why can't I?"

I let out an agitated sigh. My hands are on my hips, and I'm so tempted to walk out of his room and go home. I don't want to be here right now. He's making this so hard on me, giving me hope when I know there is none.

"Aiden, stop."

"No, Harlow. I won't stop."

I turn and walk out of his bedroom, fleeing like the coward I am. I hear him following behind me, and before I can pick up speed, he grabs my shoulder, gently pushing me against the wall. His hands are on either side of my head as he looks longingly into my eyes. I watch as his eyes turn a deep shade of blue.

"Why are you doing this?" he asks, his voice husky.

I try to stay quiet. I try so hard. "This isn't right," I finally say.

"How, Harlow? How could this not be right? It *feels* right."

"Because of Amanda. And because of California. And graduation. And because of me. I'm not the kind of girl people fall in love with, Aiden. I'm not the kind of girl *you* fall in love with."

"You're exactly the kind of girl I *want* to fall in love with."

I close my eyes and take in his words. "It won't work," I force myself to say.

"Why?"

"I told you, I'm a rock. One of us will get hurt, and I can assure you, it won't be me. I won't let that happen."

"I wasn't just quoting a song the other day."

"What?"

"When I said you've been on my mind like a drug, I meant it. I haven't been able to stop thinking about you since the very first time I saw you."

"I find that hard to believe. Were you thinking about me when you were sucking face in front of my locker?" I sneer.

His head falls to his arm. "You rejected me. That was me trying *not* to think about you. With my girlfriend. You can't be mad that I was kissing my girlfriend."

"I didn't say I was mad."

"You sound a little bitter. Maybe even jealous."

"No. I'm just making a point. And thank you for pointing out that you have a girlfriend. This is wrong, Aiden. I'm not interested in guys that are in relationships."

"Had."

"What?"

"*Had* a girlfriend. I broke up with Amanda a few days ago."

This is news to me. "Why?" I ask, wanting—no, needing—to know more.

"My heart wasn't in it anymore. It hasn't been in it for a long time. Meeting you only confirmed that."

"I think I should go home, Aiden."

"Harlow, please. Don't let California be the deciding factor here."

"Thank you for dinner," I say before I move his arm out of the way.

I hurry down the stairs and head straight for the front door. He stays at the top of the steps, his body slumped over in defeat.

My head is spinning. I don't want to hurt him. But how he feels right now isn't half as bad as what I would feel if I let him break my heart. Walking away from Aiden would be hard enough as it is. I can't let my feelings for him get any deeper. I have to protect myself.

Chapter seven

Past

He's in my driveway again Monday morning. When I get inside the car, he's acting as if nothing happened between us just a couple of days ago.

"Good morning," he says as we pull out of my driveway.

"Morning."

Things were awkward when I left Saturday night. He made his intentions clear that he wants to pursue me, and I made it known that I'm not interested in a relationship. Aiden is a relationship kind of guy. I'm not. Not with guys like him, at least.

I'd tried to distract myself from thoughts of Aiden yesterday. It was probably stupid, but I decided to finally text this guy Anthony in my chemistry class who has been hitting on me every day since I started at Liberty. For the most part, I've ignored him. But yesterday, I was desperate. I needed the distraction, and he was all too happy to oblige.

Anthony is decent-looking; tall and muscular. He's undoubtedly attractive, but he probably has the IQ of a fourth grader, which is exactly my type. I would never develop real feelings for someone like him. He's safe. Unfortunately, he didn't do a good enough job of distracting me, and I haven't stopped thinking about Aiden.

"I stopped by your house yesterday," Aiden says, pulling me from my thoughts. "You weren't home."

"Yeah. I was out."

"Oh."

After a few seconds of silence, he speaks again. "Harlow, can I ask you something?"

"Sure."

"Are you already seeing someone? Do you have a boyfriend or something?"

I feel my stomach tighten at the sudden line of questioning. Where is this coming from? "No. I don't have a boyfriend."

"Are you seeing someone then?" he asks again.

Shit. Maybe he already knows about Anthony. But how? "Define *seeing someone*."

He releases a heavy breath. I'm almost positive now that he knows. Someone must have told him. It was meaningless sex. I needed to get Aiden out of my head, and that was the only way I knew how. I know it was stupid. It didn't even work. I shouldn't have slept with him, but still, it shouldn't matter because it's not like

Aiden and I are together. Besides, Aiden's the one who's had a girlfriend the majority of the time he's tried talking to me. *He* can't be upset with *me*, though I don't know why I suddenly feel guilty.

"Aiden, it didn't mean anything."

"So, you are sleeping with someone?"

"No. Not sleeping. Slept. I had sex one time. But that's all it was: sex. No emotions. No feelings."

He nods his head in understanding. "Okay," he mumbles quietly.

We don't talk the rest of the drive to school. When we get to our lockers, he waits for me before we walk to class. Still, he doesn't say anything.

We're given the second half of the class to brainstorm the artifacts for our final project. I turn my chair around so that I'm facing Aiden, but he's looking down at his desk and playing with his pencil. He doesn't seem himself. I don't see the arrogant, cocky quarterback that I'm used to. He looks deep in thought, his eyebrows scrunched, and vulnerability is etched across his features.

"I guess I was right about your high school experience," he says softly.

"What are you talking about?"

"Sex. You apparently have a lot of meaningless sex."

I shake my head. "What?"

"Anthony," he says. "That's who it was, right? He was on my team."

"Yeah, but it was only one time, Aiden. I swear."

"So far." He shrugs, and all the while, his eyes stay fixated on his pencil. "He seems to think it's going to be more than a one-time thing."

I shake my head. "Well, it's not. But even if it was, this isn't fair, Aiden. You can't be mad at me for sleeping with someone else when you've had a girlfriend up until a few days ago."

His heavy eyes finally look at me. "I don't care that you've slept with other people, Harlow. I care that you slept with someone *yesterday*."

My face flushes, and for the second time in my life, I'm left speechless.

The bell rings, and Aiden walks out without me. I'm still sitting in my desk when the last person exits the classroom. I grab my things, replaying his words over and over, knowing full well the hurt that was behind them.

Aiden avoids me the rest of the day. I don't see him again until we get to his car after school. I try to look at the bright side. At least he didn't decide to leave me here.

He opens the passenger door for me but doesn't say a word. I decide to break the silence on our drive home.

"You scare me, Aiden."

He doesn't respond. He keeps his hands on the wheel and his gaze on the road.

"Aiden?"

"What?"

I keep my focus out the window as I'm about to admit all the things I'm afraid of to the one person who could make all my fears come true.

"I'm afraid to fall in love with you. I'm afraid to let someone in who could break my heart. I'm afraid to feel things more than I already do. I'm scared, Aiden. I slept with Anthony to distract myself, but it didn't work. You're all I'm ever able to think about. This has never happened to me before, and I'm scared for what it means. I'm scared for what you could do to me. For what I would let you do to me."

"I'm scared too, Harlow," he says softly, his voice merely a whisper.

I lean back in my seat and continue to stare out the window. We don't say anything else the rest of the ride home. He drops me off, still not uttering a single word. I've noticed that we have a lot of silent moments, and for some reason, they are the hardest. There's so much said in the silence, so much more than what could be spoken out loud.

I gave Aiden my number the night we went to the beach, but he still hasn't texted me. Not even once. I didn't ask for his number that day, and I regret it now because I really want to text him. It's been two hours since he dropped me off at home, and I feel like so much needs to be said. I told him everything I was afraid of, and he confirmed that he's scared too. So, where do we go from here? What does it all mean? What do we do about it? I no longer can convince myself that avoiding Aiden is the right thing to do, not after seeing his reaction to the news about Anthony. It hurt me more than I thought it would to see him upset. He was devastated.

After an internal battle with myself for the better part of an hour, I decide to go talk with Aiden in person. I throw on a sweatshirt and walk outside toward his house. My hand freezes right before it's about to knock on his front door. I hesitate before turning around to walk back to my house, but immediately talk myself out of the retreat and find myself back on his front step. Before I can overthink things again, I knock.

Janet opens the door, her expression pleasant. "Hello," she says.

"Hi. Is Aiden home?" I ask.

She smiles. "One moment, dear."

She disappears into the house. Aiden returns in her place, his face blank.

He opens the door wider. "Come in," he says.

He backs further into the house, and I follow him inside. Instead of closing the door, he walks directly to the staircase leading to his bedroom. I shut the door behind me and follow. By the time I get to his room, he's sitting at his desk. There's no other place to sit, so I find myself back on his bed.

"What are you doing here?" he asks.

"I need to talk to you."

"Okay."

"Okay."

He looks annoyed. I guess this is the part where I should start talking.

"I'm not going to sleep with Anthony again," I blurt, though this was not how I pictured this conversation starting in my head.

"Don't stop on my account."

My eyebrows furrow. "You're being bitter."

"You're always bitter."

I stand and walk toward his desk, stopping directly in front of him. He's tall, so when he's sitting, we're nearly at eye level.

"Please, Aiden. I'm sorry. It was stupid of me. I should have never texted Anthony. I should have never slept with him. And I know it's not an excuse, but I've never met anyone like you before. I've never met anyone that I haven't been able to get off my mind, or someone that I could see a future with. I don't know how this is supposed to work. I only know how to protect my heart and that's by doing shitty things. Sleeping with Anthony was shitty, and I'm sorry."

He has no idea how hard that was for me to admit. Thankfully, I see his shoulders relax. He grabs my hands and pulls me closer to him.

"I knew exactly what I was getting into when I met you," he says. "It was hard to hear about what you did after our night on Saturday, after I told you how I felt about you. I wanted to kiss you so bad then, but I knew it would scare you off. Then come to find out the next day you *slept* with someone. It hurt. It hurt really fucking bad."

"It would have scared me then, but it won't now. I'm going to try harder. I want to try this with you." I'm shocked by how desperate I sound, the fear of losing Aiden altogether at the forefront of my mind.

Aiden tries to hide his smile. "I'm not going to kiss you right now. Not like this. But I will kiss you. One day."

My shoulders sag, and I'm surprised by how disappointed I feel.

He pulls at my hands until they're wrapped around his back. He puts his arms around me and relaxes his head into my chest. My heart is beating so fast, I'm sure he can feel it pounding on his cheek. We stay like this for several minutes. My heartbeat relaxes as I become more comfortable being this close to him, being in his arms. I like this feeling. I like it a lot.

He lets go of me, and I immediately feel the loss of his touch.

"Do you want to watch a movie tonight, or do you have to get back home?" he asks.

I smile. "A movie sounds nice."

I feel my heart warm as he leads me over to his bed. We lie close together, his arm around me the entire time. He chose one of those end-of-the-world kinds of movies, and the next few hours fly by. Before I know it, the credits are rolling, and it's time for me to go. For the first time, I'm not in a rush to leave him.

"Thank you for coming over, Harlow. I know it probably wasn't easy for you to do," he says as he stands up.

I do the same. "It was easier than I thought." Especially because my options were to swallow my pride or lose Aiden.

He grins and pulls me in for another hug. This time, my head relaxes against his chest.

"Come on," he says. "I'll walk you home."

He grabs my hand and leads me outside. Moments later, we're standing at my front door.

This is the part where he's supposed to kiss me. I've watched enough movies to know that the guy who takes the girl home always kisses her before she goes inside. I feel anxious yet excited at the thought.

We're standing on my front porch, facing one another. He's still holding my hand. I watch as his eyes drop to my lips. *This is it*, I think to myself. *He's going to kiss me.* But much to my dismay, he laughs.

I frown. "What?"

"You look so nervous," he says. "It's cute."

"I'm not nervous," I lie, though I can feel my palms sweating beneath his.

"Yes, Harlow, you are. It's okay."

I drop my head to hide my embarrassment. He makes me so damn high-strung. When is that going to stop?

He pulls one hand away, resting his fingers softly under my chin. He tilts my head until I'm looking at him.

"I'm not going to kiss you," he whispers. "Calm down."

I nod my head, not able to form words, given our current proximity.

"Goodnight, Harlow. I'll see you in the morning."

"Okay," I say, finally managing to form words. "Goodnight."

He waits until I'm inside before he walks back to his house. I run up the stairs, directly to my room, and release all the air I've been holding for the last five minutes. Before I can fully relax, I feel my phone vibrate in my pocket. It causes me to jump.

"Chill the fuck out, Harlow," I mumble to myself.

When I pull out my phone, I see that I have a new message. My heart skips a beat when I see Aiden's name pop up on the screen. He must have saved his number in my phone while I was distracted watching the movie. I smile at the thought.

Aiden: I was accepted to UCLA.

Holy shit. UCLA is in California. Was he serious about moving there?

Me: You were serious about moving? And thanks for adding your phone number. I've been hoping you'd text me soon so I could have it.

Aiden: Oh, yeah? And pretty damn serious.

Me: When did you apply?

Aiden: The day I found out you were from California.

Me: Seriously?

Aiden: Heaven help a fool who falls in love.

Me: You're not a fool.

Aiden. Goodnight, Harlow.

Me: Goodnight, Aiden.

Chapter eight

Past

The following week, Aiden insists on driving me to school every day. I try to offer to drive some of the days, but he refuses. On Wednesday, he asks if I will come over to his house for a party the upcoming weekend.

"I'll only throw a party if you're there," he says.

We are driving home from school. I glance out the window, then back in his direction.

"Okay," I say. "If you want me there, I'll be there."

He smiles and grabs my hand. "Will you come over early? I want to see you before things get out of control."

I laugh. "Sure."

Saturday comes quickly. This will be the first party Aiden's thrown since he broke up with Amanda, and I can't help but wonder if she'll be there. Not that I care. I'm not the jealous type.

I decide to switch up my outfit for tonight. I browse the back of my closet, shuffling through each of the dresses my mother has bought me over the years. Honestly, they're so colorful it makes me sick. I want to shock him tonight, really give him something to look at, so I pick one I think he will like most. I feel stupid for even considering what he would like, but this is me trying to open up to him. I've never cared what someone else thought before, but everything is different with Aiden. I think this thing with him is worth it, even if I end up being left with a broken heart. The thought makes my stomach churn.

Please don't let him hurt me.

I choose a baby-blue dress with an open back. It dips low, so my entire back is exposed in a sexy way. It's a short dress that shows off my legs and has a small plunge in the neckline, leaving my cleavage visible. Aiden's going to love this dress on me.

After applying my tube of ruby red, I walk next door. Janet greets me before kindly inviting me in and telling me Aiden is in his room. I walk up the stairs and see that his door is slightly opened. I walk in, but his room is empty.

"Aiden?" I yell.

"Coming!" I hear from down the hall.

I catch the sound of footsteps behind me and turn. Aiden is standing in the doorway directly in front of me, shirtless. This is the second time I've seen him without a shirt, yet I still feel the need to pick my jaw off the floor.

The corners of his mouth curve up as he takes in my outfit. "Wow," he says.

"Wow is right," I say, blatantly staring at his abs before giving him a wink.

He laughs and walks into his closet. When he returns, he's wearing a shirt. Damn.

"I liked you better without it," I tell him.

He smirks. "Is that right?"

He walks in my direction, placing his hands gently on both sides of my face. My breathing hitches at the contact. We're so close, I can feel his breath on my forehead.

"I am so attracted to you," he whispers, his thumb stroking my cheek.

I blush.

"I've never seen you in this color," he says, looking down at the dress. "It suits you."

"Time for an insult."

"No. You look beautiful, Harlow," he says, and he sounds so serious, I almost believe him.

I almost believe that I'm capable of being beautiful enough for someone like Aiden. But deep down, I still know that's not me. I'm not a beautiful person. Maybe on the outside to some, but sure as hell not on the inside.

I try to put my head down so I don't have to look at him anymore, but his hands prevent me.

"Stop trying to hide. Look at me."

I look at him.

"You're so beautiful," he says again.

I give him a small smile. It's a start.

He pulls me in closer until our bodies press against each other. He rests his chin on top of my head. I can feel his heart beating rapidly against mine, though he seems so much calmer than me.

"Would you like something to drink?" he asks as we part.

"Sure."

"Is it another vodka night, or are you sticking to beer?"

I laugh. "No vodka. I was hungover for two days after that."

"Beer it is."

He holds my hand as we walk down the stairs, leading me to the pool room. I'm momentarily taken aback by how stunning it is in here. This room was full of so many bodies last time I was here that I wasn't paying much attention. My house doesn't have a pool, though there's plenty of room for one. The water shines a beautiful royal blue color as it rests peacefully surrounded by a stone pathway. There's a hot tub attached in the right corner, and several lounging chairs line the perimeter.

The makeshift bar, where I ordered way too many shots at the last party, is beside us. Aiden walks behind the bar and opens the cooler. He hands me a beer.

"Thank you."

He nods.

We take a seat in one of the lounging chairs. This one is rounded and could probably fit up to five people. It's big enough that we can lie down and get comfortable.

Being this close to him, I'm reminded about the possibilities that are yet to come. Aiden and I still haven't kissed, and it makes me nervous every time we are this close. I feel like such a prude around him. I've obviously kissed boys before, but kissing Aiden makes me so nervous.

We're lying on our sides facing each other. He is resting on his elbow, that same arm holding his beer. He places his free hand on my waist.

"Harlow," he says.

I close my eyes, trying to steady my breath after the way he just said my name. "Aiden."

He squeezes my side, urging me to open my eyes, but I don't.

"I really like you," he says.

"I really like you too," I manage.

He laughs. I open my eyes and give him an angry look.

"That was so hard for you to say, wasn't it?" he jokes.

I roll my eyes. "Don't pick on me."

He uses the hand on my waist to push me down until I'm lying on my back. Aiden makes his way on top of me, his body pressing down on mine. The second we connect, I release a small whimper. I don't mean to, but it escapes my lips. Aiden's breathing gets heavier, and his eyes fill with desire. I can feel what this is doing to him, how close we are, how badly we want each other. He's hard, and it's pressing against me exactly where I would hope it would. The tension in the air is thick. I'm convinced this is the moment he's finally going to kiss me. I want him to so badly, but a small part of me is still terrified. I'm already six feet under with him, how much deeper can I get from a kiss? I'm afraid to find out.

"Damn it, Harlow," he whispers, his forehead pressed against mine.

Our lips are so close, I can almost taste him. I feel his breath on my face.

"What?" I whisper back.

"I want to kiss you."

"Then kiss me," I say, trying to sound more confident than I feel.

Just when I think he's finally going to do it, he pulls himself away. He stands and paces with his hands laced behind his head.

I sit up on my elbows. "Are you okay?" I ask.

He's still pacing. "I'm trying to take my mind off you."

"Why?" I ask, confused.

He stops and looks at me. "If I kissed you just then, there's no way I'd be able to stop. I'm so fucking tempted to call this party off so that it's just you and me tonight."

I grin, licking my lips, suddenly feeling daring.

"Stop that," he says.

"Stop what?" I tease, biting down on my lower lip.

He releases a lungful of air. "Holy shit, Harlow. I want you so bad. I'm usually able to control myself around you. It must be that damn dress. I can't take my eyes off you." He turns around so his back is facing me. "Shit," he says again.

I stand and wrap my arms around him from behind. I feel his muscles clench beneath my touch. He turns around and wraps me in his arms. He places one hand on the back of my head and the other on the small of my back. I feel his lips brush through my hair, and it sends shivers down my spine.

We stay this way for several minutes until our heart rates slow down. Once Aiden has regained control of himself, he walks to where he set down his beer and chugs it. I follow suit, taking a sip of mine.

Once people show up, the rest of the night passes by in a bit of a blur. Surprisingly, I have a lot of fun. Aiden stays with me the whole night, reintroducing me to all his friends. My new acquaintances, as he likes to call them since I've made it clear I'm not interested in making friends.

Aiden smiles and laughs as we play drinking games and dance to music. We drink more than I can remember, and by the time midnight rolls around, I'm completely shitfaced. I think I'm more drunk than Aiden because he's being the responsible one and bringing me water. I've camped out on one of the single-person lounge chairs by the pool, making myself comfortable and trying to sober up.

An hour later, everyone is gone. Aiden finds me by the pool again and falls gracefully on top of me. His head rests on my chest, and I can tell he's more relaxed this time around, though our bodies are in the same position as before. I'm more relaxed too. Maybe that's why my fingers find his hair and weave through his messy perfection.

"Tonight was fun," I say.

"Yes, it was."

I continue to stroke his hair. "I should probably go home now."

I feel him tighten his hold on me. "Don't," he says. "Can you stay the night?"

I'm already going against everything I told myself not to do, especially here in Indiana. Spending the night with a guy is a huge no-no for me. I've never done it before and hadn't planned on doing it anytime soon. But I don't want to leave him. I also don't want to tell him no. Besides, I'm drunk. I don't want to be alone and drunk. What fun is that?

"Okay," I say. "I'll stay."

He lifts his head away from my chest and looks at me, his eyes studying mine.

"Really?"

"Sure."

He's all smiles when he stands and leads me to his bedroom. He looks more excited than I did the day he brought me to the beach, and I was pretty damn thrilled.

"What do you normally sleep in?" he asks after shutting the door behind us.

I look at him, confused. "Is that your pillow talk?"

He laughs. "No, Harlow. Do you want a T-shirt to sleep in?"

"Oh. Yes, please."

He hands me a shirt and turns around, once again allowing me the privacy to change. I take off my dress and leave it on the floor. I slip his oversized T-shirt over my head, only wearing panties beneath.

"I'm done," I tell him.

He turns around, taking off his shirt before removing his jeans. He slips on sweatpants over his boxers. I don't turn around, don't bother giving him the consideration he gave me. I watch him the entire time he changes, staring at him, at his perfect body, in awe. Then I watch as he makes his way to the floating king-sized bed.

His eyes find me, and he pats the spot next to him. "Come here."

I listen and climb into bed. He lifts the covers, and I slide underneath, joining him. He wraps his arm around me, and I naturally lay my head against his chest. His fingers stroke up and down my arm.

"Are you drunk?" he asks.

"Sort of."

"Are you tired?"

"No."

"Harlow."

I close my eyes. The closeness. His voice. My name.

"Yeah?" I whisper.

"This isn't normal," he says.

"What isn't normal?"

"Us. Relationships aren't like this. This is different."

Without warning, my entire body feels like it's on fire. Like tiny hot needles are poking at its surface. An uncomfortable warmth rolls up my neck, and I can feel my heart rate increase as panic ensues. I don't know what he means, though I have an idea, and it's scaring the hell out of me. Doubt floods my thoughts. Insecurity saturates my body. I lift away from his chest and pull myself out of bed.

"Harlow," he says. "Harlow, stop."

I don't listen, my head now taking the reins to protect my heart as it programs itself into fight or flight mode. I run for the door, but his hand grips my arm, stopping me. He shuts his bedroom door again, pushing me against it.

"Don't run," he whispers. "Listen to me."

We're close again. Close enough to smell his pine scent. Close enough to want to taste his lips on mine. Close enough to feel everything he's feeling. Close enough that everything I was just feeling—worry, fear, doubt—is dissipating.

"I've never felt like this with someone. Ever," he continues, his thumb stroking my cheek. "This is different. *We* are different. It's not a bad thing. I know you're scared. I am too. But I'm already lost to you. You have all the power in the world to crush me, and I'm openly giving it to you. I'm giving you all the power, Harlow."

His eyes move quickly from mine down to my lips. "You have the most perfect lips," he says softly.

His eyes don't leave my mouth now. He's fully entranced. "I'm going to kiss you now, okay?"

I lose my breath, and before I can answer, his lips fall into mine. He kisses me softly at first. Several small innocent pecks. Then his mouth stays on mine longer, my lips eventually parting to make way for his tongue. We continue this way, getting used to each other slowly as his hands hold my face, and one eventually finds its way into my hair. He pulls me closer to him, and our bodies collide as our mouths learn to perform together. He kisses me deeply, and I unintentionally moan into his mouth. He absorbs my sounds and kisses me harder. His hands find my waist before he picks me up, my legs wrapping around his waist as my back presses against the door. We stay tangled in each other for several minutes, his body pressing firmly into mine, only parting for tiny breaths of fresh air.

Minutes or hours later, it's hard to tell as I'm so lost in this moment, he turns and walks us toward the bed. He lays my head on the pillow gently and sinks on top of me, his lips never leaving mine. His hands explore down my side until they reach my thighs. He doesn't make a move to try and feel what's underneath his T-shirt, and when his hands return up my body, he's careful not to slip beneath my clothes.

My palms hold on tightly to whatever they can reach, his muscular frame addictive, his arms, his back. He's the definition of strong. I find every inch that I can reach and let out little whimpers as he presses himself against me. When my body moves in a rhythm against his, my shirt innately slides up. The movement of my panty line against his hardness creates enough friction to leave me desperate for more. Our kissing becomes more panicked, and suddenly, he pulls away.

"Why did you stop?" I ask, out of breath.

He reaches for the hem of the shirt I'm wearing and pulls it down until it's covering my panties completely.

"Not like this," he says, his eyes wandering over the length of my body, his voice gruff. "Dammit. I don't want to be drunk our first time."

We're both breathing heavily, and I can tell by the look in his eyes that stopping is the last thing he wants to do, yet he's the one who pulled away.

"Okay," I tell him.

He's still hovering over me, his face stricken. I can practically read the thoughts going through his head, whether it was a good idea for him to stop or if he should have kept things going.

I scoot out from beneath him, resting my head on a pillow. He does the same, his body facing me.

"That was incredible," he whispers.

He reaches one hand out, resting it on my hip. He squeezes gently, a small smile tugging at his lips. I want to tell him that was the best first kiss I've ever had. That he's right, this isn't normal. That everything he's feeling, I'm feeling too. That not only is he giving me the power to crush him, but that I am giving him all the power to shatter me. But I don't. Instead, I smile. I place my hand on his cheek and lean in until our lips meet again. I kiss him slowly, softly. I don't want to stop, but I know if we continue, we will end up in the same predicament we were just in. I pull my lips away from his. He wraps his arm around me, and I can feel his heart beating against my palm.

Eventually, he reaches across the bed and turns out the light. He places a gentle kiss into my hair. "Goodnight, Harlow."

"Goodnight."

I fall asleep in his arms, and it's the best night's sleep I've ever had.

Chapter nine

Past

    I wake up the next morning on my stomach. The T-shirt I wore to bed has inched its way up, and my entire ass is out. Aiden lies next to me with his arm draped across my back. I reach slowly to pull my shirt down, hoping not to wake him, but his hand squeezes my waist.

    "Nice ass," he mumbles, half yawning.

    I yank the shirt down and roll onto my back. He scoots closer to me, his arm still wrapped around my body.

    I can see the light from the morning seeping through his curtains, and I wonder if my parents care that I haven't come home yet. I reach for my phone on the nightstand. No missed calls. They knew I was next door; they must not be too worried. I put my phone down and relax, getting closer to Aiden.

I must have fallen back to sleep because when I open my eyes again, we're in an entirely different position than I remembered. I'm lying on my side facing the window. Aiden spoons me, one arm beneath my neck and the other covering my waist. It feels natural being with him. It's almost like I've woken up every morning in the same bed as him. I feel him scoot closer and he pulls me in, my back flush against his chest, my ass rubbing against the hardness in his pants.

I giggle at how easily I can affect him.

Aiden lifts his head to see what I'm laughing at, which only makes me laugh harder. He throws his head back in defeat.

"What do you expect when your entire ass presses against me like that?"

I roll over and face him. "I won't let it happen again," I tease.

He moves me again until I'm on my stomach. Then he climbs on top of me and presses against my ass again. His head lowers until I feel his breath on my neck, his lips close to my ear.

"I want it to happen again," he whispers.

Oh.

His head drops to my neck, and his mouth presses against my skin. Chills cover my body. He sucks on my neck, all the while he's moving himself on top of me. I lift myself a bit, pressing myself firmly against him. His breathing grows heavy. One second, I hear him grunting in my ear, the next, he has me flipped on my back, creating the same type of friction between my legs. I pull him closer to me, his lips falling to mine. He kisses me in a frenzy, like he's running out of time.

Our bodies move together, and the pressure between my legs builds. It doesn't take long for him to make me orgasm, and it's the most intense sensation I've ever felt. With clothes between us, our bodies simply rubbing against one another, I wonder how it's even possible for him to make me feel this good. My body trembles beneath his, and before the pleasures absolve, Aiden joins me, my name falling from his lips as he reaches his release.

In that moment, I forget that I ever tried to avoid Aiden. I forget about all the boys that came before him, how I would sleep with them without allowing any feelings to get involved. I can't deny that my feelings for Aiden have multiplied in the last twelve hours. I also can't deny that being with him feels better than anything I've ever felt before. Without even sleeping with him, I know that my world has changed. I know that Aiden has changed me and that I will never be the same. Nothing will never be the same.

An hour later, we're lying in his bed again. It must be the middle of the day by now.

"Are you hungry? Should we get lunch?" Aiden asks.

"Yes. I'm starving."

Aiden gets out of bed and pulls on a shirt over his head. I look down at what I'm wearing then glance at my dress on the floor. Considering the two options I have for clothing right now, it's probably better that I go home and change.

"Maybe I should stop at home and change first," I say.

Aiden laughs.

I walk home wearing Aiden's shirt and a pair of sweatpants he let me borrow. Both are huge, and I'm basically drowning in the cotton.

When I get home, I'm not surprised to find that no one is around. My mom is probably at the spa again, and my dad is in his study.

I change quickly, slipping on a pair of jeans and a T-shirt. When I get back downstairs, Aiden's waiting for me in the driveway. As always, he gets out to open the passenger side door for me before I climb it. Once we pull away, I wait for him to tell me where he's taking us. It doesn't come as a shock when he refuses to say.

"Does everything always have to be a surprise with you?" I ask.

"You don't like surprises?"

"The beach was a nice surprise, but the buildup to surprises suck."

He rolls his eyes. "We're here."

He pulls into a tiny lot of a Middle Eastern restaurant. He says it's his favorite spot in town. When we walk in, I notice how the employees know him by name. We're seated in a small corner booth, Aiden directly across from me.

"So," he says, his tone suddenly serious. "About earlier."

"What about it?" I ask, afraid that maybe he's regretting what happened this morning.

"I'm sorry if I took things a little too far."

I smile. "You didn't," I assure him. We easily could have taken that a lot farther than we did.

"I want to know more about you, Harlow," he says, now smiling back at me.

"What do you want to know?"

"Where do you want to go to college?"

"I don't know yet."

"What do you think about UCLA?"

I know he's probably asking because this is the school that he was recently accepted to, though I still don't believe he's serious about moving to California after graduation. That's where a lot of my doubt comes in. He says all these wonderful, amazing things to me, but I have a hard time believing them for myself.

"I think it's a great school," I answer him honestly.

Aiden nods his head. "Would you consider going there?"

I think for a moment. UCLA wasn't my top pick, but now that I know there's a chance Aiden might attend, it makes me want it to be my top choice. I don't want to tell him that, though. I don't want to get my hopes up and think that this entire relationship will somehow stand the test of time. That's unrealistic. The odds are against us. We're seniors in high school, and I shouldn't allow my future to be dictated by a boy, even if that boy is Aiden.

"I don't know."

Aiden looks disappointed before changing the subject.

Once we've finished eating, he stands to leave. "Ready?"

I nod.

We drive home in silence, not bringing up college again until we're back in my driveway. I'm about to get out of the car when he grabs my hand to stop me.

"Wait," he says.

I sit back down and close the door, waiting for him to say something. Eventually he does.

"Does it freak you out that I want to move to the West Coast because of you?"

Everything regarding Aiden freaks me out. But all I say is, "Yes." Though the truth is, I'm more afraid that he *won't* move to the West Coast.

"Okay."

"Okay."

I get out of the car, silently screaming at myself to say something else. To tell him why it scares me. To tell him that I want nothing more than for this thing to work out between us. That even though we still hardly know each other, he knows me more than anyone else ever has. I don't let people in, and I'm afraid if I let Aiden into my world, my other world on the other side of the country, that there will be no going back. What if it doesn't work out? What if everywhere I turn back home ends up reminding me of him? What will I do then? I know I'm acting crazy. I know that there's no reason I should feel this strongly about a guy I just met, but I can't explain it, I just do.

Aiden doesn't text me for the rest of the day, and I can't help but wonder what he's thinking, what he's doing.

I tell myself that it's normal for me to feel this way about going to college with Aiden. We've only been officially together for a week. How can I base the next four years of my life on a one-week anniversary? I convince myself I'm being rational, that this isn't another one of my ploys to protect my heart. But I know I'm lying. I know that Aiden's the kind of guy who could convince me to stay in Indiana, and that's really saying something.

I know that I'm already in deep with Aiden because I miss him when I don't hear from him. When I'm not with him, I want to be. I can't take this silent treatment any longer. I decide that I'll text him, no longer wanting to wait. Whoever made that stupid rule anyway that guys have to text a girl first? It's bullshit.

Me: Hey. Is everything okay?

Aiden: Depends.

Me: On?

It takes a few minutes before he answers, and I find myself staring at my phone like a crazy person as I wait for his reply.

Aiden: I'm trying really hard not to scare you away, Harlow, but sometimes when you know, you know. And in this situation with us, I just know.

Me: What do you know?

Aiden: You're it for me. I've known for a while now. But the question is: Am I it for you? Are you going to let me in all the way so that I even stand the chance?

The lingering doubt I have inside won't let me take his words in wholeheartedly. I want to believe him, I really do. But how can he know? How can he know so soon that he wants to spend forever with me? What if we don't even make it past next week?

Me: Aiden, if this is about school, I don't want you to commit the next four years of your life somewhere if you're not sure. I can't commit to that yet, either.

Aiden: I didn't ask you to commit to UCLA, babe. I asked if you would consider it. But you don't want to, not even for me.

Me: I'll consider it.

Aiden: I think the bigger issue is that it terrifies you that I would want to move across the country for you.

It scares me how badly I *want* him to move across the country for me.

Me: We've only been talking for a week, Aiden. Don't you think it's a little too soon to be making grand gestures like that?

Aiden: You're leaving in less than three months. I don't think it's soon enough. I'm not going to be able to walk away from you, Harlow. I told you, you're it for me.

I stare at his words for several minutes, eventually deciding to turn off my phone and bury my head in my pillow. I can feel myself shutting down, my walls building back up after all the hard work it took to tear them down, all because I'm scared. I frustrate myself. He's trying to commit to me in the most serious way, and I still find my insecurities getting in the way. If I'm not careful, I'm going to be the reason I lose him.

Chapter Ten

Past

Come Monday morning, it feels like we took five steps forward and ten steps back. We drive to school in silence, walk to class together in silence, we meet at our lockers between classes in silence, and before I know it, we're back in his car driving home *in silence*.

It's moments like this that I wish I were more like other girls. That I wish I were more willing to give someone my all. I know I want to be with Aiden. I know that I want him to come with me to California, for us to beat the odds. I know that I've never felt this way about someone, that he says he hasn't either. I know that what we have is different. So, then, why do I continue to give him a hard time about California? Why can't I just be like other girls?

Aiden Walton is the most popular guy in school, something I didn't know when I first met him, but it doesn't surprise me in the least. Not only is Aiden popular, but he's also kind to everyone, and by far the most attractive guy in the whole school. Couple that with the fact that he's the quarterback who apparently won our school back-to-back state titles, and you've got yourself a triple threat. He's a big deal here, and I'm the stupid girl playing with his heart. I have no friends at Liberty. I'm a nobody. A guy like Aiden doesn't belong with a girl like me.

Something needs to change. *I* need to change. I need to prove to him that I want to make this thing between us work. The truth is, his simple acts of compassion that show me he's in this are typically the kinds of situations that make me run for the hills. The last guy to buy me flowers? I broke up with him in front of everyone at lunch. The last guy who tried to hold my hand in public? I pretended to go to the bathroom on our date and left.

I'm a heartless bitch, and the second someone lays their heart out there for me to pick up, I step on it and make it crumble. It's what I do because I'm selfish. It's what I do so as not to develop feelings. I must get that from my mother. I would rather someone else's heart break than mine. But I don't want to break Aiden's heart, and I sure as hell don't want him to break mine. Something's got to give here, and I have a feeling that something is me.

The rest of the week goes by, and we don't bring up California again. Luckily, things feel normal again as time passes, though there's still that lingering spout of worry taking shelter in the back of my mind. I don't want to lose Aiden, but I can't seem to tell him exactly how I'm feeling just yet.

A few more weeks go by, and I realize the end of the school year is only two months away. Things seem better between Aiden and me, excluding the huge elephant in our relationship that is what the hell will happen after graduation. There have been numerous times where I've almost brought it up in conversation, but then I'm reluctant to do so. I don't want to start another argument, to feel like I might lose him again, especially when we've been doing so well.

On our five-week anniversary of being together, Aiden takes me out to dinner. He hasn't asked me to be his girlfriend, but he introduces me as such, and I can't help but feel lucky to be his. After a nice steak dinner, I'm convinced it'll be the day we finally have sex. Much to my disappointment, it's not. Aiden has been adamant about waiting, about making it special. I don't know how he doesn't see that everything we do together is special to me.

Aiden's ex-girlfriend Amanda has tried on several occasions to get back together with him. I should be annoyed at her persistence, but what I really feel is bad for her. I know it's out of character for me to pity anyone, but I can't imagine what it's like to lose someone as special as Aiden.

Tonight, Aiden's friend Matt is having people over at his house. Aiden and I are in the basement playing drinking games when Amanda walks down the stairs. All eyes turn to Aiden, then to me, before they look back at Amanda. Everyone wants to know what Aiden's reaction will be, what my reaction will be. It's not like this is the first time we've been in a shared space with her, but it is the first time she's showed up to a party where she wasn't invited.

Amanda walks right up to Aiden, stopping directly in front of him, not even acknowledging my presence. It's as if I'm invisible to her.

"Aiden," she says.

Aiden places his hand on the small of my back, moving his fingers in slow, comforting circles. Before he responds, he looks over her shoulder to see who she's come with, but she's alone.

"What are you doing here, Amanda?" he asks.

"It's a party. Am I not allowed to party since you broke up with me?"

"That's not what I meant."

"Can we talk?" she asks him.

"We are talking."

"In private?" she asks again, her tone reluctant.

"No, Amanda. There's nothing more to talk about."

I watch as her shoulders drop, her lips pout, and the waterworks begin. The entire room silences, the music has since stopped, and everyone watches as this disaster plays out. She continues to cry into her palms and between sobs, tells Aiden that she's in love with him and that she doesn't want to live without him. Aiden does his best to get her to calm down, and eventually one of her friends shows up to take her home. The minute she's out of the house, the basement erupts in laughter. But Aiden and I aren't laughing. Aiden scowls at his friends before he asks if I'll go outside with him.

We find a bench in the backyard. Aiden sits and pulls me onto his lap. The weather has finally warmed up, but it's still chilly to me. Aiden positions his arm around me to keep me warm.

"I'm sorry she keeps doing this," he says.

"It's okay."

He sighs, pressing his forehead against my shoulder.

"Does it make you sad?" I ask. "Seeing her that upset?"

"No. It makes me worried I'm going to lose you."

I cock my head, not sure why he thinks he would lose me because of Amanda. If anything, it's the other way around. Maybe one of these times, she's going to convince him to go back to her. The thought that he might take her back if she begs enough has crossed my mind more times than I can count.

"Why?" I ask.

He drops his head. "I hurt her, Harlow. I don't want you to think I'm going to do the same to you."

"Oh."

He squeezes his hold on me and pulls me in closer.

"I'm scared as hell to lose you," he whispers.

I don't say anything because I don't think he's as scared as I am. But I don't want him to know that. He's had his heart broken before; I've never allowed mine to break. I'm a rock and he's a hammer, and if he wanted to crush me, he could.

A few nights later, I am working on homework after having just finished eating dinner. I take a shower before I get ready for bed. I wrap myself in a warm towel and walk down the hall to my room.

I have one of those closets any girl my age would dream of. There are floor-to-ceiling shelves filled with shoes, one wall devoted to clothing, and another with floor-length mirrors facing the door as you enter. In the center is a circular cushion I like to throw outfits on that I choose not to wear. Rosa usually hangs them back up for me after I've left for school.

I walk into the closet, holding my towel tightly and opening the bottom drawer that holds my pajamas. My mother prefers to sleep in satin; therefore, all the pajamas she buys me are satin. I'm not complaining because they are extremely comfortable, but it is definitely one of those things I know I could live without. Just as I'm about to pull the blue satin gown over my head, I hear a noise come from my bedroom.

"Mom?" I yell, knowing full well my dad would never walk into my room without knocking.

She doesn't answer. I quickly dress myself before I walk out of the closet. I'm startled when I see Aiden climbing through the window.

"What are you doing?" I ask, immediately walking to my bedroom door to shut it.

"I texted you and told you I was coming. I wanted to see you."

"I have a front door! You just scared the shit out of me."

"Sorry. It's late. I was afraid your parents would tell me to go home."

I snicker. I highly doubt my parents could care less, but it's cute that he made the extra effort.

He walks toward me, wrapping his arms around the satin gown before he pulls me in closer. He presses his lips against mine, my mouth parting instantly. When he pulls away a few moments later, he takes a single step back before allowing his eyes to wander over my body. I watch as a shameless grin appears on his face.

"You are so sexy," he whispers into my ear, closing the gap between us again.

His lips press against my neck, and he kisses me there, tenderly sucking on the sensitive skin. Aiden walks me back toward the bed. We climb onto the quilted comforter, his body hovering over mine. His lips make their way to mine once again, his tongue slipping in effortlessly. One hand tangles in my hair, and the other presses firmly against my hip, holding me in place so as not to let me slip away. We continue to kiss until we both need to escape for air.

"I love kissing you," he says, smirking.

"I love kissing you," I say back.

We lie this way for a while. Neither of us talking, but sporadically kissing before parting again for air.

"Do you want to sleep over?" I ask sometime later.

Aiden's head falls into the crevice of my neck. He places soft kisses there until he finds my ear.

"Yes," he whispers, sending shivers down my spine.

He continues to leave a trail of kisses until his lips find my mouth. Kissing Aiden is one of my favorite things to do, and I'm not sure I'll ever get used to it. We kiss a lot. I can't even imagine kissing anyone else now. I don't want to kiss anyone else.

As our kissing turns more intense, I trail my hand down his flat stomach, reaching for the hem of his shirt so I can take it off. The feel of his muscles beneath my touch are another thing I'll never quite get used to.

I push Aiden onto his back and pull my lips away from his as I take his place and hover over him. I brush my lips down his neck, as he did mine, before I scatter playful kisses across his chest. His head falls back as he mumbles something unintelligible under his breath. I continue to kiss him until my lips touch the tense muscles just above his pants. They're firm and so fucking sexy. I find the button of his jeans and slide them off gracefully, then bring myself back on top of him. His eyes are light blue and full of hunger. My lips quickly find his in a frantic effort to continue what we've started. As our kissing becomes more possessive, I reach for every place on his body that I can manage. Aiden holds me tight, my body pressed firmly against his.

My fingers tangle into his hair as his hands rest against my ass, still pressing me into him. I can feel his hardness, feel everything this does to him. I know he's enjoying this every bit as much as I am. The next time we part to catch our breath, I attempt to take my gown off, but Aiden quickly places both of his hands on top of mine, preventing the satin from moving any further up my body.

I'm straddling him, my legs on either side of his hips. I frown. "What's wrong?"

He's out of breath, and he moves one hand to cover his face. His eyes are closed, and he won't look at me. He won't answer me. He's ignoring me. I slide off him, unsure of what the hell just happened.

I'm overwhelmed, not understanding what is happening, but feeling the need to get away. I don't know what I did. I don't know why he won't look at me. I don't know why he stopped me from taking off my clothes when he was nearly naked himself. Does he not want this? Not want me? I don't know where to go, but I know I want out.

My eyes fixate back to my closet, my feet following through and leading me there quickly. I shut the door behind me, throwing myself onto the cushion in the center.

It only takes a few seconds before I hear Aiden following, the closet door soon opening.

"Why are you in the closet, Harlow?" he asks as he takes slow steps toward me.

I try my hardest to hide the lack of confidence I suddenly feel, but it's no use. I dip my head. "I don't know what I did," I say softly.

He walks toward me with purpose and bends down so we're at eye level. He's still only wearing his boxers. He grabs my hands, kissing each of my knuckles before speaking. "Baby, you didn't do anything. I was trying to calm myself down. That is all. I didn't want to take things too far."

"Why?" I ask.

One of his hands moves to cup my cheek, his thumb stroking lightly. "You're beautiful, Harlow, and I already have a hard time controlling myself around you. The thought of you taking off your clothes and straddling me like that. Fuck, I have self-control, but not that much."

"Why can't you just let it happen? Do you not want to have sex with me or something?"

"Of course, I want to. Just not yet. I want it to be special, Harlow. More so than me climbing in through your window on some random ass night of the week. I want you to remember our first time. I want you to know how much I love you the first time I make love to you. I want to prove this to you in more ways than showing up unannounced on a school night. I'm sorry. I didn't mean to upset you. You didn't do anything wrong. You deserve so much more, Harlow."

I hear him. I hear every word. But the one that stands out the most—*love*. Did he just tell me he loves me? I can count on one hand how many times someone has said that to me. I know my parents love me; they don't need to say it. And believe me, they don't. I'm a daddy's girl, but he shows his love through gifts and cards signed 'with love'. My mother, too, though more so at the request of my dad. *To our favorite, and only, daughter: your first car. How about a new wardrobe? You want to go to Paris for your sweet 16? Of course, baby girl!* That's the kind of love I get. The materialistic kind.

I don't know how to process this new information. Does Aiden love me?

"Harlow," he says.

I squeeze my eyes shut.

"Harlow, look at me."

I open my eyes again, taking in the deep blue of his irises.

"Say something," he begs.

"Do you love me, Aiden?"

His expression doesn't change. He doesn't hesitate when he says, "Yes."

My lips part to say something, anything, but words don't escape me. I know I love him, too. I want him to know that I fell in love with him a long time ago but was too afraid to admit it. I want to tell him that falling for him was easy, that loving him is easy, but also the scariest thing in the world. There's so much I want to say, but I can't. Eventually, all I can manage is, "Okay."

"Does that frighten you?" he asks, his thumb still grazing my cheek.

I nod.

"Good," he says. "It scares me too."

Aiden grabs my hands, motioning for me to stand. He leads me out of the closet and back toward my bed. He's careful not to lose my grip, probably afraid I might run again. He sits at the end of my bed, parting his legs slightly so that I can stand between them.

"Harlow," he says. "I love you. I know that's a lot for you to take in, and believe me, I've been trying so hard not to say it. I knew what it would do to you. I knew it would freak you out, but I couldn't have you thinking that you did something wrong, okay? It doesn't change anything between us. Nothing has to change."

I nod.

"But now that you know, what do I need to do to make you okay with it? Because I'm never going to stop loving you."

There's nothing he has to do, nothing more he could ever possibly do. Aiden is patient, he is kind, and he *loves* me. He is everything I'm not, and everything I need. I need to stop being so afraid. I need to trust Aiden, trust him with my heart as he trusts me with his.

"I love you, Aiden," I say.

His expression changes within an instant. His eyes change from dark to light. His mood changes from afraid to hopeful. And suddenly, his lips are back against mine. He kisses me with so much want, so much love, keeping his arms wrapped around me as though he's never going to let me go.

When we part, his eyes gaze into mine. "Have you ever said that to someone before?" he asks quietly.

I shake my head.

He smiles, the biggest, cheesiest grin I've ever seen. "You love me."

I smile back. "I do."

He kisses me again. "I love you, Harlow. I love you so much."

"I love you too."

And I know I'll never love anyone like this again.

Chapter eleven

Past

 The senior class camping trip is coming up. Honestly, I had no idea schools even did this. My old school definitely did not have any type of senior class trip. Normally, I would think this type of event was stupid and probably wouldn't go. However, I'm excited to spend more time with Aiden, even though I have to spend that time with the rest of the senior class too.

 I don't own any camping things, so naturally, my mom asks if she can go shopping with me. What should have taken thirty minutes turned into a four-hour-long shopping spree, and we only spent twenty minutes finding camping equipment.

 I almost end up with a Louis Vuitton sleeping bag, but I convince my mom against it at the last minute. She settles for a black luxury silk sleeping bag instead. I also have to buy hiking shoes and other camping trinkets I never thought to own. It's safe to say I've never considered I'd ever go camping.

My mom drops me off at Aiden's house on our way back. He has the house to himself with his parents out of town again, and he gave Janet the weekend off.

"Aiden?" I call out as I walk through the front door.

"In here!" I hear him yell from somewhere in the back of the house.

I find him in the pool room swimming laps. I sit on one of the lounge chairs and watch as his back muscles are exposed with each stroke. He would look damn good in the ocean.

He swims toward me and stops at the edge of the pool. He drapes his arms over the side, and water spills over.

"Come swim," he says.

"I didn't bring a swimsuit."

Aiden smirks. "You can either run home really quick or take off your clothes. You pick."

I shrug my shoulders. Bra and panties it is. I set down my purse and pull my shirt over my head. I'm wearing a black lace bra that makes my breasts look at least one size bigger. *Good choice, Harlow,* I think as Aiden groans and pushes himself back into the water.

"Maybe this was a bad idea," he mumbles as he resurfaces.

I laugh. His reluctance to have sex makes seducing him all the more fun. I enjoy tempting him and seeing how far he'll let me take it.

I turn around so my backside faces him. I unbutton my jean shorts and slowly push them down my legs. I'm wearing a matching black lace thong, so my entire ass is out as I bend seductively to pull down my pants.

"Fuck," he moans.

I step out of my shorts one foot at a time, still not facing him. I can hear his heavy breathing behind me. I can almost sense the heat of his gaze on me. I smirk to myself, loving the way he reacts to my body.

I turn around and slowly pull the ponytail out of my hair. My long dirty blonde hair falls in waves, draping over my shoulders. I can see his chest moving as he takes quick, shallow breaths. He hasn't taken his eyes off me.

I walk toward him unhurriedly and stop at the edge of the pool. His hands find my waist as I bend down, and he pulls me into the water. We're in the deep end, and Aiden has several inches on me, so he doesn't let go as I wrap my legs around him.

Our faces are so close our noses are practically touching, and my hair hovers around us like a curtain shield. I feel his hands as they grip my ass. I know what my striptease has done to him as I can feel him pressing between my legs. Aiden backs himself against the side of the pool and leans his head back. I've had enough teasing him for one night because now I've gotten myself worked up too, and I know there's no way he'd let our first time be in the pool. But that doesn't mean we can't do other stuff.

I brush my lips against his, and he kisses me hard in response. His hands squeeze my ass tighter and pull me in as if there were any possible way I could get closer. Our mouths never part, we never gasp for breath. He continues to move my body against his, creating enough friction to know how this will end. My breathing becomes heavier as our kisses grow more desperate. I'm moving against him faster and with more force. I feel him pressing himself into me as he continues to pull me in. I can feel myself reaching the edge, so I pull my lips away from his and tuck my head into his neck.

"Harlow," he grunts.

I let out a small whimper to let him know I've heard him. It's about all I can do at this point when I know my body is so close to its release.

"I want to watch you."

I lift my head to see him staring intently at me. The friction becomes too much for me to take, and I quickly reach my climax. I shut my eyes, my head falling back as my entire body trembles in his arms. He never lets me go, and he never stops watching. When I'm brought back from that exhilarating high, he gently kisses my forehead. I open my eyes and see him still looking at me as if I'm the only person that exists on this earth. I love the way he looks at me. I love the way he loves me.

"You're amazing, Harlow Brooks," he whispers.

I kiss his lips and smile. "I love you, Aiden Walton."

Aiden carries me out of the pool, settling both of us on one of the larger lounge chairs until I'm left straddling him. I could kiss this boy for hours and never grow tired of it. I'm wrapped in a towel, lying on the multiperson lounge seat with Aiden, and we continue where we left off in the pool. I move myself over him, his fingers digging into my waist, his eyes locked on me.

I'm already sensitive from my last release, so it doesn't take much before I'm moaning his name as yet another wave of pleasure moves throughout my body. This time, Aiden finishes too. He squeezes my waist tighter, his lips part ever so slightly, and he grunts as he comes.

Aiden leaves for a few minutes to clean himself and change, and when he returns, he has a dry T-shirt for me to throw on over my bra and panties. I thank him, pulling the shirt over my head and inhaling the smell of him. I love wearing his clothes. I love being this close to him.

We make ourselves comfortable on the chair again, and I rest my head on his chest.

"I really enjoyed that striptease," he says.

"There's plenty more where that came from."

He kisses my cheek before I feel his body shift beneath me. I glance at his face, noticing the serious look that has taken over his features.

"I wanted to talk to you about something," he says when he sees that I've sensed his change in demeanor.

"Okay."

"It's been over a month since we've talked about it. We've come a long way, so please don't walk away or shut me out. I want to talk it through this time, the right way."

It doesn't take a genius to figure out that he's talking about California. Though I haven't had the courage to bring it up myself, I have thought a lot about it, and I have something I've been wanting to tell him.

"I got accepted to UCLA last week. I was going to tell you on the camping trip," I say.

His eyes light up. "You applied? So, you're considering going there?"

I smile and kiss his lips. "I didn't just consider it, Aiden. I've already submitted my acceptance letter."

He sits up. "You're going to UCLA?"

I nod. "If that's still where you're going."

He's all smiles.

"God, I love you so much," he says. He gives me several sloppy kisses because he can't stop smiling the entire time. Seeing him this happy made waiting to tell him worth it.

"I love you too," I say in a more serious tone. "I'm sorry that it's taken so long for me to see what you see in us, but thank you for never giving up on me. I trust you with my heart, and I'm done being a bitch about it."

He tucks a strand of hair that's hanging in front of my face behind my ear. "It's been worth every moment, babe. Even the hard ones."

He kisses me again before asking more questions.

"When do you plan to move back to the West Coast?"

"Originally, I was going to be on the first flight out of here the day after graduation. I had plans to stay with my best friend Jolene until I could move into the dorms in the fall. But now, I don't know.

I thought if we were both going then maybe we could talk about it and figure it out together?"

Aiden caresses my cheek with his palm, grinning. "I'd like that."

"Are you going to send in your acceptance letter now?" I ask.

"I already did."

"What?" I ask surprised. "You did? When? Even with how our conversation went the last time?"

"Yes," he says. "I knew that you were going to California no matter what. At least I could be in the same state as you. It sounds kind of stalker-ish now that I think about it. Love makes you do stupid things."

I give him our line. "Heaven help a fool who falls in love."

"This fool fell hard."

We spend the rest of the night laughing and kissing, and I fall more in love with him than I ever thought possible.

Less than a week later, it's time for the senior class camping trip. The trip isn't technically put on by the school but rather the student body president. Basically, it's one long weekend of getting drunk with your classmates in the middle of the woods. A few parents volunteer to chaperone, but from what I'm told, they're always the kind of parents who drink along with the rest of us.

The campground is an hour away from Portlet. Aiden's driving us and a few of his friends, but we're taking my car since it's bigger. Aiden's best friend Max and his girlfriend Jess are sitting in the backseat with Matt. Aiden's other friend Nick drives separately with a few of their other friends.

Jess and I have gotten close over the last two months. She's always around whenever we go out, and I've found that I actually like her. She isn't ditsy or annoying like most girls I've seen at parties. I think it's safe to say that she and I have become friends. Max, Nick, and Matt have grown on me too. They're Aiden's closest friends. I'm surprised by how happy it makes me to see how close they all are. Aiden deserves to have good people in his life.

Aiden showed me last night the giant tent he bought for the two of us to share. He also packed an air mattress with pillows and blankets, so we don't have to sleep in our separate sleeping bags. Knowing I won't be using that stupid silk sleeping bag makes me regret the four-hour shopping frenzy I had to endure with my mother.

Aiden blasts our favorite band and sings completely off tune as we drive the open roads toward the campground. He's smiling so big. Seeing him this happy is adorable. Max, Jess, and Matt have already begun drinking in the backseat.

When we arrive, we park the car by a shade tree. Aiden pitches our tent a few feet away, and the others follow suit. Once we set up the tents, we pregame for the big first night bonfire.

"What're you drinking tonight, Black Sheep?" Aiden asks me as he pulls the cooler out of the trunk.

Jess has been drinking seltzers lately and has gotten me hooked. They're way more flavorful than beer, and I'm convinced I feel the buzz sooner.

"I'll have what Jess is having," I say.

Aiden pulls out a lime seltzer and tosses it my way. I catch it with two hands. "Thanks."

"Let's play truth or drink!" Jess yells.

The guys don't argue. Jess is the kind of girl who always gets what she wants because she never takes no for an answer. It's what I like most about her.

Max gives her an adoring smile and says, "Sure, babe. That sounds fun."

Nick and his carpool show up shortly after us and join the pregame. He's with three girls—Sarah, Natalie, Stacey—and some guy from the football team named Bryce. We all gather around the cooler and prepare for the first drinking game of the night.

"Who wants to go first?" Jess asks.

Bryce volunteers. "I'll go." He turns to Matt. "Who would you rather have sex dreams about, Jess or Harlow?"

"Dude," Aiden says, clearly annoyed.

I roll my eyes. Of course, Bryce picks the two girls who have boyfriends here. I've found that he's the asshole of the group, and I'm not sure why Aiden hangs out with him.

Matt eyes both of us, then looks to his beer. "I'll drink."

"Lame ass," Bryce mumbles.

Matt's turn is next. "Max, how many girls have you slept with?"

He knows this is a safe question. Everyone knows he's only ever been with Jess. Even *I* know that.

"Easy," he says, showing off a crooked smile. "One." He turns and kisses Jess.

I continue to sip on my seltzer as the game continues. I don't understand the purpose of this truth or drink game because we're all drinking no matter what. I guess it just gives us something to do in the meantime. We never played games like this in California. We mostly just got shitfaced and surfed.

"Sarah," Max says. "How much money does Bryce have to pay you for you to make out with him?"

Everyone in the circle laughs.

Sarah answers confidently, "At least $200."

Bryce rolls his eyes. "Yeah, right. We made out last week, and I didn't pay her shit."

Natalie and Stacey gasp.

Sarah throws her empty can at Bryce. "Asshole!" she yells.

After the laughter dies down, I notice Sarah making eyes at me. Great. "Harlow, who was the last guy you slept with?" she says with ease.

My smile fades. I turn to look at Aiden, who also frowns. He knows my answer, but they don't. I don't know what to say, don't know what to do. If I drink, what will they say? I'm sure they'll still question if I've slept with Aiden or not. Maybe they'll think I'm cheating on him. Shit. I need to say something; everyone is staring at me.

"Anthony," I say, surprising both Aiden and myself by spitting out the truth.

Everyone in the circle looks at me shocked, their gaze momentarily locked on my face before turning to Aiden's to see his reaction to this news. I follow up my answer before anyone can assume anything.

"It was before Aiden," I clarify. "We haven't slept together. Yet," I add.

"Not that it's anyone's business," Aiden says, eyeing Sarah, annoyance evident in his tone.

Sarah shoots me an apologetic stare. "I am so sorry. I thought I was giving you a safe question. I'm sorry, girl."

"It's fine."

Now it's my turn. Hopefully my question will ease the awkwardness, or at the very least get the attention off Aiden and me.

"Nick," I say. "What's your guilty pleasure?"

"Watching porn," Bryce coughs out.

Nick ignores him. "I think it's hot as fuck when a girl lets you choke her."

"Jeez, you sadist," Jess scoffs.

Nick shrugs and looks to Aiden. "Aiden, my man," he says. "Have you ever stolen your best friend's girl?"

Aiden's face falls, and I'm alarmed by how guilty he looks. Stealing his best friend's girl? Where did that come from? That doesn't sound like Aiden. Not my Aiden.

"Really, dude?" he asks, his fingers brushing through his hair.

Nick shrugs his shoulders again. Maybe they don't have as solid of a friendship as I thought. Did Aiden really steal someone from Nick? That's the impression I'm getting. Still, that seems so unlike him.

"I'll drink," Aiden says after a few moments.

I frown, wondering what he's keeping from me and why he won't answer the question.

The mood is dead after that. No one wants to break the silence, so I think the game is over.

Jess approaches Nick and is the first to speak, her words coming out in a hushed tone. "That was shitty," she says.

"He steals my girlfriend, and *I'm* the shitty one?" Nick replies, a little too loudly.

"That was three years ago. Get over it," Jess says.

I look next to me to where Aiden was just sitting, but he's no longer there. I look around for him, spotting him walking back to the tent. I get up and follow him.

"Hey," I say. "What was that all about?" I reach for his arm, but he brushes me off.

"Nothing."

"Aiden, come on. Everyone else seems to know what he's talking about. You're not going to tell me?"

He sighs. "I was convinced she was dating the wrong guy. I really liked her at the time, and I let her know. She chose me over Nick. I thought I was in love, but I was wrong. She wasn't the girl for me, but in my defense, she wasn't the girl for him, either."

"Who?" I ask.

He avoids eye contact, releasing a deep breath. "Sarah," he mumbles.

Chapter Twelve

Past

I've always known that Aiden dated other girls. He admitted that he's had his heart broken a few times, and for that to happen, he's had to have loved other girls. Apparently, Sarah is one of them. We've hung out with her almost every weekend since we started dating, and I had no clue. How did I not know? I can't help but wonder how many of the other girls I've met have dated Aiden. How many of them has he loved?

I leave Aiden in the tent alone. I don't know how to feel or what to say about what he told me, so I walk away.

Typical Harlow.

I'm drinking by myself at the bonfire after grabbing an entire case of seltzers so I wouldn't have to keep going back to the cooler by everyone else. Aiden didn't follow me. He hasn't even stepped foot near the bonfire. Truth is, I don't know if he'll come at all. He was so excited for this camping trip, and I feel bad that it's starting this way, but I need time to process what I found out and accept that one of the girls Aiden fell in love with is someone we've hung out with so often. I don't want to say something to him that I might regret because my instincts are telling me to run right now. It hurts that he kept something like this from me, that I had to find out from a stupid drinking game. And come to find out, not only did Aiden fall in love with Sarah, but he also did so by taking her away from one of his best friends.

I continue to drink alone, sitting on a stump near the fire. Jess has checked on me quite a few times, but nothing she can say will make me feel better. There isn't anything anyone can say. I know Aiden and I will have to talk this out when the time is right, but that time is not now. I just want to be alone.

I catch Sarah's glance in my direction, and I worry that she's going to try and talk to me. If she knows what's good for her, she won't. Not right now.

I can't help but wonder if she still loves Aiden. I can't imagine how someone could stop loving him.

I notice Nick walking in my direction. I wouldn't mind the company any other day, but he's the last person I want to talk to right now. Second to Sarah.

"You okay?" he asks, sounding surprisingly sincere for what he just did.

I shrug my shoulders. "That was a pretty shitty thing for you to bring up," I say.

"Did you already know about that?"

I shake my head.

"I see," he says, digging his shoe into the dirt. "Sorry. I guess I never got over it."

"What happened?" I dare ask.

Nick sighs. "Sarah and I started dating the summer before high school. Aiden and I have always been best friends, since first grade. Anyway, we started dating, and after a few months, I noticed Aiden always asking about her. Like if she was going to hang out with us, or if she'd be joining us on the lake that day. Out of nowhere, he had a lot of interest in my girlfriend. I didn't question it because he was my best friend, and she was a lot of fun to be around. Eventually, she started acting different toward me. Both of them were suddenly busy all the time, and I wasn't seeing much of either of them. I found out they were hanging out behind my back, and then she dumped me and got together with Aiden."

"What the hell?"

"Aiden and I weren't friends again until a year later, after the two of them broke up. He apologized a bunch of times, but I guess I've never really forgiven him."

"I don't blame you," I say. "Why did they break up?"

"I don't know all the details, but I think she broke up with him."

"Oh."

"If it makes you feel any better, Aiden is crazy about you. Crazier than he ever was about Sarah."

It doesn't make me feel better. I've never felt real jealousy toward anyone before, but I sure as hell feel it now, and it's all directed toward Sarah. How could she be the one to break up with Aiden? Who would ever want to end something with a guy like him? I can't help but wonder if he would still be together with her now if she'd never left him. If he would still love her.

Nick puts his arm around my shoulders. "I know how you feel," he whispers softly.

"Get the fuck away from her," Aiden yells from behind, appearing out of nowhere.

I jump at the booming tone of Aiden's voice. I've never heard him sound so angry. He's fuming, his face beet red. I notice a vein sticking out of his forehead that I've never seen before. He's really mad.

Nick takes his arm off me and stands up. "Chill, bro."

Aiden walks with aggression to where Nick stands, but Nick doesn't back down. He stands up straighter and puffs out his chest. Nick's big, but Aiden is bigger. Aiden would kick his ass if this turned into a fist fight.

"Don't touch her again," Aiden says.

"Are you scared I'm going to steal your girl like you did mine?" Nick bites back.

The next ten seconds somehow move in slow motion. I watch Aiden's fist meet Nick's jaw. I hear Jess yell for Max. Max appears out of nowhere, pulling Aiden back. Matt finds Nick and drags him in the other direction. Nick yells something at Aiden, and Aiden yells back. Before I know it, everyone is gone, and I'm standing alone. I sit back down on my stump as the rest of the senior class wanders around the open field lit up by the giant fire, oblivious to what just happened. I grab another seltzer and chug. Once it's empty, I grab another.

A long while later, I hear footsteps behind me. I try to turn around to see who it is, but my body feels heavy, and I'm scared if I move, I'll fall over.

I recognize Jess's voice when she says, "Come on, Harlow. Let's get you to bed."

I try to speak, but I can't. Words aren't coming out of my mouth, though I think a series of slurs escape at some point. I've lost count of how much I had to drink and am way drunker than I intended to be.

Jess holds onto my hands, helping me stand, but the world around me spins, and when I try to take a step, I realize I can't walk straight. All of my weight is on Jess. Her arm wraps around my back, the other holding the hand hastily thrown over her shoulder. She leads me toward my tent, where Aiden probably is. I know full well that I don't want to see him right now.

"No," I manage to mumble as I fight against Jess's grasp and try to get away.

Ultimately, I'm too weak to get away from her. My struggle seems to get a few people's attention because now, I see three or four bodies in front of me. Or maybe I'm seeing three or four of Jess. I can't tell. I think I just need to take a seat.

I sit down in place, falling ungracefully onto the dirt and grass. Jess doesn't try to fight me or get me to stand back up. Instead, she walks away and returns seconds later with a bottle of water. I hear Max's voice somewhere before it disappears.

The water seems to be helping, and I think I'll be able to stand on my own soon. I wish I was one of those people who threw up when they got too drunk. That would sober me quickly, but I've never gotten sick from alcohol before. I can't tell if that's a blessing or a curse. Right now, it seems like a curse. Who knows how long it's going to take for me to sober up?

Suddenly, the hairs on the back of my neck stand as I hear Aiden's voice, his footsteps approaching.

"Baby, are you okay?" he asks, sounding worried.

I look up and see him for the first time since he punched Nick.

He studies my face before he glances at Jess. "I've never seen her like this before."

"She's okay," I hear Jess say. "She was upset and got drunk. It happens. She'll be fine, Aiden."

Aiden nods and looks at me. "Can you walk?" he asks.

I shake my head no.

He puts one arm under my legs, the other behind my back, and scoops me up. My head falls against his chest as he walks us to the tent. I hear the sound of a zipper before he sets me down on the air mattress. He takes off my shoes and pulls off my jacket. I hear him shuffling around in one of our duffle bags for a few seconds before he returns to my side. He unbuttons my shirt and takes off my bra. I know I'm drunk, but I'm fully aware that Aiden has never seen me fully naked. Right now, he's getting a full view of my bare breasts.

He slides one of his T-shirts that I packed over my head, unbuttoning my jeans next, and sliding them off. He lifts the covers to pull them over me. I hear more shuffling before I feel him get into bed next to me. He wraps both of his arms around my small frame and pulls me in close to him. I close my eyes because it makes everything stop spinning.

He presses his mouth to my ear. "I am so sorry, Harlow. This is my fault. I am so sorry," he whispers.

It's the last thing I hear before I fall asleep.

When I wake up the next morning, Aiden and I are in the same position we fell asleep in. I turn to the side, searching for my phone to see what time it is, but instead grabbing my head and realizing that I have a pounding headache. I move away from Aiden and turn over to find some Advil. There's a bottle of Tylenol lying next to the air mattress with a water bottle. Did Aiden put that there? I take two and chug the water.

I hear Aiden scuffle behind me. I turn over and see that he's waking up. When his sleepy eyes open a little and he sees that I'm awake, he sits up.

"Harlow," he says, wiping the sleep from his eyes.

Every damn time he says my name, I think my heart stops. Will I ever get used to that?

"Yeah?" I manage, my eyes focused on the water bottle in my hand.

"Look at me," he says.

I do and see that his eyes are full of sadness.

"I'm sorry about last night. I shouldn't have left you alone. I should have gone after you so we could talk about it."

"I don't want to talk about it," I tell him.

"We need to, babe."

He reaches his arm out and pulls me back to him so we're lying in the same position we fell asleep in. He kisses the top of my head.

"I was a shitty friend to Nick back then. I regret what I did, but I knew he was messing around with other girls while he was dating Sarah. She started coming around more when Nick would hang out with us, and I thought she was cool. She was showing interest in me around the same time I started to feel things toward her. I convinced myself that what I was doing was okay because I would treat her better than Nick ever did. It still wasn't okay, Harlow, and I know that now. I knew it then, but it still took me time to admit that to Nick."

Nick conveniently left out the part where he'd cheated on Sarah when he told me his version of things. Still, it doesn't make what Aiden did okay.

"She broke up with you," I say, not as a question because I already know the answer.

He lays his head on mine. "Yes."

"She's the one who broke your heart?"

He sighs. "Yes."

"You were in love with her."

"I thought I was, but what I feel for you, it's so much stronger than any feelings I ever had for her. I'm in love with you, Harlow. The two don't even compare. It's not even close."

"How do you know? She broke up with you. It could have gotten there. Why are you convinced that we're so special?"

He moves his head away from mine and forces me to look at him.

"I dated her for almost a year. You and I have been together for two months, and I felt more for you in the first day than I did the entire time I dated her. I could never love her the way I love you. Yes, she broke my heart at the time, but it wouldn't even compare to what you could do to it. I probably haven't even experienced real heartbreak, Harlow, because I've never given myself to somebody like I've given myself to you. That's how I know we are special."

He doesn't let me look away as he waits for my response, but I'm not sure I have one.

"I'm jealous," I finally admit.

He cocks his head. "Of what?"

"That she broke your heart. That you loved her enough to get your heart broken in the first place. And that you might still be together with her if she hadn't broken up with you."

He kisses me softly, his lips staying on mine for a few seconds. "Even if she hadn't, I would have left her the second I met you."

He kisses me again. After a few minutes, I ask him something that's been bugging me.

"Why did you punch Nick?"

"He had his arm around you," he says as though it's obvious. "When I saw the two of you together, it felt like my heart had been ripped out of my chest."

"It wasn't like that."

"But that's what it looked like."

"I'm sorry."

He shakes his head. "Don't be sorry. It was my fault. I handled everything wrong, and I'm sorry for that."

"I shouldn't have had so much to drink. My head is throbbing."

Aiden nods. "I've never seen you that drunk. Not even after the first time you came to my house for that party."

"I was pretty drunk that night."

"Yeah, I know. You passed out on my couch."

"What? No, I didn't. I woke up in my bed."

"I carried you home," he says, surprising me.

"You did? Why didn't you tell me? What did Amanda say?"

"I couldn't tell you because you wouldn't speak to me then. And I didn't care what she had to say. I knew I needed to get you home so that was my only priority."

"Did you kiss her in front of me on purpose in the hallways?"

Aiden's head falls back on the pillow. "Sometimes, yeah. Sometimes I kissed her because she was my girlfriend, and it's what I was supposed to do, but I found myself being way more affectionate when you could see. I wanted to know your reaction, to see if you were jealous."

"I hated it."

Aiden tucks a loose strand of hair behind my ear. "I know, baby. I'm sorry I did that, too."

"Is there anyone else I should know about?" I whisper, afraid for the answer.

"You want to know who else I've dated?" he asks.

"I want to know if I know anyone else you've dated," I correct him. "Like Natalie or Stacey. Please don't say Jess."

"No, baby. None of them. And even if I did, none of them come close to you."

"Okay."

I close my eyes, and we lay in silence as Aiden strokes my arm with his fingers, tiny goose bumps emerging.

"You saw me naked last night," I say, remembering how he undressed me before we fell asleep.

His fingers continue to caress my arm. "I wasn't concentrating on that, babe. I just wanted to get you comfortable so you could sleep. And you weren't *completely* naked."

"You saw my boobs."

He smiles. "You have great boobs."

I bury my head in his chest, embarrassed that I was so drunk he had to undress me.

"I love you, Harlow," he whispers into my hair.

"I love you more."

Chapter Thirteen

Past

 The following week is spring break and so happens to also be my birthday. My parents take me on vacation every year to celebrate during the week I have off school. This year, my mother has chosen Bali. My birthday has always been an excuse for her to travel somewhere exotic. It's nothing to her but a reminder of what her body went through and how hard she worked to make sure she fit back into a size two. It has absolutely nothing to do with celebrating another year of my life.

 After school, I head straight to my room to pack. Our first flight leaves tomorrow morning. Aiden knows about the trip, but I haven't told him that my birthday is in a few days. Either way, we won't be able to spend it together. I've never celebrated my birthday with my friends, though I shouldn't complain because I've spent it in a different country every year. I guess you never really know what you're missing if you don't have it. I've never had someone like Aiden. He'd probably make my birthday special, but now I won't have the chance to find out.

I glance at the time. Aiden should be here any minute. I pull my Bottega Veneta luggage from the closet and cram every swimsuit and cover-up I own inside. Aiden walks in just as I start filling my second bag.

"Shit, how long are you going to be gone for again?" he asks, staring at my six-piece luggage set.

I look at all the bags lying around my floor. "Only a week," I say. "I guess I could limit it to three bags."

He laughs. "Hey, you should model some of your swimsuits for me," he says, wrapping his arms around me and kissing me. "You know, since I can't be there to check you out myself."

I see this as another opportunity to test his willpower. I smirk. "Gladly."

I pull out one of the swimsuits from my bag. "Stay here," I say.

I close the closet door behind me as I stare at the swimsuit I chose. It's the most revealing one I own.

The bikini is black with small triangles that hardly cover my C-cup breasts, tying in the back with a small string. The bottoms crisscross over my pubic bone and wrap around the back. It's a thong bikini that reveals my entire ass. I check myself out in the mirror, grinning as I think to myself what Aiden will think when he sees it.

I crack open the closet door. "You ready?"

"Hell yeah."

I step out, doing a full spin, and stop directly in front of Aiden. His lips part as his eyes wander the length of my body, pausing in the places the bikini barely covers.

"Do you like what you see?" I coo.

He nods, reaching one hand out, and pulling me closer until I'm standing between his legs. His hands grip my bare ass as his lips place a soft kiss on my stomach.

"This one is not going back in your suitcase," he whispers against my core.

"Why is that?" I ask.

He glances down and back up my body, looking at the small layer of fabric barely covering me.

"For my eyes only," he says, his voice husky.

"But I might need to wear it for the wet T-shirt contest," I joke.

His forehead falls to my stomach as he shakes his head.

"What's wrong, Aiden?" I'm tormenting him, I know it.

"I'm a guy, Harlow. Do you know what seeing you in this kind of swimsuit does to me?"

"Nope."

He takes a deep breath and lies back on the bed, his hands covering his face. I use this as my opportunity to climb on top of him. There's no way he'll resist me now. I've waited long enough to have sex with my boyfriend. I want something to remember him by this week, something to look back on.

I move his hands away from his face, holding them above his head as I kiss his neck. I soon find his lips, and they part for me immediately. He frees his hands, and they fall to my waist, gripping me tightly.

"Harlow," Aiden mumbles between breaths.

I ignore him and try to take his shirt off. His hands quickly find my wrists to stop me.

"Harlow, no."

I sit up, still straddling him. "Why, Aiden? Why not now?"

"You know I want it to be more special than this. You know that. What you're doing is working. Believe me, it's working. But this isn't how our first time should be. The wait will be worth it, I promise."

Annoyed, I get off him and stand beside the bed. I've never wanted someone so bad in my life. His game of playing hard to get pisses me off. It's cute that he wants our first time to be special, but it's just sex. It'll feel just as great now as it will whenever he finally decides to fuck me.

I've got one move left before I've laid it all out there. I reach behind my back and pull at the tiny strings holding up my top.

He watches me closely. "Harlow, please don't."

I don't listen. My top comes untied, and I drop it to the floor. My breasts are completely bare and exposed to him, but he's not looking at them. His eyes fix on mine.

"Aiden, look at me."

"I am, baby," he says, his voice sounding hoarse. His eyes never leave mine.

I wrap my fingers around either side of my bikini bottoms and slowly push them down until they're wrapped around my ankles, and I'm left standing in front of him, completely nude.

Aiden squeezes his eyes shut.

"Aiden, look at me," I say again.

His eyes slowly flutter open. I can see them struggling to stay fixed on my face. I get back on the bed and straddle him.

"Can you still say no to me?" I ask, my voice barely a whisper.

He rests his hands on my waist, and I notice the fast pace of his chest as he breathes. He still hasn't looked away from my face.

"Why are you doing this?" he asks, his voice strained.

"I don't want to wait any longer."

"*Why*, Harlow?" His expression is pained.

"I want you."

"You already have me."

"No. I want you in the ways I haven't had you yet," I clarify. "You slept with your other girlfriends. Why won't you sleep with me?"

Tears sting at my eyes, and I will them away quickly. I've never cried in front of anyone, and I don't plan on starting now. But I'm so frustrated. I've never been more vulnerable in a situation. I feel like I'm begging my boyfriend to have sex with me, which I guess I am.

Before I can comprehend what's happening, Aiden flips me over, and I'm left lying flat on my back with his broad body hovering over me. For the first time, his eyes stray from my face. He looks down, checking out my body slowly. *Finally.*

His eyes wander my curves when he says, "If I have sex with you right now, it's going to be because you performed a striptease that got me horny as fuck. It's not going to be because we're in a special moment together that you'll look back on and remember forever. It's not going to be because we're so wrapped up in being in love that we want to be tangled in every part of each other. It's going to be because you want me to fuck you like I fucked my ex-girlfriends."

"I don't want you to fuck me like you fucked your ex-girlfriends."

He sighs. "Then can we please wait, Harlow?" he begs.

I roll out from underneath him and walk to my closet, shutting the door behind me before dressing myself. I want every part of my body covered after that.

Seconds later, Aiden knocks on the closet door.

"What?"

"Can I come in?" he asks softly.

"Sure."

He opens the door and looks at me with those damn blue eyes, eyebrows furrowed. "Babe," he starts.

I hold up my hand. "Just stop, Aiden. I've heard enough."

He nods and takes a seat next to me on the cushion.

"I didn't want our last night together before you leave to be like this," he says.

And neither do I. We have spent every single day together since we started dating. It's the first time we're going to be apart, and instead of having something amazing to remember him by for the next week, I have this to look back on.

"Yeah. Me neither."

"What can I do to make it better?"

I shrug, feeling stubborn and pissed off. "I think what's done is done."

Aiden places his hand on my knee. "I love you, Harlow."

I've let my ego get the best of me. I don't respond.

"Do you want me to leave?" he finally asks.

"Yes."

Aiden hesitates for a few moments before he stands up. "I'll see you when you get back, okay?"

He kisses me on the forehead and walks out.

Chapter fourteen

Past

    Today is my eighteenth birthday. Now I can get a tattoo without a parent's permission, vote, enlist in the military, play the lotto, and hell, I can even sue someone if I feel like it. Too bad all I can think about is that I still can't get my boyfriend to sleep with me. Just to spite him, I packed the black bikini he forbade, and I'm flaunting it for my big day.

    There are a lot of cute boys staying at this resort that I couldn't help but notice—spring breakers looking for a no-strings-attached one-night stand. My swimsuit provokes them, as they've been sending drinks my way all morning. But the truth is, I have no desire to sleep with anyone else, no desire to flirt even. I'll have to swallow my pride and wait patiently for Aiden to find the perfect moment for us so he can finally let go.

After another round of tequila shots, courtesy of the rowdy bunch across the pool, I feel a buzz and decide to send Aiden a selfie. I dip myself in the water so that my chest glistens from the reflection of the sun. I hold my camera up to get the best angle, show him what he's missing, and show him what bikini I'm in.

Me: Your girlfriend misses you.

I press send with the attached photo. He responds almost immediately.

Aiden: Not as much as I miss her. I thought I told you to leave that bikini at home?

Me: It's my birthday. I don't have to listen to you.

Aiden: What?

He sends another text before I can respond.

Aiden: Is today actually your birthday, Harlow?

Shit. It slipped.

My phone rings. Aiden's name flashes brightly across the screen with a picture of him smiling at the camera from inside our tent on the camping trip.

I answer. "Hello?"

"Harlow, is today really your birthday?"

"Yes."

He exhales. "Why the hell didn't you tell me? Did you not think I would want to be with you on your birthday? Or that I might want to celebrate with you?" he asks, sounding both irritated and desperate.

"I was going to be on vacation whether you knew it was my birthday or not."

"That doesn't make any sense. Why wouldn't you tell me?"

"I don't know."

"Shit, Harlow. I feel like an asshole."

"Why?" I ask.

Why the hell would he feel like the asshole for not knowing my birthday? I'm starting to feel like an asshole for not telling him. I didn't think it would matter this much.

"I should have asked when your birthday was. It should have come up in conversation at some point."

There's silence on the line as I don't know what to say.

"Harlow, I hate this."

"I'm sorry."

"Fuck!" he yells. "I want to be with you today. This is a special day, and I'm not even in the same damn country as you."

"It's not a big deal, Aiden. I'm out of town on my birthday every year."

"It's a big deal to me, babe." I can hear the frustration in his tone.

"I'll be home in a few days," I say. "We can celebrate then if you want."

"Yeah. Okay."

After he wishes me a happy birthday, I hang up. My buzz is long since gone, and I don't end up hearing from him the rest of the night. I hardly hear from him the rest of the trip.

It takes nearly an entire day to get back to Portlet from Bali at the end of the week. I've been home now for two hours and still haven't heard from Aiden. He knew what time I'd be home, and I thought we had plans to see each other once I got back. Finally, I decide to text him.

Me: Hey. I'm home.

Aiden: Welcome back. How were the flights?

Me: Long. Where are you?

Aiden: At Matt's.

Me: Will you be home soon?

Aiden: Not sure.

Oh. I don't know how to feel right now. For some reason, I thought Aiden would be on my doorstep waiting for me to get back. I thought that he'd miss me like I've missed him and would want to see me right away. I know that he was upset after missing my birthday, but I'm home now, and if it mattered to him that much, wouldn't he be here now trying to celebrate?

I switch my phone to silent, not wanting to dwell on the fact that I haven't seen my boyfriend in over a week, and he doesn't seem to be in any hurry to rectify that. If he wants to see me then he will make the effort. I know how girls are, and I refuse to be one that gets upset that her boyfriend isn't paying enough attention to her.

I spend the rest of the night catching up on lost sleep. When I wake up, I check my phone. There's an empty feeling in the pit of my stomach when I see that Aiden didn't call or send any texts.

At this point, I don't expect him to pick me up for school, so I grab my keys and head out the door. But as I do so, his car pulls into my driveway. I stand still for a few seconds, confused as to what's going on. We've hardly spoken since my birthday, and he bailed on the plans I thought we had yesterday. Still, I put on my brave face, not wanting him to see how hurt I actually feel as I walk toward his car and get in. I notice right away that he doesn't get out to open the door for me like he normally does. That's yet another sign that something is wrong.

"Hi," I say.

"Hi."

I don't feel like playing our typical game of who will address the issue first, so I volunteer.

I keep my tone even when I say, "I thought you would have wanted to see me yesterday."

"Did you want to see me?" he asks.

"Yes, obviously."

"Who was it obvious to, Harlow?"

What? Of course, I wanted to see him. How was that not obvious to him? This was the longest we've been apart, and we were both counting down the days until I got back. He was excited for me to come home, until he wasn't anymore. Maybe something happened while I was gone. Maybe this isn't just about missing my birthday.

"Did something happen this week that I should know about?" I ask hesitantly.

His gaze turns to me for a quick second before he focuses back on the road. For the few seconds he met my gaze, I noticed something off in his eyes. What was that about?

"I had to drive Amanda home from a party on Wednesday," he answers.

Wednesday. Wednesday was my birthday. We barely spoke after that, and I thought it was because he was mad at me. Maybe I got this all wrong. Maybe something happened with Amanda. Did she finally convince him to get back together with her? Is that what's happening? Is he going to break up with me?

"Is that why you didn't want to see me yesterday? Is something going on with her again?"

His eyebrows furrow. "Seriously?"

I give him a look to let him know just how serious I am.

"No, Harlow. Nothing is going on with her. And I *did* want to see you yesterday, but honestly, I'm pretty pissed at you."

"What did I do?"

"How could you not tell me that your birthday was last week?"

So, this whole thing *has* been about my birthday.

"I already apologized for that, Aiden."

He shakes his head slightly. Clearly, he didn't accept my apology.

"Things were good before you left, then you basically begged me to fuck you. You've been so focused on us sleeping together that you obviously forgot to tell me something that was super fucking important, like the fact that you were turning eighteen in a few days. I don't know how I can be in a relationship with someone who doesn't want to share the special moments in life with me."

He doesn't know how he can be in a relationship with someone who doesn't want to share the special moments in life with him? Is he serious? This is the whole reason I didn't want to have a boyfriend in the first place. I'm not the serious relationship type. I'm the sleep with me and move on a few months later type. Aiden made me believe that maybe I could be both. He made me believe that I could be good enough for him, that we could figure this out. But I'm not what he wants anymore.

I've opened myself to the possibility of forever with him. I've committed myself to a college for him. I started dating him after I was clear about not wanting any ties to this town, to this state, after I said I would never stay. And I've tried to be patient while waiting to sleep with him, but I will never beg anyone to stay with me, not even Aiden. If he doesn't want me, fine. If he doesn't know how he can date me, then he shouldn't. I don't need him.

"Then don't be. Break up with me," I hiss.

"Harlow, stop. That's not what I meant, and you know it."

"No, Aiden, I don't. I never even wanted a boyfriend. I didn't want to make friends here. Six months. Six months for me to finish school and get the hell out of Portlet. I never asked for you. I never asked for this. If you don't know how to be in a relationship with someone like me, then don't fucking be in one."

Aiden swerves suddenly, pulling the car over on the side of the road. We aren't at school yet, so I don't know why he's stopping. He puts the car in park and turns to face me, grabbing my hands and squeezing them tightly. I'm fuming, almost on the verge of tears because I'm so mad, but the second I look over at his pleading eyes, I feel a sense of calm.

"Please stop," he says softly, his thumb stroking my palm.

I nod, staying quiet. I take deep breaths as I try to relax.

"I was hurt," he says. "I've given myself to you, Harlow. You have all the power in the world to hurt me and you unintentionally did. I can't blame you for that, but that doesn't mean I don't get to be upset. I sometimes feel like I'm setting myself up for failure with you. I don't want us to fail, Harlow. Our love may be rocky, but it's still love. The most real love I've ever felt. I want to give you everything, but I want you to give me everything in return. I want to spend birthdays, holidays, anniversaries, whatever it may be, I want to spend them with you."

He takes a breath before continuing.

"I was hoping you would ask me to come home last night. I needed to feel like you wanted to see me as much as I wanted to see you. That wasn't fair of me. I can't expect you to read my mind, and I'm sorry. It's been a hard fucking week without you, and Wednesday was hell. The only place I wanted to be was wherever you were, and instead, I was at another stupid fucking party. Amanda showed up again and caused a scene, but for the first time since you and I started dating, she made me feel something. I don't care for her like that, and I don't want to be with her, but she made me *feel* loved. She loves me the same way I love you. But, baby, I need *you* to love me like that. Birthdays, holidays, anniversaries; I need that from you. Do you think you can give that to me, Harlow?"

Tears. Real actual fucking tears sting at my eyes. I nod my head as Aiden takes his thumb and wipes away the tears as they fall.

A few minutes go by before he speaks again. "Can I take you somewhere?"

"What about school?" I ask, sniffling. I can't stop crying, and I wonder when I became so damn emotional.

"Let's play hooky. I want to show you something."

Chapter fifteen

Past

Aiden pulls into a parking spot in front of Oliver's, a small café in downtown Portlet. I recognize the place immediately. My mom and dad brought me here when we first moved to town.

"I've been here before," I tell Aiden.

"I know."

Confused, I open my mouth to say something, but he cuts me off before I can get a word out.

"Come on. Let's go inside."

He steps out, walking around the car to open the door for me. He stretches out his hand, offering it for me to take. It's a small gesture, one of the many that I've come to love.

We walk inside and order breakfast at the small counter. Aiden orders French toast with coffee, and I decide on avocado toast and chai tea. When our order is ready, Aiden takes the tray of food and leads me to a table near the window.

"I thought you wanted to show me something?" I ask.

"I do," he says. "I was sitting in this exact spot on New Year's Day. I had a New Year's Eve party the night before and was hungover as shit. It was one of the worst nights of my life."

"Why?" I ask.

"I know you might not want to hear this, and I've argued with myself about telling you any of it, but I want you to know. It was a shitty night because of something that happened with Amanda. She had brought up graduation and college that night at the party. She's set on going to New York and asked if I would go with her."

I frown, wondering what could be so bad that he didn't want to tell me. "What did you say?"

"I told her that I wanted to stay here and work for my dad."

"I thought you didn't want to work for your dad's company?"

"I don't," he says firmly. "But I didn't want to go to New York with her even more, so I lied."

"Oh."

He nods. "If Amanda is anything, it's determined. When she wants something, she sets her mind to it, and she doesn't stop until she gets it."

"I've noticed," I say, thinking back to how many times she's tried begging for Aiden to come back.

"I had already decided that I didn't want to be with her anymore, whether she left for New York or not. She didn't do anything wrong, but I couldn't get myself to feel for her the way she felt for me. I tried time and time again to break things off with her, but she was so insistent on making it work. Again, nothing is wrong with her. Anyone would be lucky to date her. She's an amazing girl, and she's obviously beautiful."

I roll my eyes at that remark.

"I did something stupid that night," he continues. "I've never cheated on anyone before, Harlow. I meant what I said the night I told you that isn't me, that I'm not a cheater. But I just felt so stuck. I drank enough that night to convince myself that if I hooked up with someone else, that would be the last straw, and she would finally leave me."

"You cheated on her so she would break up with you?"

He nods. "I drank too much and picked some random girl at the party. I don't even remember her name, but I slept with her. I was going to tell Amanda afterward, but she walked in on us still half naked."

"Oh, my God."

"It was bad. She was a mess." He shakes his head, probably thinking back to that night. "I felt like such a shitty person. She was so upset; she couldn't stop crying. I felt so bad for her, Harlow. I didn't know what to do, so I convinced her it was a drunken mistake. A one-time thing. That I'd never do it again. The only way I could get her to stop crying was if I agreed to stay with her, to work things out. My plan completely backfired."

"I still don't understand what that has to do with this café," I say.

"Obviously, Amanda and I didn't break up. It was the first day of the new year. You know the saying; *New year, new me*. Well, I told myself that staying with Amanda was what was best. She is a really good person, and if I stayed with her, I would probably end up marrying her one day. We would be happy enough. Life would be good enough. It wouldn't be great, but it would be good. And maybe I didn't deserve that once-in-a-lifetime love that I had been waiting for. I definitely didn't think I deserved it after what I did to her."

He sighs, taking a sip of his coffee.

"I dropped Amanda off at home the next morning after I was up all night apologizing and wiping away her tears. I walked into this coffee shop afterward, ready to start the year off fresh, having convinced myself that I would make this thing with Amanda work, that I would do anything to make her happy after what I had put her through. You can't date someone for a year and not care about their feelings. I was determined. I ordered this exact meal and sat at this exact table trying to come to terms with the mistakes I made and what I needed to do to right my wrongs. I was certain that I would be able to give her what she wanted. And then guess what happened?"

"What?"

"You see that table over there?" He lifts his chin, nodding his head to a small table pushed against the wall under framed black-and-white pictures of Oliver's history.

"Yes."

"Then I saw *you* sitting right over there."

I look over at the table again, thinking back to that morning, trying to remember if I saw Aiden sitting here alone. It was New Year's Day, but I can't remember ever seeing him, can't remember anything other than feeling miserable about being here in the first place.

"When I saw you, all I could think about was how beautiful you were. The most beautiful girl I had ever laid eyes on. Everything about you was different, I could just tell. The way you dressed, the way you did your hair, the way you carried yourself. You were captivating, Harlow. In that instant, I knew I couldn't commit myself to Amanda. That was all it took. Looking at you. Seeing the way you moved around with confidence, you were unlike anyone I had ever seen before. I *needed* to know you. I hardly ate my breakfast that morning because I was too busy staring at you.

"When you left, I almost followed you, but you were with your parents, and I needed to break up with Amanda for good before I could pursue someone else. I wasn't going to make that same mistake twice. I came back to this café every day for a week after that hoping to run into you again, and I stopped the day you walked into my first period class. I had almost lost hope of ever seeing you again. But there you were, introducing yourself in front of the entire class. *Harlow.* The new girl from California. The beautiful girl I couldn't take my eyes off at the café. The one I hadn't been able to stop thinking about. Right away, I knew I was done for. I knew Amanda and I were over.

"Then that same day, you showed up at my house for dinner, as if fate had a funny way of playing tricks on me. I went to that damn café every day for a week hoping to see you when you were right next door the entire time. You were reluctant to pay me any attention at first, so I tried to work things out with Amanda. But still, I couldn't stop thinking about you. I knew I had to break up with her and not take no for an answer, even if you didn't want anything to do with me. And that's what I did. I have wanted to know every part of you, Harlow. The good, the bad, the bitchy, everything from the first moment I laid eyes on you.

"I've fallen in love with you in everything that you are. I love who you make me, even when you make me furious, even when you drive me crazy. But you're worth being mad over. I care enough to be hurt when you don't tell me when your birthday is. I care enough to want the first time I make love to you to be something you'll never forget, for it to be special. I've never cared about those things before. I'm so in love with you, Harlow. I never want you to doubt that. I will want you forever. I will *love* you forever."

For the second time today, my eyes fill with tears. I look at him through a blurry fog. I've never cried for anyone. I don't even remember the last time I shed a tear before today. What is this boy doing to me?

Aiden gets out of his chair when he sees that I'm crying again. He kneels beside me, wiping my tears with his thumb.

"I didn't think you could cry so much," he teases, bringing my hand to his lips. He kisses my knuckles, his eyes focused on me.

"I didn't think I could either," I say. "I don't know what's wrong with me."

"You're in love with me."

I nod because he's right. I'm in love with him, and there isn't a damn thing I can do about it.

We spend the rest of the day walking around downtown Portlet, visiting parks, and even checking out one of the museums. In the early afternoon, Aiden and I walk down the path outside of the museum. It leads to a quaint pond where ducks float on the water's surface and kids fish across the way. We take a seat on a nearby bench.

"Did you ever go to any school dances in California?" he asks.

"No. They were never really my scene."

"I figured," he says. "But I would really love to take you to our school's prom."

"Is this your way of asking me?"

He smiles. "Unless you want me to make a big spectacle of it. I could fill your bedroom with rose petals or write 'prom?' in the sand."

I shake my head. "Hell no. Prom-posals are so cheesy."

He laughs. "So, will you go with me?"

I smile. "Yes. I'll go with you to a lame school dance if it'll make you happy."

"Oh, it won't be lame. I can assure you of that." He winks, grinning from ear to ear.

Prom isn't far away. I'll have to find a dress. My mother is going to freak out when she finds out we need to go dress shopping. I'm already dreading the hundreds of dresses she's going to force me to try on.

"My mom is going to be so excited," I say sarcastically.

"That you're going to prom or that she gets to go shopping with you?" he asks.

"Shopping."

Aiden smirks. "I can't wait to see what you choose." He kisses me on the forehead. "Let's get out of here."

Chapter sixteen

Past

I text Aiden that I'm on my way over to his house. I spent most of my Saturday listening to my mom gossip about the other moms she meets for weekly lunches. They're other housewives, likely only married to their men for money. It didn't surprise me when she told me how one of them is having an affair with her plastic surgeon.

Aiden's parents are flying to Costa Rica this weekend, which comes as no surprise to me since they're seemingly out of town every other weekend. He texts me that the door is unlocked.

I walk in, confused as to why all the lights are switched off. I'm used to the bright space, typically lit by the extravagant light fixtures that hang from the cathedral ceilings. I reach for the switch by the door. I hear the flick of the switch followed by loud yelling as the lights turn on.

"Surprise!"

I jump, startled. I've never been so close to having an actual heart attack in my eighteen years of life. My heart beats a million miles per minute as my eyes search frantically for Aiden. At last, I spot him stepping through the crowd of people. He's grinning from ear to ear when he reaches out for me, pulling me in.

"Happy Birthday, Black Sheep," he says as he kisses my forehead.

I place my hand to my chest. "I think my heart stopped."

He laughs and drags me through the crowd of people.

Jess appears out of nowhere, handing me a drink before wrapping her arms around me, hugging me tight. "I can't believe you didn't tell us it was your birthday!"

I shrug. "It never got brought up."

"You're a better girl than me. I have to remind Max weeks before just to make sure I get a present. I'm that petty."

We laugh. "Let's go get blow jobs," she says.

It takes me a few seconds to register her words. Did I hear that right? *"What?"*

"It's a shot. Come on!"

She pulls me away from Aiden and toward the pool room with the makeshift bar. Some vodka chocolate concoction is made and poured into a shot glass topped with whipped cream. It's called a blow job shot because we have to drink it by placing our lips around the rim of a shot glass, tilting it up, and downing the entire shot using nothing other than our mouths. We both put our hands behind our backs and carefully place our mouths over the rim of the shot glass. I tilt my head back until the entire shot goes down, surprised by how tasty it is. Jess follows suit.

"Hell, yeah, babe. All that practice has finally paid off!" I hear Max say.

Jess pushes herself into him as she laughs hysterically. I think she's drunk already. I have some catching up to do.

Aiden joins us, placing his hand on my lower back as he talks to some of the guys. I love how he always makes sure his attention is on me, even when he's in conversation with someone else. He's always touching me in some way, even in public. If anyone else would have done that to me in the past, I would've run for the hills. Aiden is kicking the bitch right out of me and turning me soft.

Minutes later, after the guys walk away, he turns his full attention back to me. "I have a present for you," he says.

"A present? Like a birthday present? Isn't a surprise party enough?"

"No."

He leads me upstairs to his bedroom where it's quiet. He walks into his closet and comes out holding a small box.

"Open it," he says, handing it to me.

I take the silver wrapped box out of his hands. I untie the ribbon and lift the lid.

"Concert tickets?" I ask, holding the two tickets in my hands.

He smiles and nods. "To see the Lumineers. They play at the Hollywood Bowl in July."

My eyes grow wide. "The Hollywood Bowl?" I repeat. "The one in Los Angeles?"

He puts his lips on mine. "Yes," he whispers. "That's the one."

I didn't think this night could get any better. My dream concert at my dream venue with my dream guy.

"You're amazing, Aiden. Thank you so much. This is the best gift I've ever gotten." I cling to the tickets tightly.

"You're welcome, babe."

I don't want to go back downstairs. Right now, I just want to savor this moment with him a little longer.

"Can we stay up here for a few minutes? I didn't know I could love you more than I already did, and I need some time to come to terms with that before I start to socialize again."

Aiden smirks. "It's your party. We can do whatever you want."

I grin. "*Whatever* I want?"

"Careful what you wish for," he warns.

"I just want you to hold me for a few minutes," I surprise us both by saying.

He wraps his arms around me, and I bury my head into his chest. He rests his chin on my head and strokes my back with one of his hands.

"Harlow," he says.

I squeeze my eyes shut, the fluttering in my chest multiplying. "You know I can't handle it when you say my name like that."

He ignores me and says it again. "Harlow."

"Yeah?"

"I'm going to marry you one day," he says with confidence. He places a soft kiss in my hair. I can't see his eyes right now, but I can imagine exactly the way they look. A merging of blues, like the shallow ends of the ocean meeting the deep. Light mixed with dark.

"That would make me really happy," I say softly.

The rest of the night goes by in a blur, almost too quickly. Time is never enough with Aiden; I'm always wanting more. We spend the night dancing, singing, and drinking a lot. I feel lucky to be spending my senior year here with these people, with Aiden, something I never thought I would say a few months ago. If you would have told me I would fall in love in Indiana, I would have told you that you were fucking crazy. But life is so good right now.

For an instant, I consider staying here for the rest of my life. But I'm not ready to commit to that, though I wouldn't rule it out anymore. After college, I would be willing to discuss with Aiden where he'd like to live, and if he says Indiana, then I would pack my bags and be on the next flight out with him. I would go anywhere with him. I *will* go anywhere with him, just like I know he will follow me to the ends of the earth. We're in the deep end, and there's no turning back now, no life jacket to get us back to shore. It's just Aiden and me, keeping each other afloat.

It's almost three in the morning, and Aiden and I are lying in his bed. I can't hide that I've once again gotten drunk, though not nearly as bad as I was on the camping trip. Even still, Aiden had to help me up the stairs and get me undressed for bed. I'm coherent this time and can still form sentences, but walking was hard. Undressing was even harder. I'm in another one of his T-shirts that smell like him, and I never want to take it off.

"Let's get married on the beach," I say, picturing a tan Aiden wearing khakis and a white button-down shirt.

"You'd want to have an actual wedding?" he asks.

"I guess. Wouldn't you?"

"I figured we'd elope. You think prom is stupid. I thought you'd think weddings are worse. It's an expensive prom for adults."

"You're right," I agree. "It *is* an expensive prom for adults. What was I thinking?"

He chuckles. "A beach wedding sounds nice, though."

"Any wedding where I get to marry you sounds nice."

"You're turning soft on me, Harlow," he teases.

"I know. I need to say something bitchy now."

"Go for it."

I think for a minute. "I can't think of anything. Oh, my God! Am I not a bitch anymore? What have you done to me?"

Aiden's laugh gets louder, and he pulls me on top of him. Our stomachs are pressed flat against each other and the tips of our noses touch.

"Please don't leave me, Harlow," he whispers.

"Never," I whisper back.

Chapter seventeen

Past

Jess tags along with my mom and me to dress shop, and I'm thankful for the buffer because without her, my mom would no doubt make me try on the brightest and puffiest dresses and drive me absolutely crazy.

We drive to a small bridal boutique on the outskirts of Portlet. The exterior is lined by floor-to-ceiling windows with wedding gowns of various designs on display. When we walk in, one of the saleswomen greets us. She asks what brings us in, and my mom takes the poor woman to the side to explain the exact type of dress her daughter will be wearing to prom before assigning her the task of finding it. The woman looks afraid. She smiles nervously as she heads to the back. I give Jess a look, telling her 'I told you so' without saying 'I told you so.'

The formal dress section is in the back of the store, hidden by the several mannequins displaying even more elegant wedding gowns. The dresses are sorted by colors on the racks, and I immediately flock to the black section.

"Harlow, you are not wearing black to prom!" my mother says, appearing out of nowhere.

"Why?" I jeer.

"Your mom's right, Harlow. You look so beautiful in colors. Let's find one that shows off that tanned skin of yours."

My mouth parts in shock that Jess agrees with my mom. Maybe she's right. Aiden loved when I wore that blue dress to his house.

"Fine," I agree.

I walk away and eye the racks filled with colors. It's so bright it's almost nauseating. After trying on every single dress my mom had the saleswoman pick out, and hating every single one, I find a soft pink gown tucked away in the corner. It has a deep V-neckline with a cinched waist. The dress flows gracefully to the floor with a slit cut to about mid-length. The dress has gold sequins sprinkled throughout, delicately placed on top of dusty pink tulle. It's the most beautiful dress I've ever seen.

"This is the one," I say with confidence.

Jess turns in my direction and eyes the dress. "Wow! Aiden is going to *love* that!"

My mom walks over and takes the dress out of my hand. She eyes it for several minutes before nodding in approval. Of course, she makes me try it on before we can leave. Thankfully, it's as though the dress was made for me.

My friends and I used to make fun of girls that went to dances, the girls that got all dressed up and took awkwardly posed photos in front of a pond in a random neighborhood. I've never wanted to even attend a school dance, much less having to buy a couple hundred-dollar dress so that I can dry hump my date in the school's gymnasium. Well, look at me now. I'm the girl I used to make fun of.

Aiden rents a limousine for us to take to the dance. Liberty's prom is held at a local convention center, much classier than a school's gymnasium. Apparently, they serve dinner in the ballroom before everyone moves to the dance floor. Prom is already a step up from the sweaty dances I had imagined.

I see the limo pull onto our street through the front window. Aiden steps out and walks toward my door before ringing the doorbell.

I laugh quietly to myself. He's never rung my doorbell before.

"Mom! Dad! Aiden's here!" I yell.

They both shuffle into the foyer promptly.

"Harlow, you look like a woman!" my mom exclaims.

"You're stunning, sweetie," my dad says with kind eyes.

I open the door, losing my breath as I take in Aiden standing in front of me, all six foot two of him. I didn't know it was possible for him to be better looking, but a tuxedo suits him. He's wearing a dusty pink tie to match my dress, though I don't know how he knew what color I wore. I suspect Jess had something to do with it because it matches perfectly. Aiden's hair is in its perfect mess on top of his head, and he grins from ear to ear, his eyes fixed on me.

"Wow. You look absolutely beautiful, Harlow," he says.

I blush. "You don't look so bad yourself."

My dad waves us over so he can take some pictures. Aiden slips a corsage filled with dusty pink roses and white baby's breath over my wrist. I notice the light blue flower that appears beneath the roses. He even has a matching boutonniere. I'm almost positive *I* was supposed to give him that, but he obviously has everything covered. I thank him for remembering before we head out the door.

We walk with our hands intertwined toward the limousine. The driver opens the door for us, and we slide in. A bottle of champagne rests inside with several champagne flutes. Though neither of us are of age, Aiden pours us both a glass and raises his for a toast.

"Cheers to my having the most beautiful date to prom."

I smile, clinking my glass to his before taking a sip.

Our limo stops in front of Jess's house, where we're meeting up with Jess, Max, Matt, and Natalie, Matt's date. Jess and Max are already outside taking pictures, Jess flaunting a beautiful lilac mermaid dress that shows off her petite figure. Matt and Natalie arrive shortly thereafter.

The six of us pose for pictures in the back of Jess's house. Though this is the part of prom I dreaded most, it doesn't suck so bad when Aiden's the one holding me.

Jess's backyard is beautifully decorated with flowers, a garden her mother no doubt takes pride in, which makes for a nice backdrop. When Aiden's parents arrive, he excuses himself from the group to greet them. I follow behind, not sure what else to do.

"Harlow!" Monica says. "You're a beauty queen!"

I thank her, giving her a hug hello. Aiden's dad gives us an approving head nod. We return to our group and continue with pictures, Aiden's mom requesting a few of just the two of us. After the hundredth picture is taken, Aiden can sense I've had enough.

"Want to sit in the limo until they're done?" he asks, referring to our friends who planned on riding to prom with us.

I give him a look that says, *Yes, please save me!*

He nods and takes my hand, leading me toward the limo after saying goodbye to his parents. Once we're comfortable inside the limo, he pours us another glass of champagne.

"I have a surprise for you later tonight," Aiden says.

"You really like surprises."

"I think you're really going to like this one."

"I like all your surprises."

The rest of the group piles into the limousine a few minutes later. We all sip our champagne while the driver takes us to the dance. When we arrive, a mock red carpet is set up for couples to take pictures on as they enter. Aiden and I wait in line until it's our turn. After even more pictures are taken, we make our way into the ballroom and find a table. The tables are round and seat up to ten, so we can sit together with a few open chairs.

I see Nick walking in with his date. It's Sarah. He fucking brought *Sarah* as his date. After what I found out at the camping trip, I'm surprised he'd even want her as his date.

"Mind if we sit with you?" he asks, staring at me.

I shrug and look to Aiden. He doesn't say anything either. Max jumps in and tells him to have a seat, though we've already made it awkward.

"Didn't expect to see you two here together," Jess remarks, speaking out loud what we're all thinking.

"Sometimes things happen that bring two people back together," Nick says with a smug grin.

Sarah rolls her eyes. "We're here as *friends*."

Bryce and Stacey join the table next. Bryce's eyebrows raise when he sees Sarah, noticing that she came with Nick.

"He had to pay you to come with him, didn't he?" Bryce asks.

Sarah picks up a roll off the table and tosses it at Bryce's head.

We're served dinner shortly after we arrive: baked chicken, pasta, and vegetables. It's decent. I've gotten so used to Rosa's cooking over the last few months that I'm not sure anything else can compare.

Once we've finished eating, we make our way to the dance floor. I've always liked dancing, and we dance a lot at Aiden's parties, but I quickly realize it's not the same way people dance at prom. There are poufy dresses everywhere, and it's hard to get around without stepping on them. Aiden and I try out the dance floor for two songs before he suggests that we get out of here.

I laugh. "You want to leave already? I thought you were excited for prom. You're the one who said it *wouldn't* be lame. You think it's lame, don't you? I told you!"

He shakes his head. "I *am* enjoying prom, and I *don't* think it's lame, but I'm more excited for the after-prom surprise."

I'm excited for Aiden's surprise as well. So we both agree to leave.

After we say our goodbyes, Aiden calls for the limousine. It drops us off at Aiden's house before heading back to the convention center to wait for the rest of our group. Aiden walks right to his car and ushers me in. We're on the freeway in less than five minutes.

"Are you taking me back to the beach?" I ask, recognizing some of the exit signs we pass.

"Something like that."

We drive for what feels like several hours, but I'm not actually sure because I keep dozing off. I wake up as Aiden steers the car onto an uphill gravel road. I look around and see nothing but forest.

"This isn't the part where I find out you're a serial killer and you've come to chop up my body and bury the evidence, is it?"

Aiden laughs. "You have quite the imagination there, Black Sheep."

The road is bumpy, but eventually turns to asphalt. When we reach the top of the hill, I notice a white timbered house tucked away in the woods. It sits beside a lake.

"What is this place?"

"My family's lake house."

He parks in front of the house, and I watch him through the rearview mirror as he opens the trunk and pulls out two duffel bags.

I open my door before he can and look at him curiously. "Did you pack us bags?"

"Yes."

"You went in my closet?"

He looks guilty. "Maybe."

I laugh, following Aiden inside. The moment he opens the door, my eyes are drawn to the perfect view of the lakefront through the floor-to-ceiling windows. The entire back of the house is made up of glass that makes you feel like you are actually on the water. The ranch-style home overlooks the lake with a deck that has steps heading down to the water.

I make my way outside and follow the steps to a path that leads me to a small private beach. The familiar feel of sand beneath my heels fills me with joy. Aiden follows behind, and I feel his hands wrap around my waist. We're still dressed in our clothes from prom. We slip off our shoes and sit near the water's edge.

"Have you ever been skinny-dipping?" I ask.

Aiden's eyes are static on the water ahead. "I can't say that I have."

I stand up. "Unzip me."

"Babe, the water is probably freezing."

"Aiden, unzip me!"

He gets up and slowly loosens my zipper. I step out of the dress until I'm left wearing only a beige pair of lace panties. I couldn't wear a bra with my dress, and I don't think Aiden expected me to be nearly nude underneath, though it's nothing he hasn't seen before.

I slowly walk into the water. It's not freezing like Lake Michigan, but it's not warm either. It's bearable. The ocean in California isn't always warm, despite the milder weather, so I'm used to this temperate. I wait until I'm waist deep before I slip off my panties and toss them back onto the beach.

"Come on!" I yell.

Aiden loosens his tie before unbuttoning his shirt. He strips until he's left in nothing but his boxers. He walks into the water, though he has to walk deeper than I did for the water to reach his waist. I follow him into the deeper end. He maneuvers under the water, bringing his hand up to show me his boxers are off. He wads them into a ball and tosses them into the sand. This is the first time Aiden's ever been naked in front of me. I can't see anything, but knowing what's beneath the surface causes my lips to tremble. Suddenly, I'm nervous.

"Are you cold?" he asks.

I shake my head no.

He smirks. "Do I make you nervous, Harlow?"

He must be able to read my thoughts. I don't know why I'm so nervous. I nod my head.

"This was your idea."

"I know."

Aiden walks closer to me, our bodies nearly touching when he places his hands on my face. He pulls me in gently and kisses me. My hands find his back, which instantly tenses beneath my touch.

He's nervous too.

We pull each other closer until there's no space left between us. He kisses me passionately, and with so much love, I can feel it in every part of me. His hands move from my face to my waist, his touch sliding down my body. My legs curve around him, and I grip onto his shoulders. Every muscle on his body is tight right now. He keeps one hand on my waist to steady me, and the other returns to my cheek. The whole while, he never stops kissing me. We never part lips. We hardly catch air.

I can feel his heartbeat on my chest become more rapid as our kissing becomes more fervent, if that's even possible. I've never been kissed like this before. He pulls his lips apart from mine for the first time, but they instantly return to my skin. He leaves a soft trail of kisses from the corner of my mouth, up to my ear, and back down my neck. I arch my head to allow him more access. His mouth continues until it's covered every inch of my exposed skin above the water.

He moves us slightly into shallower waters, exposing my chest, and his lips fall to my breasts. He runs his tongue across my pebbled nipples, and I let out a small whimper. He responds by taking in more of me. My head falls back; the feel of his mouth on such a sensitive part of my body sends me into a spiral. I never want this moment to end. I never want him to stop.

Several minutes later, Aiden walks us back to the shore. He carefully lays me on top of his jacket in the sand, his body covering mine.

"I love you, Harlow," he says, his voice deep.

I rub his face with my hand while looking deep into his lake-colored eyes. "I love you more."

His lips return to mine. He falls beside me, with only half of his body still pressed against me. His fingers glide down my body and stop between my thighs. They softly trace me, tease me, causing my back to arch and my lips to part.

He lifts his head as he watches the effect his touch has on me. My eyes are forced shut as he pushes two fingers inside me, already nearing me closer to the edge. His mouth falls to my stomach and his lips brush against my skin in all the places he could not reach before, his tongue soon sliding against my center.

"Aiden," I moan.

His tongue continues to work. My hands move to his perfectly imperfect hair, pressing him harder into me. It doesn't take long for the orgasm to take over. I let out several uncontrollable whimpers as waves of pleasure soar through me. Aiden waits until I've caught my breath before he kisses me again.

"You taste so good," he whispers.

His lips fall back to mine, both of our mouths parting as he allows me to taste myself on his tongue. He moves on top of me, pressing his body against mine. I'm shortly pushed over the edge yet again from the friction. I whimper into his mouth, my body trembling beneath him. The kiss, the movement, Aiden leaving me breathless.

"I have condoms inside the house," he says.

"You don't need one. I'm on birth control."

His eyes soften as he takes in this moment, as I take in this moment. *This* is what he's been waiting for. A moment neither of us would ever forget. A moment so perfect, we'll remember it for the rest of our lives.

His fingers stroke gently through my hair. I can feel sand everywhere, and it doesn't even bother me.

"I'm going to make love to you now," he says, staring so deeply into my eyes.

I nod, because I've somehow lost the ability to speak.

"Never forget this, Harlow. I've never loved you more than I do right now, and I will love you more tomorrow than I do today. Every day, I will show you how much I love you. Every day, from now until forever."

"I'll never forget," I whisper.

He gently pushes himself inside of me, my eyes closing when I feel the fullness.

"Open your eyes, baby. I want to see you."

I open my eyes and stare into his as he moves himself on top of me. I'm quickly sent into my third orgasm, my body already overly sensitive and in overdrive. The pressure of him and the quivering of my body causes me to moan louder than the two times before. I feel this orgasm in every part of my body. I hear Aiden grunt as reaches his peak shortly after. He finishes inside of me, and it's the most intimate thing I've ever felt. I've always made guys pull out, never allowing them to finish inside of me. But I want this with Aiden. I want to feel all of him inside me, let him feel all of me. Making love with Aiden is everything he said it would be. Nothing can be better than this moment. I want him to love me like this for the rest of my life.

Part Two

Or will it cause them to sink under pressure?

Chapter eighteen

Eight years later (Present)

I'm on a red-eye from LAX to IND. I haven't been back to Portlet since I left eight years ago. There are very few things that would bring me back to the place where I had my heart broken. I don't want to be reminded of how cruel the world can be. One would think eight years would be enough time to allow someone to get over their first love. Their *only* love. If only it were that easy. If only time really did heal all wounds. I only spent six months of my twenty-six years of life in that town. Six months was enough time to change my life forever, yet eight years wasn't long enough for me to get over him. Him being *He Who Shall Not Be Named.*

Back to why I'm on this flight in the first place: My dad is getting married. Remarried, actually. I'm flying back to the place I promised myself I would never return to because of a damn wedding. I love my father too much to not be there for him, especially because he's asked me to be his best man. *Best woman.* My mom moved back to the West Coast after the divorce seven years ago, but she's dating a hotshot actor now, so she'll be just fine. I'm honestly shocked it took my dad as long as it did to leave her. But he's planted his roots in Indiana, and I don't see him leaving anytime soon. How unfortunate for me.

There's another two hours left in this flight. I drink wine and keep my AirPods in to avoid any unwanted conversations with strangers. I'm already stressed out enough as it is, and making small talk is not something that will make me feel at ease. This wine, however, seems to be helping a little.

My dad bought my plane ticket to make sure I showed up. He even went as far as putting me in first class. I stood at the gate until they announced *final boarding call* over the intercom back at LAX. Everything in me said not to step foot onto this flight, but my dad's sweet voice telling me how excited he was to see me played in the back of my mind on repeat. I couldn't run away again. Not from him.

A baby is crying somewhere on the plane. I can hear it over the podcast playing in my ears. The sound sends chills up my spine. I wonder when it will get easier. A lot of my girlfriends back home have had babies. I avoid them all. I don't want to, but I have to. In all honesty, part of me enjoys it when the little ones refer to me as Auntie Harley. I love spending time with them, loving on them. But at the end of the day, when I'm home alone, that happiness goes away. Kids don't bring me joy once they're gone. They bring me pain. Their cute dimples and smiley toothless grins—every adorable thing about them jabs a knife into my heart. I can't be around them. So, I choose to avoid them as often as I can. Being around them, it hurts almost as much as the thought of Aiden. *Shit.* I mean, *He Who Shall Not Be Named.*

I bought a house on the beach, right off the Santa Monica Pier, last year. It's a beautiful, quaint two-bedroom home that looks out over the water. I avoided the beach for the first seven years after moving back to California, so buying that house was a big step forward. I used to love the beach and the sand. I used to love how the sand felt beneath my toes, how the air smelt of salt water and ocean life. But now, the water only reminds me of his eyes, and the sand reminds me of a love I can't get back.

When I first moved in, I broke down in the living room, tears spewing from my eyes at an alarming rate. It was our dream to live on the beach in California, our dream to go to college together, to start a life together. Somehow, I had done everything we had set out to do, but I did it alone.

Over time, looking out onto the ocean became easier, eventually giving me a sense of calm, though his piercing blue eyes wouldn't be a far-off thought. That first day, I noticed a wooden sign hanging above the door that said *Rocky Top Retreat*. I kept that sign, wondering how I had not noticed it before. That home is my retreat, my safe space. I thought it could be my fresh start. I had to overcome my hatred for the beach, and what better way than not being able to escape it?

Unfortunately, in the time it took me to set foot in the sand again, I've returned to being a rock of a human. It used to be my best quality because it protected my heart from dark-haired boys with eyes that I could get lost in for hours, from guys that would do and say everything I wanted them to. But I crumbled. I'm still trying to pick up the pieces he broke, what's left of them anyway, and I think it's been working. Sort of.

There's a male flight attendant who has been bringing me wine for the last hour. He's cute, and I can't help but be thankful for the eye candy on this flight. The ratio of male to female flight attendants is very antifeminist. I once read there are only twenty-six male flight attendants to every hundred females. Twenty-six percent. This man is part of the twenty-six percent, and I'm thanking the high heavens that we are flying through for putting him on my flight. Why? Because I appreciate the distraction. He's brought me four glasses of wine already, and I'm eyeing him for another. He notices, winking at me, as he pours another from the cart and walks it over to my seat in 3A.

"Here you go, hun," he says, winking again as he hands me the wine with a smile that's nearly blinding.

I take in his appearance once more. The perfectly chiseled jaw. The gelled-back hair. The flawlessly straight and white teeth. The beauty of his effortlessly smooth skin. The tight pants that show off his perky ass. I sink back in my seat, watching as he struts away, realizing that this man is gay.

"Thanks," I mumble once he's already gone.

I don't even pour this bottle into a cup. I chug it, noticing the woman in seat 2C staring across the aisle at me, judging me. Who is *she* to judge *me*? I move my gaze and ignore her. I'm too busy internally punching myself for wanting to sleep with a gay flight attendant to deal with some rude and nosey passenger.

I'm emotionally unattached to all the men I've had sex with over the last eight years. Eventually, I had to decide that enough was enough and that I needed to get back out there. I wasn't looking for another relationship like the one I had with *He Who Shall Not Be Named*, just something that would distract me from the never-ending downward spiral I seemed to have fallen into. If I couldn't be with the one person I wanted in this world, then I'd just fuck everyone else.

The flight goes by more quickly than I'd hoped. Once I'm off the plane, I walk through the other gates before riding down the escalator with my carry-on luggage toward baggage claim, though I only have one small suitcase with me because I don't plan on staying in Portlet any longer than I need to.

As I walk through baggage claim toward the pickup area, I glance out the windows. My past life stares back at me in the form of chilly weather and Midwest accents.

I notice my dad right away, waiting right outside the door for me in arrivals. My future stepmom is with him.

"Harlow!" he shouts when he sees me, instantly reaching to grab my only bag. "It's so good to see you. You only brought one bag?"

I nod. "I'm leaving the morning after the wedding."

"I was hoping you'd consider extending your trip, but you can't get out of here soon enough, huh?" He puts my bag in the back and kisses my cheek. He leads me toward a bubbly blonde, my soon-to-be stepmom. "Honey, this is Tammie. My fiancée."

I try to give Tammie a friendly smile. Too bad I don't believe for one second that she's the real love of his life, only the second woman who's been attracted to him for his money. She's probably just like my mom, and he's buying it. Again. Literally.

I wave. "Hi."

"It's so nice to finally meet you!" she says, full of enthusiasm.

I force a smile as I get into the car. The sooner we can get this weekend over with, the sooner I can leave. I'm dreading every moment I have to be here.

A long drive later, we pull up to the familiar row of houses. One *his* and one *mine*. Well, not mine anymore, per se. I'm not even sure if it's his anymore. I try not to look, but I can't help but notice that there's a new front door. It's green. I liked the old one better. My dad's house looks exactly the same as when I left, and when I walk inside, I see that he hasn't changed the inside at all either. Everything looks precisely as I left it, even my room.

My room. I think back to every memory I have there, and each one that I remember involves him. Too much happened. I had too many nights with him. Too many memories. I can hardly even look inside. I shut the door, not taking one step inside, and proceed down the hall to one of the guest rooms. I throw my bag onto the bed. There are no memories in here. Nothing that can make me remember the pain. This is where I'll sleep.

I lie on the bed, studying the miniscule details in the ceiling, trying my damn hardest not to cry. I'm pathetic. How could being in this town make me feel this sad?

Not seconds later, I begin to cry. Tears fall uncontrollably from my face as I remember everything that happened here, every moment, every feeling, just *everything*. He wasn't just another guy. He was *the* guy. He was *my* everything. *My* guy. All this time apart has only confirmed one thing: how madly and deeply in love I was. It's scary to realize I'm still in love with him, that it wasn't just young love. It was an all-consuming, all-encompassing love. The kind that is supposed to last a lifetime. I'm afraid it still will, even though that love isn't reciprocated. I'm afraid I'll never be okay again.

Chapter nineteen

Past

    Our final project is due today in first period. Aiden and I spent the last week narrowing down our artifacts that would best describe the last four years of high school. We even bought a small chest from a thrift shop to keep our treasures in. For fun, we agreed to open the artifacts again in ten years, no matter what happens between us, as a way to remind us of the time we fell in love. The assignment was meant to be artifacts that described our high school experience, but the only part of high school we want to look back on are these last few months that brought us together.

    Aiden's first choice was a Lumineers CD. He places it in the chest.

"The first band I played when you drove me home. I was so relieved that you didn't like shitty music."

I laugh. "Seeing them at the Hollywood Bowl is going to be unreal."

"It'll be our first Californian date," he says with a smile.

Aiden and I booked a pair of one-way tickets to LAX the Monday after the Fourth of July. We figured we could spend one last weekend with our friends and family before we jetted across the country together. Our dorms at UCLA are only a five-minute walk from each other.

I'm still rooming with one of my old friends, Jolene. We met when we were only three years old and have stayed friends ever since. She balances me out because she is the complete opposite of a bitch. She's the sweet, innocent kind of girl who catches a lot of guys' attention. If you know her, then you're lucky. Jolene is someone you want to know because she makes you feel special. We didn't go to the same high school because her family moved to San Diego when we were ten, but we've always kept in touch, and she will forever be my best friend.

Aiden is rooming with a random, but they've talked on Facebook. His name is Luke, and so far, all I know about him is that he's from Texas and he plays football. At least they have football in common, so I'm not worried about Aiden and him getting along.

Aiden's second artifact is a football. This one doesn't have much to do with him and me, but it has everything to do with him. I never got to see him play because I transferred to Liberty too late in the year, but he's talked about it with me a lot since I found out he was the quarterback. He is very passionate about the sport and has already been in talks with the coach at UCLA. He's good enough to play division one. I only know that because I've heard his friends say so.

Aiden places the football inside the box. "Should I autograph it in case I play professionally one day?" he jokes.

"You mean *when* you play professionally one day?"

He smiles.

I pick up the next artifact, looking at it with a newfound appreciation. It's a rock. It's everything that describes me. My name. My personality. My heart. My emotions. I was a rock. Aiden managed to break me in the best way possible, and I love him for that, but I wouldn't be here without the rock that has protected me all this time. Who knows what kind of person I would be if I let my heart fall for someone willing to break it, for someone who isn't Aiden.

"I Googled your name the day you told me it meant a pile of rocks," Aiden admits.

"You *what*?"

"I kind of didn't believe you."

"And what did you find?" I ask.

"That your name does, in fact, mean a pile of rocks."

I laugh, placing the rock inside the chest.

"Our final artifact," I say, holding a small glass tube filled with tiny granules of sand.

We collected it the weekend of prom, right after we made love for the first time. I've always treasured the beach, but Aiden and I can appreciate the sand and the water in a different way than most are capable of understanding. It was *our* moment. A moment we could never neglect. And now the beach is something we both cherish together.

"I will never forget that day, Harlow."

"Neither will I."

I place the glass tube carefully inside the chest.

We had to type out a report explaining each of our artifacts to turn in, though we had to bend the truth a little, especially when it comes to the sand. God forbid our teacher finds out we actually had sex on the very sand inside that tube. That would be mortifying.

Unfortunately, our artifacts don't win, meaning we aren't exempt from the final. But Aiden and I are okay with it because the entire project was more for us. A way we can look back and remember the days we met, the days we fell in love, and some of the happiest moments of our lives.

Before I know it, it's graduation day. The day I've been looking forward to since I arrived in Portlet. I thought I would be more excited. I mean, I *am* excited. But not as much as I thought I'd be. The rest of my senior year here ended up being the best months of my life, all thanks to Aiden. I never thought I could be happy here. I never thought I could be happy with a boyfriend. I was so wrong. Aiden makes me giddy, and I can't help but get butterflies in my stomach every time he looks at me.

Aiden gifted me a dress for graduation. When I got home from school the other day, a box wrapped in black and silver ribbon sat on my bed. The card beside it read:

A gift before we start the rest of our lives.
I'll love you more then than I do now. Happy graduation, baby.

I love you,
Aiden

When I opened the box, my mouth dropped at the beautifully sewn black lace dress. As I look at myself in the mirror today, wearing the very dress Aiden chose, I admire the way it hangs off my shoulders, clinging to my body in all the right places. It falls to about mid-length, showing off my long legs. It's absolutely perfect.

Aiden is coming over before we head to the high school. Our ceremony is in a few hours, then we will officially be part of the Liberty High School Vikings graduating class of 2012.

I'm in my room curling my hair when I hear him walk in.

"Hey, babe," he says. He kisses me on the lips, then sits on my bed.

"Hey. Are you ready to graduate?"

He shrugs his shoulders. "I already feel like we graduated. Finals ended two weeks ago. Technically, we're already in college."

I roll my eyes. "Then why are we going to the ceremony?" I ask, mostly joking.

But Aiden doesn't take it that way. He thinks for a minute. "I don't know," he says before his eyes light up. "Maybe we shouldn't."

I put my curler down and turn my chair so I can see his face fully. "Aiden Walton," I say.

"Harlow Brooks," he says back with a sinful grin.

"We're going to play hooky again, aren't we?"

He laughs. "Only if you still wear that dress." His eyes roam down the length of my body.

"On one condition," I say.

"Anything."

Chapter Twenty

Present

I've cried enough tears for one day. I need to get out of this house. I decide to go for a walk, hoping maybe that will clear my head. One of the first things I figured out upon arriving at my dad's house is that he and Tammie got a dog. It has long droopy ears and a kissable nose. I've never known my dad to be interested in having pets. In my eighteen years of living with him, we never had so much as a fish to take care of. Tammie must have talked him into Ernie, the dog, and right now, I'm grateful for his company, for the excuse he's about to give me to get the fuck out of this house. Maybe I'll even bond with my new brother.

"Dad, I'm going to take Ernie on a walk!" I yell from the front room.

He waves his hand in acknowledgement. He's watching the horse races and is too occupied to care where his new pet is off to.

Tammie hears and claps her hands in excitement. "He loves walks! Have fun!" she exclaims.

That girl has too much energy. How does my dad put up with that?

I put on a smile and hook the leash to Ernie's collar. "Let's go, brother," I mumble to the dog.

The second I walk outside, my phone rings. I see Jolene's name flash on the screen. She knew how much I dreaded this trip. That girl has seen me at my absolute worst, and I don't think I would have ever gotten through what happened if it wasn't for her. She was strong for me when I couldn't be. She did all the things a best friend should do.

"Hey, Joey," I answer.

"Harley, what's going on? You already sound so sad."

I sigh. "I broke down when I saw my old room. I couldn't even walk in. I have to sleep in the damn guest room."

"You knew this was going to be hard," she says. "But it's been eight years. Do what you need to do to keep your mind off him."

"Sleep with someone?"

"Well, that's not what I meant. But that works too." She laughs. "I was thinking more along the lines of going for a run or planning a trip to Paris with your best friend."

"Paris is the city of love, you asshole."

"I *love* you, Harley!"

I snicker. "Love you too."

"So, what are you up to?"

"Taking my brother for a walk."

"What? Since when have you had a brother?"

"Just met him. He's furry and has four legs."

"Oh, my God, your dad got a dog! How precious. What's-her-face must have really done a number on him."

"Tammie," I say. "She's so over the top, Joey."

"You think everyone is over the top. Even me."

"That's because you are."

"And you love me for it. It's why I'm your best friend."

She's right. I wouldn't change anything about her.

"Are you planning on meeting up with any of your old high school friends?" she asks.

"The only person I would even consider seeing is Jess, but I might run into him if I go and see her."

"You think he's going to magically appear anywhere you go. You're nuts."

"It's a small town. He could be anywhere."

"You're staying next to his house, Harlow. If you're going to run into him anywhere, it's going to be on those sidewalks you're walking right now."

I freeze. She's right.

"Harley?"

"Yeah, I'm here," I say.

"Are you okay?" she asks.

"Yeah, but you're right. I can't be out here. I have to go back. I'll call you later, okay?"

"Don't hide inside the whole weekend. That's not what I meant! Let loose, Harlow!"

"Yeah, yeah," I say. "Okay, bye."

I hang up the phone and turn the dog around so that we're walking in the direction we came from. Shit. Why did I think this was a good idea?

We hardly make it anywhere when Ernie decides to take a shit in one of the neighbor's yards.

"Really, Ernie?"

I didn't bring any bags. I've never walked a dog before. I've also never picked up poop before, and I don't plan on starting now. I wait impatiently. When he finishes doing his business, I pick up a handful of mulch that's surrounding a decorative tree and place it on top of his poop.

I smile to myself. "There. No one will ever know."

"What are you doing?" I hear a voice ask from behind me.

My first reaction is *shit, I've been caught. Literally, with shit.*

But my second reaction. Oh, my second reaction is exactly what I was afraid of. It's the entire reason I've never come back. The hairs on the back of my neck stand up. I have an instant knot stuck in the back of my throat. My chest beats uncontrollably. My palms are sweaty. My eyes fill with tears when I thought I'd cried them all out already. They're betraying me. Again. Why am I such an emotional mess? Bitches don't cry. Come on, Harlow. Be a bitch. The one time it matters most, be a fucking bitch.

Chapter Twenty-One

Past

    The rest of the senior class is participating in the commencement ceremony right now. Our valedictorian is probably giving some cheesy speech about how we're about to start the rest of our lives and that this is only the beginning. That after one door closes, another opens. They're all the same. Every year. I went to my friend's older sister's graduation last year and it was b-o-r-i-n-g. I know we aren't missing much. However, people are missing us. Jess and Max are blowing up our phones because no one has heard from us in several hours. The only person we told where we were going was Rosa. I kind of can't believe we skipped graduation.

    "Aiden, what are we doing? I can't believe we just left."

He grabs my hand and squeezes. We're still in the car driving. "You're not having regrets already, are you, Black Sheep?"

His smile comforts me. Life with Aiden is a wild ride that I never want to get off. "Hell, no."

We have the windows down, the Midwestern air finally warm like the West Coast. We're still dressed in our graduation ceremony outfits. His dress shirt is unbuttoned, revealing his undershirt beneath. He looks so hot.

"How much longer until we get there?" I ask.

"Soon enough, babe. Soon enough."

Another hour or two passes. The sky has turned different shades of orange and pink as the sun sets in the distance. We passed a *Pure Michigan* sign a while back, another part of the Midwest I've yet to see until now. If there's anything I've learned since moving here, it's that people underestimate Middle America. Sure, the weather is shitty half the year, but there's so much to see here, and the cool air of a summer night is something I could get used to.

Aiden pulls the car onto a dirt road. There are no streetlights to guide us as we maneuver through the trees. When we decided to ditch graduation, Aiden quickly found a log cabin on a small lake courtesy of Airbnb. He rented it for the entire week. One whole week of alone time with the love of my life is exactly how I want to celebrate officially being high school graduates.

I see a roof peaking over a narrow hill. When we reach the top, we have the perfect view of our cabin, nestled near fresh water. I saw in the listing there was a hot tub and Jacuzzi bath. I have a feeling we will spend the entire week in the water in some way or another, which is perfect for what I have planned. The thought makes me grin.

"What are you smiling for?" Aiden asks.

"Just imagining what kind of activities will take place at the cabin."

Now Aiden's smirking. "What activities did you envision in that beautiful head of yours?"

"I could show you better than I could tell you."

Aiden laughs as he parks the car, unfastening his seat belt in a hurry. This is what I love about us. We are simple. Our relationship is simple, but at the same time, it's the most intense, deep, and powerful connection I've ever had with someone. Small things make us happy. We don't need to go on fancy dates to expensive restaurants or fly to exotic places around the world. Materialistic favors are nice, but place us in the middle of nowhere with water and sand, and that's when we are happiest. Whenever we are somewhere together in this big world, we have everything we'll ever want or desire.

Aiden leaves our bags in the car. He tucks his arms beneath me, carrying me like a bride on her wedding night into the cottage.

"Where to first, babe?" he asks.

I look around. There's a stone fireplace near the sofa, and furnishings of different shades of wood. It's cozy and small and perfect.

"Let's find the hot tub."

Aiden's smile grows wider as he carries me through the cabin onto the back deck overlooking the lake. The sundeck is made with a dark wood, a circular hot tub tucked in the corner. It sits in beautifully finished wood that matches the deck beneath us. There are lanterns placed sporadically, lighting up the scene in the night in a very romantic way.

Aiden sets me down so that I am standing right beside him. "What's your one condition?" he asks.

I look at him with eyes full of longing. I place my hand on the shoulder of his dress shirt as I slide it down his arm. "Whenever we are in water," I whisper, "I want it to touch our bare bodies."

Once Aiden's dress shirt has fallen to the floor, I lift his undershirt above his head. His abs are exposed, illuminated in the light of the lanterns. I brush my hand softly across them. His body is sexy as hell. I'm mesmerized by his perfection.

When I reach to unbuckle his belt, his hands stop me at my wrist. I look up.

"My turn," he says softly.

I nod and turn around so the has access to the zipper of my dress. I look back at him over my shoulder. "Are you upset I didn't get to wear this dress longer?"

He shakes his head. "I'll like it better off you."

I turn my head forward again. Aiden's kissing the back of my neck as he slowly unzips the dress. It falls to my ankles, and I'm left wearing my strapless bra and panties. I turn around to face him, his hands immediately finding my face before his lips fall to mine.

As he's kissing me, I reach again for his belt. This time, he doesn't stop me. I unhook it and reach for his button. My fingers move along his waist band, pushing down at the polyester until it falls to the floor. His boxers aren't hiding the effect of this moment. He can't physically see what his touch does to me, but I whimper when I feel how hard he is.

He pulls me closer, allowing me to feel his erection against my body, his hands leaving my face for the first time. He finds the hook securing my bra, and I hear a snap as my breasts are revealed. He pulls our bodies even closer until my breasts press against his bare chest. He finds my panties, and he pushes them down my legs in one swift motion. Before I have the chance to do the same to him, he reaches between my legs. His fingers gently caress the sensitive skin and leave me moaning louder into his kiss. My head arches back when the touch becomes too much, but he never stops kissing me. One hand has found my cheek, keeping my lips pressed into his and his other never stops the intentional motion making my head spin.

"Aiden," I moan into his mouth.

The kissing doesn't end. Neither of us gasps for air. When I reach my climax, my legs become weak, and I almost collapse. He moves one palm to the small of my back as he holds me up while simultaneously bringing me down. My legs quiver as I moan from the pleasure. He takes in all my sounds, absorbs them, keeping them forever. Once I can stand on my own, he pulls his hands away and removes his boxers.

He's eyeing me as he ushers me toward the hot tub. "After you, my love," he says.

I squint my eyes at him and try to look serious, but I can't fully hide the smile on my face. "Don't look at me like that."

"Like what?" His face doesn't change.

"Like you can control me."

"But I can control you, Harlow. Did you not witness what I just did? I made that happen, and I loved every damn second of it."

Aiden has been arrogant since the day I met him. It makes him more attractive, if that's even possible. And he's right, he *can* control me, which is no easy feat. I would do anything he asks. *Anything.*

"Are you ever not cocky, Aiden Walton?"

"When you're good at something, what fun would it be to hide it?"

"So, you think you're good at making me feel good?"

"Am I?"

I roll my eyes. "Well, obviously…"

He winks at me. "Exactly."

I walk ahead of him and step into the hot tub.

"Nice ass," he mumbles as he follows me in.

He tries reaching for it, but I turn, avoiding him because I'm not finished with this conversation yet. I take the seat opposite him in the hot tub.

"I think I can control you, too," I say.

"Is that right?" he says, crossing his arms over his chest.

"Remember when I tried on my bikini for you?"

Aiden's head falls back, and his eyes close. He remembers. It didn't end well.

"Yes," he whispers.

"If I would have kept pushing for it, you would have slept with me, right?"

"Yes."

"Would you say I have control over you?"

"Yes, Harlow. You have complete control over me. There's never been any question about it."

I stand, feeling satisfied at his admission, and walk through the water until I'm in front of him. My breasts are exposed, the water ending at my waist. He lifts his head and looks at me. I can see his struggle to not look down, to not see my body that's being presented right in front of him. He's a gentleman, trying to control his urges as his eyes stay focused on mine.

"Look at me," I demand.

"I am looking at you, baby," he says, his eyes staring intensely into mine, his voice gruff.

I shake my head. "No. I want you to look at *me*."

His head does a slight nod, as though I've permitted him to follow his impulses. I watch his eyes as they fall down my neck, my collarbone, and eventually stopping at my breasts. He lets out a soft grunt, his hands finding my waist and trying to pull me in closer.

"No," I say. "Just look at me."

I know what he wants to do to me, and I sure as hell know what I want him to do me, but right now, I need this. I need to see that I have the same power over him that he has over me. He does what I say, admiring me, my body. The parts he can see, anyway. His hands have already tried to work their way up and down, to touch me in the places I'm craving to be touched, but I stop him every time. When I can see that he's had enough, I tempt him further. I straddle him beneath the water, hovering over him as I balance on my knees. He reaches right below my ass, slowly inching up.

"What do you want to do to me?" I whisper.

Aiden's still looking at my body, his hands beginning to inch around to my hips. Right now, his eyes focus on the space between my legs.

His voice is raspy when he looks at me and says, "I want to make love to you, Harlow."

And we do. We make love in the hot tub. And again in bed.

Best graduation ever.

Chapter Twenty-Two

Present

I'm staring at the pile of shit I just covered with mulch. I'm trying so hard to make Ernie's feces my sole focus. Do you know how hard it is to try and think about shit for that long, the undigested particles and bacteria of whatever fancy food Tammie feeds him that he eliminates out of his ass? He shits shit. It smells.

I try to ignore the voice and start walking back toward the safe confined walls of my dad's house. Who am I kidding? Nowhere is safe here. My house is safe. I need to get back to my beach.

"Come on, Ernie," I say.

I tug on his leash, and he walks with me. I walk faster. Ernie tries to keep up, his little legs shuffling frantically. I hear footsteps catching up behind us.

"Harlow," he says.

I squeeze my eyes shut. How can he still say my name like that after all these years? When my eyes close, my feet stop moving. Ernie is probably relieved to catch his breath. My pulse races. If he could see my chest right now, he would see how spastically my heart is pumping to keep the blood flowing. I try to contain my tears.

I slowly turn around. It's time to face the inevitable.

When I see him, my heart flutters out of my chest. How can my heart still love him when my head knows what he's done? Why do my eyes produce tears when I've already cried over him enough? It's all too much to handle.

He's still so insanely attractive. His hair sits on top of his head in the same imperfect mess, just a little shorter. His eyes are as blue as the ocean back home, maybe bluer. No. Fuck. I'll be damned if he ruins my safe haven for me too. His skin is tanned, like he's spent several hours being kissed by the sun. He's grown into his muscles, too. He's a man now. A very, very good-looking man. I notice the facial hair, and how he can pull off the scruffy look so well. He's wearing running shorts and no shirt, his abs more defined than the last time I saw them. How is it possible for someone to get better looking with age? He's glistening in sweat. If he tried to take me right here, right now, I can't say that I would stop him.

I realize what I'm wearing—still my outfit from the airplane. A giant T-shirt that does nothing for my chest and a tan pair of biker shorts. My hair is dirty and greasy and sits in a giant messy bun on top of my head. My hair is longer than when he saw me last, leaving my bun to look like a bird's nest.

"I haven't seen a black sheep around here in quite some time."

"Don't call me that," I snap. It's the first words I've spoken to him in God knows how long.

He looks down and puts his hands in his pockets. I look down at the ground too. The sidewalk is cracked every ten feet or so. I try to focus on the cracks and nothing else. I've moved on from thinking about dog shit to sidewalk cracks. Perfect.

"Harlow," he says again. "You look really good."

I almost choke on my spit. I look really good? In comparison to the last time he saw me? Sure. I was a bit of a mess, so of course I look better than that. But to say I look good? He's lying.

I let out a small cackle. "We can't all take care of ourselves as well as Aiden Walton," I say, pointing out his glistening abs.

He looks uncomfortable now. "I'm glad I ran into you," he says hesitantly. "I've been trying to get ahold of you for a really long time now."

I blocked his number and every social media site he has when I moved to the West Coast. I needed a clean slate. I deleted him from every aspect of my life. If only I could delete the memory of him too.

"The only reason I'm here is because my dad's getting married," I point out.

"I know."

Of course, he knows. Small town.

"All right," I say.

He takes a step forward, so I take a step back. I don't want him any closer to me. If anything, I want us to be farther apart. Eighteen hundred miles apart should do the trick.

"Harlow."

"Stop saying my fucking name!" I yell. Finally, my inner bitch is coming out.

His shoulders drop, and he lifts his hands slowly in surrender. "Can we talk?" he asks.

"No, Aiden. There's nothing for us to talk about."

He shakes his head. "There's a lot for us to talk about," he says, his voice a little deeper, demanding.

I've had enough of this. I turn around and attempt to start walking back to my dad's house. I feel more anger right now than anything. I'm fuming. My skin is hot, and it's not from the sun that's beating down. But before I can take two steps, his hand is on the back of my arm, stopping me. I turn around, his face only inches away. I want to scream. I want to yell. But my eyes betray me because their first reaction is to look at his lips. His beautiful, plump, pink kissable lips.

I quickly regain control and bring my gaze to his eyes. I scrunch my nose, and my eyebrows arch. "Let go of me, Aiden."

"I will if you'll talk to me."

"Or else what?" I ask. "Are you going to hold me captive for the rest of my life?"

He lets go of my arm. "No."

"Okay, then let me fucking go. You've done it once before, what difference does it make eight years later? You should be a pro at it by now."

His head falls, and I know I've hurt him, but I don't care. I can't fall victim to Aiden Walton. Not again.

I turn back around and walk away. I don't need to look back to know he isn't following. I don't hear his footsteps. There's no sound at all.

When I get home, Ernie runs inside toward Tammie. She talks to him in a high-pitched, squeaky voice. "Did you have a good walk, my little peanut?!"

I roll my eyes and walk past their love fest. I sit on the couch next to my dad. Until now, I hadn't seen him since he helped move me in a year ago. Our lives keep us busy. After college, I didn't know what I wanted to do with my life, so I decided to go to law school. Three years later, I passed the bar and had a job lined up at the firm my dad used to work for. I followed in his footsteps, becoming a lawyer. I enjoy working there, and it helps pay the bills.

My dad and I talk about work and the wedding tomorrow, though my mind is elsewhere. I had hoped that talking with my dad would allow me to forget the little encounter I had with Aiden, but it does the opposite. Aiden and I probably would have been married by now. Weddings make me think of love, and love makes me think of Aiden.

Before I know it, I'm in my dad's car, driving to the nearest bar I can find. I need a few shots. I text Jess when I find one, telling her to meet me. I'm going to have to drink my way through this weekend if I want to survive.

Chapter Twenty-Three

Past

By day two in the cabin, we have to shut off our phones. We both have hundreds of missed calls and texts. It's Aiden's idea so that we can enjoy our time together away. Before we shut off our phones, I did talk to Rosa, who had to be the one to break it to our parents that we went out of town and wouldn't be home until the following weekend. Aiden thinks he will get grounded, but I'm not worried. I've never been grounded before, and I don't expect my parents to start being strict now. The way I see it, the day I turned eighteen, I could do whatever I wanted. I no longer have to live under my parents' roof if I don't want to, thanks to the trust fund I gained access to on my birthday. That's the positive part about coming from a rich family—trust funds.

We found a small trail behind the cabin when we checked things out this morning. We go inside to change so we can see where the path leads, though neither of us packed enough clothes in our haste to leave, so we're stuck wearing our pajamas. My satin gown wasn't exactly made for walking through the woods, so Aiden gives me one of his T-shirts. I'm putting on a pair of leggings when I eye Aiden walking over, smirking like he's up to something.

"What are you doing?" I ask.

"Don't wear pants."

"What? What do you mean don't wear pants?"

"I made a bucket list."

"What does that have to do with whether or not I wear pants?" I ask, confused.

He smirks. "A bucket list of places I want to make love to you." He pulls out a sheet of paper from his pocket. "First on the list, the woods." He points to a scribbled number one.

I try to look at the other places he has written down, but he pulls away the paper before I can make out what anything says.

"No peeking," he says.

"Is that the whole reason you suggested this walk?" I ask. "Did you even want to see where it leads?"

He laughs. "Guilty."

I shake my head but can't help but smile. "I'm still wearing pants. You can take them off later."

"Fine," he agrees. "But don't wear underwear."

We're both laughing now, and I wonder if other people come up with such crazy ideas when they're in love.

A few minutes later, we're walking down the dirt path. The second we're surrounded by trees, Aiden lunges at me. He pushes me against a tree, his lips pressing against mine.

I push him back. "Not yet! I want to see where this trail leads."

Aiden's body leans into mine, and I'm stuck between his body and the tree. I can already feel that he's ready. He tilts his head back and runs his fingers through his hair as he looks at the sky.

He sighs. "I think I love you too much."

"Good." I bring his face back down, cupping his cheeks so that he's looking at me, and kiss the tip of his nose. "And you better never stop."

His hand caresses my cheek. "No matter what, Harlow. I promise I will never stop loving you."

That's all he has to say for me to lose myself in our next kiss. But when Aiden <u>tries</u> to take off my pants, I know it's time to retreat.

"Let's go," I say out of breath. "I want to see more."

Aiden's head falls. "You're killing me, babe."

I grab his hand and pull him down the path. "That tree has already seen enough action. Let's find another."

That perks him up, and he falls into step with me.

The trail leads us to a couple of different lookouts with amazing views that oversee the lake. Every break we take, we make out. The make-out sessions leave us breathless and slow down the hike. We laugh at how out of shape it makes us seem.

Eventually the trail leads us to a stream. Down the current, water brushes past scattered rocks. We dip our feet in, the water warm. It's the perfect temperature. We walk casually alongside the stream, picking up stones and trying to skip them across the water. Mine all sink, but Aiden can get his to skip two to three times each.

"Are you not good at anything?" I ask.

He thinks for a minute. "I can't surf," he finally says.

I laugh. "Have you ever tried?"

"No."

I laugh, scooping water into my palms and splashing him. His eyes get big, and his mouth falls open.

"Harlow!" he says. "You're going to regret that."

I try to run, but as I do, he pulls me into the water, soaking my clothes worse than his splash would have.

"Harlow, you're breaking the one rule you made," he says as he stands in the stream. "I thought we were only going to ditch graduation on one condition?"

Now my eyes are wide. I look down at my soaking wet clothes. He's right. When we're in the water, I said no clothes.

"Shit." I pull the T-shirt over my head and toss it near our shoes. The wet leggings are a lot harder to take off. They stick to me and don't want to budge. I fall over trying to get my leg out. Aiden runs over, laughing. The water is about three feet deep, and I find it easier to slide the leggings off under the water. Aiden takes his clothes off next and tosses them.

I can only hear the sounds of our breathing; the sound of nature and wildlife around us mute. It's only Aiden and me in this moment, no one and nothing else.

"I can't wait any longer, Harlow," he whispers.

And I don't think I can, either.

His hands find my face, and his lips crash into mine. He eventually carries me out of the water, sitting beside an old maple tree. He moves my body on top of him, guiding himself until he's inside of me.

We check off the first item on the bucket list.

Chapter Twenty-four

Present

Jess meets me twenty minutes later at a dive bar I've never been to, since I wasn't twenty-one until after I moved away. Jess and Max recently got engaged. Their love story is one of my favorites, but it's hard to think about because Aiden and I used to be that in love.

I take a seat at the bar and order a vodka tonic. My drinks have gotten classier with age, though I still hate vodka, and I only order it on days I need to forget things. Like today.

The bartender throws a lime in my glass and pushes it in my direction. "Do you want to start a tab?" he asks.

"Yup."

I hand him my card, and before Jess even arrives, I'm two drinks deep. A guy across the bar orders me a shot, too. He says I look lonely and might need a little something extra. I hold my shot in the air and give him a head nod before I down whatever the hell it is. It's awful, but I feel the buzz.

I see Jess walk into the bar. Her hair is shorter now, but she's still adorable and petite. I stand to hug her.

"It's so good to see you!" she screams as she runs in for a hug. When we separate, she's holding my shoulders and trying to read my expression.

"How are you?" she asks. "I never thought I'd see you in this town again. I thought I was going to have to fly across the country every time I needed another dose of Harlow."

I shrug. "I can't wait to get the hell out of here."

She takes a seat at the bar and sees my vodka tonic. "It's that kind of night, I see."

I nod.

Jess waves for the bartender. "I'll have what she's having, and she'll take another."

I love her.

The bartender brings us two fresh drinks. I chug the one in my hand and push it away.

"What time is the wedding tomorrow?" she asks.

"Bridezilla is making us start hair and makeup in the morning. The ceremony isn't until five o'clock at night."

"You're going to be hungover as shit."

"Yep. And then I'll just start drinking more. I need to be incoherent this entire weekend to survive. I've only been here for three hours, all of which I was sober, and I cried for the majority of that time."

She makes a sad face. "Har."

"It's okay," I say. "I'm fine."

She doesn't look convinced. "Maybe we should go dancing tonight."

"If they have vodka, I'm there."

Her eyes light up. "This is going to be so fun!"

I eye her drink. "You've got some catching up to do."

Jess slurps down the whole thing. She has a pained expression on her face when she asks the bartender for another.

"How do you drink those things?" she asks, her expression sour.

"It almost tastes worse than I feel," I admit. "Makes it more bearable."

"Harlow, it's been eight years. Are you ever going to be okay?"

I know Jess would never get over Max if they broke up. I know how much she loves him because that's how much I love Aiden, maybe even a little more.

"Would you ever get over Max?" I ask.

She shakes her head. "No," she says. "I guess I never would. I love him too much."

"I love him too much too," I admit out loud for the first time in a long time.

She tries to put a smile on. "Sorry. I didn't mean to bring it up. Let's talk about something else. How's your new house? Do you love it? I'm so happy you found a place on the beach! I have to come see it soon."

I know she doesn't mean to upset me, but I already feel the buzz wearing off just thinking about Aiden. I need another shot.

"I love it," I say. "Let's take a shot." I look at the bartender. "Two shots of whatever that guy ordered me earlier, please."

The bartender looks from me to Jess, giving her what seems to be a look of pity. I snap my fingers at him to get his attention.

"Don't look at her! Two shots! We're trying to mend my broken heart, and you're playing a significant role in that!"

He looks at me, stunned. "Coming right up."

Jess laughs. "That was amazing."

"It's my go-to line. Normally I get a few drinks for free out of it. People feel sorry for me."

The bartender brings us our shots. Jess and I each grab one and clink them together.

"Let's get fucked up," she says.

"Cheers to that."

We down the shots. I don't react to the repulsive substance that just slithered down my throat. But Jess's face is priceless.

"What the *fuck* was that?" she asks, wiping her mouth. She chases the shot with her vodka tonic.

I shrug. "I don't know."

She looks to the bartender. "What the hell did you just give us?"

"It's called a black death shot," he says. "Jack Daniels, Jose Cuervo, Jim Beam, and Jägermeister all in one."

Jess looks back at me. "What the fuck, Harlow! Never order that again!"

I laugh. "It wasn't that bad," I lie.

She's chugging her drink, desperately trying to get the taste out of her mouth. I'm still laughing. It feels good to laugh. This is why I asked her to meet me.

"I'm ordering us some food. If we're going to drink like that all night, we need something in our stomachs." She gives a dirty look to our empty shot glasses.

Twenty minutes later, the bartender brings us out what looks like a frozen pizza.

"This will soak up some of the alcohol."

"Doesn't that defeat the purpose of drinking the alcohol, then?" I ask.

She shakes her head. "We'll be able to drink more. What are you, a rookie?"

"Apparently."

Chapter Twenty-five

Past

We're sitting in the sand watching the sunrise, coffee in hand. It's the first morning we've woken early enough to see the sun awaken over the water. Aiden's sitting with his legs spread apart, and I'm nestled in between them, my back flush against his chest. It seems like each day with him gets better and better. It's almost too good to be true.

"Aiden," I say softly.

The sun peeks out above the water, the first sign of light, as it's been dark for the last half hour we've been sitting outside.

"Yes, Harlow?"

"Do you think we'll ever break up?"

"No."

"How can you be so sure?"

"Because I love you, Harlow. What more reason do I need? I will never love someone else the way I love you. Remember that, no matter what."

"Okay."

"Do you think you'd ever want to break up with me?" he asks, his voice sounding hesitant.

I'm sickened at the thought. "Never."

It's light enough now to see the trees surrounding us and the water in front of us.

"I have an idea," he says.

"What is it?"

I can't see Aiden's face, but I know he's grinning. If it's possible to sense someone's reactions, I can sense his.

"Let's bury the chest of artifacts here."

I turn around to face him for the first time since being out here. I was right, he is smiling.

"Did you bring it with?" I ask.

He nods.

I smile. "Let's do it."

We stand in a hurry, both excited to have found the perfect hiding spot for our time capsule.

"Where should we bury it?" he asks once he's taken it out of the car.

I look around the grounds, thinking back on all the memories we've made while here already. When I look at the hot tub, I remember our first night. The woods remind me of the hike and checking off the first item on Aiden's bucket list. We've since checked off another item after we rented a small fishing boat from a nearby shack. When I look out onto the water, I remember how Aiden carefully removed my clothes and made himself comfortable inside me.

When my eyes fall to a beautiful white flowered dogwood tree on the property, I point. "There," I say. "Underneath that tree."

He smiles. "Perfect. Let me check the shed for a shovel," he says. "I'll be right back."

While he's gone, I find a sharp rock on the ground. I carve our initials into the tree, marking our burial site. It reads:

$$H + A$$
$$= Forever$$

I finish by outlining our initials in a giant heart.

Aiden returns with the shovel. He looks at the tree trunk and smirks. "You're such a softy now, Black Sheep," he says.

I roll my eyes. "Shut up. It's so we know which tree it is when we come back."

He laughs. "Sure, it is."

Aiden digs a hole in front of my marking. Once it's deep enough, he places the chest inside. He shovels the dirt to fill the hole.

"Ten years," I say.

"And not a day sooner."

"What if we're not together in ten years?"

"If we're not together, then I'll bring you back here anyway to remind you of the time we fell in love. Then I'll convince you to fall back in love with me."

"What if I'm married already to someone else?"

"If you ever marry somebody else..." He pauses for a second. "I don't even want to think of that happening. Please don't do that to me."

I walk toward him and wrap my arms around his back, burrowing my head into his chest. I can feel his heart beating rapidly.

"I love you," I whisper.

"I love you too."

After a few moments, I lift my head to kiss him. His soft lips brush mine. I want to kiss him more.

"Let's check off another item on your bucket list," I say.

Aiden smiles. He takes the list out of his pocket. He still won't let me see it. I can sort of see through the paper from where I'm standing, but I can't make out any of the words. It looks like his list has grown.

"Did you add more?" I ask.

"Maybe."

I laugh. "Where to next?"

"We can do this one," he says, looking at me. "Number six."

"What's number six?"

He smirks. "Time to christen my car."

"Your *car*? That thing is so small!"

He grins. "Up for the challenge?"

I smile, and he grabs my hand, pulling me toward his small two-seat sports car.

Chapter Twenty-six

Present

The bartender gives Jess and me a blow job shot on the house, which Jess requested for old times' sake. We cover the rim of the shot glass with our mouths, throwing it back like we're eighteen again. The bartender claps in awe when we don't spill a drop, though I must have whipped cream left over because Jess laughs.

"You got…jizz…on your lip!" She hardly gets the words out because she's laughing so hard.

The words she did get out were so loud everyone could hear. Old men stare at us, and we laugh harder.

Suddenly, something changes in Jess's demeanor. Her laugh stops abruptly. Her smile fades. She's not looking at me anymore, but rather directly behind me.

"What's wrong?" I ask.

She doesn't say a word. Instead, her eyes follow something behind me. Before I have the chance to turn around and look at who or what she sees, her hands grab hold of my arms.

"I am so sorry, Harlow," she says, her face worried.

I'm so confused, having no idea what she's apologizing for. We were having such a blast that I actually forgot about what's-his-face for a while.

And that's when it hits me.

That's the only thing she could truly be sorry for.

I turn around, immediately making eye contact with Jess's fiancé, Max. He's walking toward Jess with a bashful smile on his face, though his manner changes when he sees the look on Jess's face.

And then I see him, no longer focused on the exchange between Jess and Max. He's not far behind, wearing beautifully distressed denim jeans and a light blue T-shirt that makes his eyes glow like the shallow ends of the ocean. He shaved his face. He's somehow even more attractive than he was just a few short hours ago, which says a lot since he wasn't wearing a shirt before. *Dammit.* Why does he have to be so damn sexy? It makes it so much harder to avoid staring at someone when they look completely and utterly desirable.

The guys make their way toward us. Max kisses Jess on the lips, and I see her nudge in Aiden's direction. She whispers in Max's ear, although it's hardly a whisper because of how drunk she is.

"What is he doing here?" she hisses.

Max looks at Aiden, confused. "What do you mean?"

This time Jess jolts her head at me, as though the answer is obvious because it is. She gives him a wide-eye expression, and after a few awkward moments, he finally catches on.

"Shit," he says. He turns to Aiden. "You tricked me, dude."

Aiden shrugs.

What does that mean? Did he know I was going to be here?

Max looks at me. "Hey, Harlow. It's so good to see you." He reaches for a hug, and when he pulls away, he continues, "My friend here suggested we come meet you guys out when I told him Jess was meeting with a friend," he says, referring to Aiden.

Aiden takes a seat next to me and orders a beer. I look at him, revolted.

"You're seriously staying?" I ask him.

"I'm just having a drink," he says. "That's all."

I turn my chair so that I'm facing Jess, and my back is to him. I can't stand to look at the light stubble left on his jaw, or the perfect mess of hair on his head. He looks so damn good, and I'm grateful I decided to dress up before I left. I want him to see what he's missing, what he let walk away.

I pick at the hole in my jeans, as though it's some sort of distraction that could ease the awkwardness I feel having Aiden sitting beside me. I look at my nearly empty vodka tonic. I think I'm sobering up again. When Jess sees me eyeing my drink, she gives Max a dirty look.

Max looks at the bartender. "Another round, please."

The bartender nods, and I wonder if he's picked up that the person responsible for why I'm here just walked into the bar and has placed himself right beside me. I glance over my shoulder to see what that person is doing. He's sipping on his long-necked bottle, minding his own business. His eyes fall to mine when he notices me looking at him, and he smirks. A devilish, oh-so-sexy smirk that once upon a time I couldn't resist. My nose scrunches, and I give him a dirty look. His smile fades and his eyebrows move. He looks sad, and my heart instantly plummets.

"I have to go," I blurt out.

Aiden stands. "I'll drive you home."

"No. I'll be fine." I grab my keys off the bar.

Jess jumps in. "Harlow, you can't drive. You drank enough vodka tonight to get a small army drunk." She elbows Max.

"I can drive you," he volunteers.

I smile politely. Anything is better than Aiden and me in a car. Together. Alone. "That would be great, thanks."

A few minutes later, Max is driving my car home, while Aiden and Jess follow behind.

"I'm sorry," Max says again in the car. "I wasn't even thinking when he said we should meet up."

I'm looking out the window, trying not to let him read my expression. I'm sad. Really fucking sad. It was hard to see Aiden again. Things can fall so easily back together when I'm around him because the feelings I had for him never went away. That's why I have to go back to the West Coast. That's why I had to leave in the first place. I would've taken Aiden back after what he did, that's how in love with him I was. But I didn't deserve that, and I didn't want him to feel stuck. The only way I could return to my normal life was to not see him, not speak to him, and not have anything to do with him.

"It's okay," I mumble.

"He still loves you, you know."

I don't want to hear it, so I don't respond.

"He hasn't been with a girl since you."

I know that's a lie because I caught him with one right before I left. I still don't acknowledge him.

"Harlow," he says, trying to get my attention.

When he says my name, it doesn't affect me like when Aiden says it. I turn my head to look at him.

"You should talk to him."

"I don't have anything to say."

"He has a lot to say. Believe me. I've been listening to it for eight fucking years."

My eyes water. "He hurt me, Max."

He nods his head. "I know. And he's sorry. He's hurting, too."

"Sorry doesn't mean shit to me."

"You still love him."

I don't say anything because it's true, and there's no point denying it.

"You should talk to him, Harlow. Believe me. You'll want to hear what he has to say."

I can't stop the tears from falling. So much has happened, and I've hardly been in this stupid town for twelve hours. I can't wait to leave. The wedding is tomorrow, then I'll be on the first flight out the next morning. I won't have to deal with my past coming back to haunt me any longer because I won't make the same mistake twice. I will never come back to Portlet.

"There's nothing to talk about. There's nothing he could say that will take back the past. I'm leaving Sunday morning, and he'll never have to see me again. Everything will go back to normal."

"Things haven't been normal in a long time, Harlow. Not since you left."

His words sting. I'm crying harder now, and Max reaches across my seat to pull a napkin from the glove box.

"Here," he says.

"I'm so pathetic," I say, wiping my tears.

"No, you're not."

I don't realize it at first, but we're already in my driveway. I see Aiden pull up behind us. I immediately scurry out of the car, quickly saying thank you to Max for driving my car home, before I bolt for the door. Aiden jumps out when he sees me making a run for it, tossing Max his car keys.

"Harlow, wait!" he yells.

I don't wait, but it doesn't matter anyway. Aiden's caught up to me. He moves in front of me to block the path leading to the front door.

"Stop running, Harlow," he pleads. "You've been running for years."

I wipe the tears streaming down my face. Not only can alcohol not help me with my heartbreak anymore, but it also can't stop me from crying. I'm a damn drunk crier now.

He takes a step toward me. I can hardly see him through my blurry vision of tears. He places his hands on both of my shoulders and slowly pulls me into him. I don't have the energy to fight him off, and I haven't felt his touch like this in so long. It causes me to break down even more. I'm wailing now, and I can't stop. My emotions are uncontrollable.

I notice the headlights disappear from the driveway, leaving us in total darkness. Aiden rubs my back with one hand as I cry into his chest. He tries to comfort me, whispering in my ear that everything is okay. It's not helping. It's only making things worse. My legs become weak, and I collapse to the ground. Aiden holds me, sitting on the walkway as I lay curled in his lap, his hand still moving across my back.

We sit like this for a long time. I lose track of time. I'm still crying, but it's softer now. I need to stay here for a little longer. Being near him is the only thing that relaxes me right now, though I know the second we separate, I'll be a pathetic mess again. Why did he have to break my heart the way he did? Why do I still love him?

"Harlow," he says softly.

My heart breaks a little more. "Please, Aiden. Don't say my name like that."

His shirt is soaked from my tears, and I probably have black mascara smudged down my face. It's a good thing it's dark right now. I probably look so pathetic.

"I still love you, Harlow," he says.

Fuck.

All that hard work to calm me down flies right out the window with that simple sentence. With those simple words. How many times had I heard him say that to me before? Only now, it's the last thing I need to hear. We can't be together. Too much has happened. Love wasn't enough.

"You're only making this harder," I say between sobs.

"It's been eight years, Harlow. Can't you see that it's never going to get easier?"

The realization leaves me defeated. I'm wilted in his arms, no longer having the strength or the energy to keep myself together. Not that I've kept myself together in any way since landing at IND this morning. I wish I didn't love him. I wish so many things were different.

"I have to go," I say, willing my body to move, to escape this hold he has on me both physically and mentally.

He doesn't make an effort to move, and unfortunately, neither do I.

"I need to talk to you," he says.

"Then talk."

"Not like this. Not when you're this upset. And not when you've been drinking."

"I can promise you I'll be upset either way. And if I haven't been drinking, you won't get more than five minutes with me. I'll run."

"Not like this," he repeats. "Please talk to me before you head back to California."

I shake my head. "I'm on the first flight out the morning after the wedding."

He sighs. "Stay with me tonight, Harlow. We can talk in the morning."

That's the last thing I can do. An entire night with Aiden? There's no way I could handle that. "Hell no."

I somehow find the strength to get off his lap. I stand, wiping under my eyes. Aiden stands with me, his eyebrows furrowed as he waits for my next move. He exudes the face of a broken man. But I remind myself that he broke himself. And me in the process. This is his fault. None of this needed to happen.

"Don't forget this is your fault, Aiden," I remind him. "You broke my heart after you promised you wouldn't."

"Harlow," he says, defeated.

"Stop saying my fucking name!" I yell, sounding psychotic as I reach my breaking point. It can't get any worse than this. It just can't.

Aiden jumps a little, startled.

"Goodbye," I say as I march past him into my dad's house.

I don't wait for a response, don't wait for whatever the hell else he has to say. I can see his shadow still standing outside through the window, not making any moves to leave.

Eventually he turns to go home. I watch him until he's out of view, then I run upstairs to the guest room and cry myself to sleep.

Chapter Twenty-seven

Past

We have to leave our private paradise today. Check out is 11:00 a.m., only a few hours away. We woke up early to watch the sunrise again, both feeling pretty bummed to be leaving and trying to soak up the last bit of time we have left. This entire week, we kept our phones turned off. Aiden made me promise that I wouldn't power it back on until we're back home. We want no distractions. Only each other.

Aiden's carrying our bags to the car while I stand on the wooden walkway outside of the cottage staring out onto the water. I could do this every day for the rest of my life.

I take a sip of my coffee just as I hear footsteps coming my way. Aiden's standing next to me a moment later, looking over the horizon now, too.

He puts his arm around me and kisses the crown of my head. "Did you have fun this week?"

"Yes. I don't ever want to leave."

"Then let's stay."

I look at Aiden, not sure if he's being serious. "What? We can't stay, can we?"

"No. Unfortunately, we can't. I already tried. They have someone checking in this afternoon."

I giggle because it's cute that he's already tried to extend our trip. He's enjoying this time away just as much as I am.

"But we can do this again," he assures me. "We can do this for the rest of our lives, babe."

"That would be nice."

"And soon, you will be closer to the ocean. You won't have to deal with these tiny lakes."

"*We* will be closer to the ocean," I correct him, excited that our flight leaves in only three weeks.

Aiden doesn't say anything. For some reason, I feel a pit in my stomach. Something is off, I just know it.

"Are you okay?" I dare ask.

"Yeah."

I take a step away from him, studying his features. "You don't seem okay. What happened? Are you not excited anymore?"

"I'm so excited, Harlow. I can't wait to see it all with you."

Still, his words don't convince me. "Then what's wrong?"

"Nothing. I don't want to talk about it right now. We've had a really good week. Let's keep it that way."

I take another step back. I feel a wave of heat wash over me, maybe nausea. Something is going on. Something is definitely wrong. There's something he's not telling me.

"Aiden, tell me," I demand.

"Not right now, Harlow."

"Aiden!" I yell. There's no hiding the panic in my voice.

He shakes his head, and his shoulders drop in defeat. He runs his fingers through his hair, and he's avoiding eye contact with me.

"What did I do?"

He tries to move closer to me, but I step away. He can see on my face that I want him to stay right where he is, right where I can see him. My hands grip the railing behind me.

"Harlow."

"Aiden."

"You didn't do anything."

"Then what the hell is going on?"

When he doesn't speak, I lose it. "What is the real reason you brought me here, Aiden? So I could feel like we are living in some fantasy land before you tell me whatever the hell is going on and shatter my entire world? Tell me, *now*! What the fuck is going on?"

"Babe, calm down," he says.

I storm off, my feet stomping. I am so far from calm. I walk into the cabin and shut the screen door behind me. I'm aware that we have to leave, and the last thing I want right now is to be stuck in a car with him when he's been keeping something from me. I thought he said he'd never hurt me. Why do I feel like I'm being hurt?

Our deal is off. I'm calling it off. I rush to find my phone in my purse and turn it on. I have a ton of missed calls/texts. I skim through the texts asking where I'm at, ignore the ones from my parents, but the message from Jess catches my eye. It's from six days ago.

Jess: I'm so sorry about all of this. I hope you're okay.

I immediately call her.

"Hello?" she answers.

"Jess, why did you text me that? What are you sorry for?"

She's silent on the other end of the line, and I'm so fucking sick of everyone not answering my questions. I can hear people yelling in the background. She's probably at a party.

"One second," she finally says. "Let me find someplace quiet."

I wait for what feels like eternity before she speaks again.

"Harlow?"

"What?"

"Have you spoken to Aiden yet?"

"About what?" I ask.

She's quiet again.

"Have I spoken to Aiden about *what*, Jess?" I ask louder.

"Shit," she mumbles.

"Jess, what the fuck is going on?"

"Harlow, I'm so sorry. I thought he talked with you. I thought that's why you both didn't come back after graduation. I am so, so sorry."

"*What the hell?*" I'm so angry.

"Go talk to Aiden."

"He won't tell me anything!" I scream.

"Har," she says quietly. "You need to get him to talk to you."

I hang up the phone, frustrated. I read her text over and over again, trying to figure out what it can mean. *What is she sorry for? What the actual fuck is going on? Why wouldn't I be okay?*

I scroll through my other missed messages, hoping to find some sort of clue as to what is going on, but I find nothing.

"Aiden, what the fuck!" I yell as I walk back outside. I'm holding my phone up so he can see the text message from Jess. I'm desperate at this point. I can feel myself building up those walls, the walls Aiden worked so hard to break. "What is she talking about, Aiden?"

My voice cracks. I'm not mad anymore. I'm afraid, nervous, knowing whatever he's about to tell me will change everything.

"I'm scared, Harlow," he admits. His eyes look glazed as they study me.

"I'm scared, too," I say before I cry.

I feel like I'm losing him. I don't know what's going on, but I know it's bad. This week has been a dream, and I never want it to end. But maybe that's what he intended. Maybe he wanted to throw it in my face that this is the life I could have right before it's ripped away. Now that this week is over, I'm scared my life will be over, too.

"You're going to break my heart, aren't you?" I whisper.

He doesn't respond.

Chapter twenty-eight

Present

The hangover wasn't half as bad as I expected. Tammie had her maid of honor wake me up three hours earlier than necessary. I ignored her at first, then she stormed into my bedroom like an elephant on a mission to find the watering hole.

"I'm awake!" I finally yell.

"Good," she hisses.

The maid of honor is Tammie's older sister, Tanya. Tammie and Tanya. Tanya is the complete opposite of Tammie. Tanya is aggressive, scary, and overall, not friendly. My mood is sour when I walk into the kitchen where the bridal party is sipping mimosas and snacking on fruit.

"I'm making a bagel," I announce. "Anyone want one?"

I hear one of the girls gasp. "You're going to eat *bread* before the wedding? You're going to be bloated!"

Is she serious?

I ignore her and put the bagel in the toaster. She's eyeing me like I have two heads. I have no fucking clue who this girl is, or who any of these people are besides Tammie and Tanya. When my bagel pops out, I take it upstairs to eat. I sit on the bed chewing all the toasted carbs with the satisfaction those girls wish they had.

For a second, I forgot about the horrid day I had yesterday. I should have known it would be impossible to avoid Aiden while I'm here.

I lie back on the bed, rubbing my hands over my face in frustration. Why is this happening to me? I've been content with living in my misery thousands of miles away. It's so much harder to actually see the person that caused me all this pain. It's really fucking hard.

I grab my phone off the nightstand. I have several missed messages, and the first I see is from Jess that she sent last night.

Jess: Love you, Har. Sorry about tonight.

I respond right away.

Me: Love you too. I'll be out of this town soon. It's fine.

I notice a missed text from Max next. He and I never text, so right away, it catches me off guard. My stomach drops when I realize it's not really from Max.

Max: Harlow, it's Aiden. I stole Max's phone so I could send you this. I wish you would unblock my number, but I understand why you haven't. I fucked up. I was young and stupid, and I know that isn't an excuse, but I need to explain what really happened. You've been running from me for so long now, please don't run anymore. Please. You're not going to be happy to hear this, but I wanted to tell you instead of it being a surprise. I'll be at your dad's wedding. He and I have stayed in touch over the years. It was my only way to know you were doing okay. I hope you know how proud I am of you. But I would be lying if I said it doesn't fucking hurt to hear about all you've accomplished without me. I wasn't there for your graduation, when you passed the bar exam, or when you landed your first job at a firm. I want you to know that I've always celebrated your successes, and I've been cheering you on from here. Please don't avoid me at the wedding, I have so much more to say to you. My life hasn't been the same since you left, I hope you know that. If you've made it this far in the message, thank you for not stopping. Thank you, Harlow. I don't deserve anything from you, but you do deserve to be loved by someone the way I love you. If you still don't want anything to do with me after I get the chance to explain things, then I promise I will leave you alone. But I will never stop loving you. I will never

move on. And that's okay, as long as you're okay. I love you so much, Harlow, and I always will. I'll see you soon.

A tear lands on my phone screen. I have flutters in my stomach, and my breathing is labored.

He's coming to the wedding.

Does my dad not know how heartbroken he left me? He can't, or he wouldn't be inviting him to the wedding.

I don't know what to do, if I should respond or not. But curiosity gets the best of me, and I wonder if Aiden still has Max's phone.

Me: Max?

Max/Aiden: No. Still me.

Now I don't know what to say. Maybe I should just unblock Aiden's number for today, then block it again when I leave tomorrow. If I have to be around him at the wedding, maybe I should at least hear him out so I'm not distracted by him later. Then I laugh to myself because who am I kidding? Aiden has a way about him that makes me lose my train of thought, makes my brain feel scattered. Even still, I unblock his number and text his phone.

Me: I unblocked your number, so you can return Max's phone.

Aiden: I will, gladly.

I ask him a question that's been on my mind because I don't understand after all these years. After everything that's happened to him, after our lives have been lived completely separately.

Me: How can you still love me?

Aiden: How could I not? I've always loved you. I can't just stop.

Me: But haven't you been with other people?

Aiden: Sure. Nothing serious. Have you dated other people?

Me: Yeah. A lot.

Aiden: Ouch.

Before I can respond, my phone chimes with another message.

Aiden: Did you love any of them?

I answer honestly.

Me: No.

There's a knock at the door. Bridezilla's evil assistant walks in before I have a chance to answer.

"It's your turn for hair and makeup," Tanya says flatly.

"Coming," I say.

I look down at my phone. He hasn't responded yet. I sigh, disappointed, though I try not to care.

I chose a sleek jade color gown for the big day; it hugs tightly at my curves. My hair is pinned back in loose spirals with pieces hanging around my face, giving my appearance a gorgeous but effortless look. My makeup is subtle, but enough to know it's there. It is both agreeable and elegant.

Tammie and my dad's ceremony is taking place in a courtyard at a prestigious country club. My dad frequents the golf course. I've seen Tammie post pictures of her lying poolside with her girlfriends and sipping on skinny girl margaritas. Her skin is fair in comparison to mine and easily becomes an unflattering shade of pink. In all honesty, she should probably avoid the sun.

A tacky party bus filled with champagne ushers us to the venue. Thankfully, I can separate from Tammie and her minions once we arrive. I meet my dad in one of the waiting areas. He doesn't have anyone else standing on his side for the ceremony. He's done the big wedding thing; he's only going along with this façade to please his new wife. He told me I'm the only one he needed to be here.

It's supposed to be a short ceremony, and it's at the start that I realize how much my dad really loves Tammie. I notice a small tear fall as his bride walks down the aisle, escorted by her father. I've never seen my dad cry, not for anything. And for that reason alone, I try to have a more positive outlook on the day. It was important to him that I be here, and although he didn't need another fancy wedding to marry his new love, he's making it a special day for her regardless.

In all the bustle of wedding prep, I forgot about my conversation with Aiden. I even disregarded that Aiden was supposed to be coming to the wedding. It's in the middle of the vows that I eye the crowd and noticed he isn't here. Of course, I left my phone in the waiting area. I'll have to find it when the ceremony is over so I can check if he's responded.

The happy couple says their 'I do's,' and my dad kisses the bride. Wedding bells chime as they walk up the aisle, hand in hand, beaming from ear to ear. I sneak away during the cocktail hour to find my phone.

I frown. No missed messages.

Aiden never responded.

I walk back out to the crowd of people slurping the free booze and stuffing their faces with hors d'oeuvres. I eye every person in the courtyard, trying to find Aiden in the crowd. Why am I so concerned about where he is? I need to forget about him again, distract myself with this wedding. It worked earlier.

I order two vodka tonics and down them faster than I care to admit. I order two more and socialize with the friends my dad has made in the place I can't wait to leave. Dinner is being served, and there's still no sign of Aiden. He must have changed his mind. He must not be coming after all.

By the end of dinner, the alcohol still isn't diverting my thoughts from Aiden. I need a better distraction.

There's a very handsome man sitting at table six. His muscles bulge through his suit coat, his hair is jet black, and he has dark, mysterious eyes. I see no ring on his finger, which means he's fair game. I notice his manly hands, unable to concentrate on much else other than what those hands could probably do.

I down another vodka tonic and make my way toward the attractive stranger after the dessert is served. He's ordering a drink at the bar when I walk up next to him, placing my empty glass on the bar mat. He turns to face me, not even hiding the fact that he's checking me out. He eyes my legs that peek through the slit in my dress. He makes his way up to my chest.

I clear my throat. "Hi there."

His eyes quickly jump from my boobs to my eyes. He half smirks. "Hello."

"You must be a boob guy," I say.

He's taken aback. "Excuse me?"

"Your eyes were glued to my breasts for just a moment too long. You must be a boob guy."

"As opposed to what?" he asks.

"An ass guy. Guys are either into boobs or a great ass."

"How would I know if I'm a boob guy or an ass guy? I haven't even seen your ass."

I laugh. "It's a great ass."

He smiles. "I'll bet it is. What are you drinking?"

"Vodka tonic."

The bartender appears with what looks to be a bourbon for Mr. Tall, Dark, and Handsome, who proceeds to order a vodka tonic for me.

"Bourbon?" I ask, eyeing his drink.

He shakes his head. "Scotch."

"Impressive."

"Is it?" he asks. He takes a sip.

The bartender brings my vodka tonic. I thank him and walk away as I wait for Tall, Dark, and Handsome to take the bait.

"You have a great ass!" he yells from behind.

I stop in place. I can't hide my smile, though I try when I turn back around.

"So, what's the verdict?" I ask.

"I have to pick just one?"

I nod.

"I think I may have always been a boob guy, but I've never seen an ass like yours. I think I've been converted."

I give him a smirk. "What's your name, and who do you know here?"

He walks closer to me until our glasses touch. I can feel his breath on my forehead. He's at least half a foot taller than me.

"James. Tammie is my cousin. How about you?"

"Harlow," I say. "Your cousin just married my dad."

"It is very nice to meet you, Harlow. Are we technically family now?"

I give him a dirty look. "No. That would make it extremely inappropriate for you to be checking me out the way you have been."

"Who says I've been checking you out?" he smirks.

"You're not very good at hiding it, James."

"It's not easy to look away from you, Harlow."

I grab his tie and pull him in a little closer. "Should we get out of here?" I ask.

He doesn't hesitate when he grabs my hand and leads me out.

Chapter Twenty-nine

Past

The ride home is three hours. In the time it takes us to leave the cabin and get home, Aiden and I don't exchange a single word. Not since he finally told me. As far as I know, Aiden hasn't kept anything from me. Until now. He broke down when I confronted him about my message from Jess. He had to tell me what was going on because I wasn't backing down.

"She's pregnant," he finally whispered as a single tear fell from his eye, his head bowed. He couldn't even look at me.

My body went numb. My tears stopped falling. I felt nothing. No sadness. No anger. I had zero emotion.

"Who?" I asked.

"Amanda."

"Why do I care that Amanda is pregnant, Aiden?" Though I already knew what he was saying.

"She says I'm the father."

We got in the car a few minutes later to drive home.

When Aiden pulls up to my house, he tries to follow me inside. I don't let him follow. Instead, I slam the door in his face. I don't know how long he stays outside or how long it takes him to leave and finally go back home, and frankly, I don't care.

I didn't cry after he told me. I haven't shed a single tear since. I'm a rock of a human again, going into protection mode once I realized Aiden was going to break my heart. But I'm afraid it's not working. I'm afraid it might be too late.

As I sit at home, I still feel nothing, stuck in an emotionless state, though I can't help but wonder how many other people knew about this big secret before me.

Amanda is pregnant.

Aiden is the dad.

I wonder how far along she is. She can't be too far because I haven't noticed a bump at school, but I don't pay much attention to her. Maybe she wore loose clothes? If she's only a few weeks, that means Aiden has been cheating on me. If he didn't cheat, then it's been months since they've been together. How long does it take someone to start showing?

I search Amanda on Instagram. She hasn't shared any photos of her bump, and her Facebook doesn't show any indication that she's pregnant either. She definitely seems like the type that would post a picture of the ultrasound in some pathetic public announcement. I feel sick at the thought of her and Aiden having a baby together. Maybe I do feel something? Nauseous. This is repulsive.

The next day, I find out through Jess that Aiden is grounded for a week for ditching graduation. I simply get a mere slap on the wrist.

You only graduate high school once, Harlow. It was important you be there. And that was it. My parents haven't brought it up again.

Aiden's parents take his phone and don't let him leave the house. Again, I only know this because it's what Jess told me. She says Max stopped by and Aiden had to send him away. I wonder if his parents know he got a girl pregnant. Will they ground him for that, too? Missing a graduation ceremony seems like such a moot point compared to impregnating your high school ex-girlfriend.

A week goes by, and I'm not in the least bit surprised when Aiden knocks on my door first thing in the morning. I haven't even gotten out of bed yet when Rosa tells me he's looking for me.

"Tell him I'm sleeping," I say.

Rosa gives me a look. "Harlow, you haven't seen him in a week. Is everything okay?"

"No. And I'm not ready to see him."

Rosa nods and returns to Aiden. I can hear mumbling through the floorboards followed by the front door closing. I relax in bed, satisfied with my lack of emotion in the matter.

Way to take care of yourself, Harlow, I think to myself.

I've almost fallen back asleep when the sound of my window opening frightens me.

Oh, no, an emotion. I quickly sit up in bed.

Aiden climbs through the small opening and appears in my room. My emotions fall flat again.

False alarm, they're not back.

"Go home, Aiden," I mumble, turning over so my back faces him. I pull the covers over my head. I can feel the pressure of the bed change as he sits near my feet.

"Harlow."

Nothing. I feel nothing. Not even when he says my name like that. What the hell is going on?

"Can we talk?" he asks.

I remove the blanket from my head, annoyed. "What's there to talk about?" I spit. "You're going to be a dad. Congratu-fucking-lations."

He shudders at the carelessness in my voice. "Are you okay?"

"I'm fine, Aiden. Dandy. Just trying to sleep."

He puts his hand on my leg. The blanket is the only thing separating his touch from my bare skin. I look at where his hand sits then look back at him.

"Don't touch me," I say.

He retracts his hand, the look on his face showing his pain. "Harlow, we can work through this."

"I don't want to work through anything. I'm moving soon. I don't care, Aiden. I really don't."

"Yes, you do."

I sit up, my face falling flat. I look at him so he can fully comprehend what I'm about to say. "I don't care that you are about to have a baby with your ex-girlfriend. *I don't care.* I haven't cried. I haven't wanted to see you. We are obviously over, so there's nothing left here to say. You can go now." I gesture toward the door, shooing him away.

"Harlow," he begs with desperation. "I'm going to figure this out. I'm going to make this work. I know you love me. You don't just stop loving someone."

"Yes, you do."

His face falls into his hands. He doesn't say anything.

Eventually, he stands and walks back toward the window, finally taking the hint. He pushes back the curtains as he makes his way outside. But before I let him leave, I have one last question.

"Aiden?"

He turns around.

"Were you cheating on me?"

This time his face is blank. He doesn't have his usual cocky persona, and the sadness that was there a few moments ago has since vanished.

"Would it make a difference, Harlow?" he asks.

I shake my head. "No," I say. "I suppose it wouldn't."

Chapter Thirty

Present

Turns out, James isn't from here. He's from Utah, which is about all the information I learn before we started making out in the Uber. We can hardly keep our hands off each other. The drive isn't fast enough. We can't get up the hotel steps quick enough. The time it takes for us to ride up the elevator to when he finally finds his key card and swipes it seems like an eternity. Though I'm not complaining, because his lips never leave mine.

I like the way he kisses me. He kisses like a man. His firm hands hold onto me tight, feeling every part of me. He moans into my mouth. Things escalate quickly as I move to unbutton his shirt. We're momentarily interrupted when my phone rings loudly from inside my purse. I ignore it, continuing with the task at hand. His shirt falls to the floor, and my tongue clings to his six pack. When I begin to remove his belt, my phone rings again.

"Should you answer that?" he asks, out of breath.

"Just ignore it."

I remove his belt, but before I can take off his pants, he's lifting me to his level. His lips press to mine as he lowers the strap of my dress over my shoulder. Then my phone rings for a third time.

I sigh into his mouth. "One second."

By the time I find my purse, my phone stops ringing. I'm tempted to ignore it again, but at this point, I know another phone call is inevitable. My call log shows I have eight missed calls and ten unread messages. The messages and three of the missed calls are from Jess. I don't recognize the number that called me the remaining five times. I open the messages from Jess.

Jess: Harlow, you need to call me.

Jess: I know you're at the wedding, but this is important.

Jess: It's about Aiden.

Jess: Harlow??????

Jess: Pick up your damn phone.

Jess: For fuck's sake, Harlow.

Jess: ANSWER YOUR DAMN PHONE!

Jess: Aiden was in an accident.

Jess: Call me back.

Jess: Fuck, Harlow. I need you to get to the hospital right now. I don't know if he's going to make it.

I can hardly comprehend the messages after seeing the words *Aiden* and *accident* before I grab my purse and head straight for the door. On my way out, I catch sight of a suitcase filled with men's clothes.

Shit.

For a second, I forgot all about James.

I turn to look at him before I walk out, my face more panicked than apologetic.

"I'm so sorry. There's an emergency. I have to go."

Before he can answer, I'm in the hallway. I rummage through my purse looking for my keys in the elevator. Once I'm in the hotel parking lot, I realize I don't have a car here. *Shit. Shit. Shit.* I order an Uber that arrives a very long five minutes later and call Jess once I'm on my way. She answers on the first ring.

"Harlow," she says, sounding relieved.

"Yes. Hi. It's me. I'm on my way. I'll be there in ten minutes."

"Okay."

"What happened?" I ask.

"He was on his way home when someone swerved off the road and hit him. We just found out an hour ago and rushed here."

Is that why he never texted me back? Why he didn't show up to the wedding? Has he been at the hospital, fighting for his life this entire time?

She continues, "They've been trying to call his emergency contact, but we don't know who it is since both of his parents are dead."

I'm quiet. Too quiet.

"Hello? Harlow, you still there?"

Is that who the other missed calls are from? Am I his emergency contact? Everything happened so long ago. Has he had me as his emergency contact this entire time?

"Yeah," I say. "I'm here. Jess, I think I'm his emergency contact. I have a bunch of missed calls from an unknown number."

Now she's quiet.

I swallow. "I was at the wedding. I didn't have my phone on me and then I went back to James's hotel room and heard the phone ringing and after the third time I finally checked. Shit. I can't believe this. Fuck!"

"Who is James?" she asks.

"Some guy I met at the wedding—I was trying to distract myself because Aiden didn't show up."

I squeeze my eyes shut.

He didn't show up because he was in a car accident. And I reacted by trying to sleep with the first guy I could find that was attractive.

"I hate myself. Oh, my God," I say between sobs, realizing for the first time that I've been crying.

"It's okay, Harlow. You didn't know. I'll see you soon, all right?"

"Okay."

I hang up. The Uber driver hands me Kleenex, and I offer a pathetic smile as I accept.

We arrive at the hospital a few minutes later. I run inside to the waiting room, immediately spotting Jess and Max. Jess's eyes are bloodshot, and Max looks pale as a ghost.

"Where is he?" I ask.

Max steps forward. "He's in surgery."

I walk past them to find the nurse's station. I need more information.

"Hi, my name is Harlow Brooks. I'm the emergency contact for Aiden Walton. What's going on?"

"Ms. Brooks," she says. "We've been trying to get ahold of you all day."

"I know. I was at my father's wedding. I'm here now. Where is he?"

"He's in surgery right now. He had several broken bones when he was brought in and was bleeding internally. He suffered from an intracranial hematoma. I'll let his doctor know the family of the patient has arrived, and he will be out as soon as he can to give you an update."

Jess stands over my shoulder, listening to everything. I'm not sure how much information they told her before I got here, but she seems more shaken now than when I spoke with her on the phone.

"Are you okay?" she asks.

"No," I say. "I'm not. I've been running from the man I love for all these years, and he kept me as his emergency contact. What does that mean? I'm the only person he has left that he considers family, and I haven't even given him the time of day? I've been avoiding him since that shit went down with Amanda eight fucking years ago. Then his parents died, and I still avoided him. I'm such a selfish bitch."

Jess strokes my back. She knows I'm right, but she's too good a friend to admit it.

"He hurt you, Harlow. After the initial shock of what he told you, you can't blame yourself for the way you reacted. He broke your heart, even if you didn't want to believe it at the time. But that's not what landed him in the hospital. And the important thing is that you're here now."

I cry the tears I should have cried the day he told me Amanda was pregnant. I cry for all the times I sheltered myself from feeling anything. As time passed after I left, it became harder and harder to remain emotionless. I missed Aiden more than I wanted to admit, but I had to keep reminding myself that what he did hurt me more than I could handle. I did what I needed to do to finish school and start my life. I did it all without Aiden, and it was the hardest thing I've ever had to do.

He's once again removed the hardened parts of me in the short time I've been back, and now, I might not even have an Aiden to love anymore. The thought shatters any remaining walls I had up. I love this man. The past is in the past, and its time I stop lying to myself. He bruised my ego back then more than anything. He never told me he didn't want to be with me. He never said he stopped loving me. I assumed those things after what I saw. I assumed he wouldn't want me at his parents' funeral. I assumed his life would be better off if he stayed in Indiana, and I moved across the country where I belonged.

I was so wrong. About everything. Our lives were always better with each other. I don't want to live in a world where Aiden Walton doesn't exist. We've hurt each other, but we've loved each other more. I need him. He can't die. I can't live another second without him.

Chapter thirty-one

Past

Another week goes by, and I've still been avoiding Aiden. He's probably busy picking out baby names and cribs with Amanda. We haven't talked about California, not that we'd have a chance to since we still aren't talking, not since I found out he's going to be a dad, so I don't know when it would have been brought up. I'm leaving in a few days, and I already know Aiden won't go to UCLA now. He will end up working for his dad and raising his family here. He's too good of a person, he'd never leave his own child behind.

I started packing already, which is very unlike me, but I guess I'm anxious to leave. There's nothing here for me anymore. I've been ready to get back to the West Coast since I arrived in this stupid town. Aiden only clouded my judgement. Now that he isn't holding me back any longer, I want to board the first flight into my future.

There's a big Fourth of July celebration tonight. Usually Aiden hosts the big parties, but with his recent predicament, Nick offered his parents' place. I didn't want to go, and I definitely wouldn't have if it was at Aiden's, but Jess drags me out of the house.

Decked in our red, white, and blue, Jess and I are driven to the party by Max. We're drinking spiked seltzers in the back seat out of water bottles because there's no way I can show up to Nick's sober.

"Have you talked to Aiden recently?" Jess asks.

"No."

"You should."

"There isn't anything more to say."

"Harlow, you're moving soon. You can't leave things unresolved. You love him."

"Loved," I correct. "He has someone else to love now. Someone he's having a baby with."

"Maybe so, but that doesn't change the way he feels about you."

"It changes the way I feel about him," I say. "I have no feelings toward him anymore. None at all."

Jess rolls her eyes. She knows it's a lie, but she doesn't push the subject further. "Well, let's have fun tonight. Forget boys. They're stupid."

Max looks at us through the rearview mirror. "Hey!"

Jess laughs. "Oh, come on. You know you're stupid sometimes."

Max and I both laugh, though his laughter is more genuine than my own.

Nick's house is smaller than Aiden's, but it's still larger than the average house. He has an outdoor pool and a big backyard. When we pull up to the house, we can hear the bass booming from the speakers. We walk around to the backyard until we're greeted with familiar faces. I instantly see Matt and hug him. I scan the crowd to see if Aiden's here, though not discreetly enough, because Matt catches on to what I'm doing and immediately assures me that Aiden isn't coming. I'm relieved, but also slightly disappointed. I'm confusing myself with my emotions, or lack thereof, I should say.

I spot a group of guys doing body shots off girls in their bikinis. Jess and I roll our eyes at how desperate they are for attention. We join in on drinking games, ones that don't involve drunken mouths slurping out of our belly buttons, and eventually the buzz grows stronger. We find ourselves swimming drunkenly in the pool with Matt and Max.

We're laughing about something Max just said when I notice Nick walking toward us. I don't want to talk to him, but of course his eyes are laser focused on me when he joins us in the pool.

He's grinning. "Hey, Harlow."

"Hi," I say.

"You look sexy as hell in that little bikini of yours." He sounds drunk. And pathetic.

Max interjects. "Lay off, dude."

The dynamic of the group has changed a lot since the camping trip. The most interaction we've had with Nick was when he sat at our table at prom. Other than that, we haven't really been on the best of terms.

"Can't a guy compliment a pretty girl?" he says, his eyes still on me.

"Thanks." I turn away from him, hoping he can sense my disinterest when I start a conversation with Jess, but he doesn't get the hint.

"Where's Aiden?" he asks me. "With his knocked-up ex?"

Before I can respond, Jess splashes him. "Quit being a dick. Harlow doesn't deserve that."

She's right. I've never done anything to him, so what's his problem?

"I know. What I wanted to say, was that I'm sorry on behalf of that idiot. He had a great thing going with you. What a fool for letting you go."

I agree with him, but I don't like the way his words come off. Like I'm a pet that Aiden didn't take care of and is giving away to someone else. I'm not anyone's to give.

"I need a shot," I say, ignoring Nick altogether.

"Me, too," Matt agrees.

Matt and I make our way to the cooler. Our options are limited to UV blue and Jägermeister. Matt and I settle on the Jäger.

"Gross," I say after throwing back the shot.

Matt laughs. "It wasn't all that bad."

We walk back toward the pool. Jess is in the middle of an intense game of water volleyball, though it's mostly just a lot of splashing and drinks spilling, and not so much of volleying the ball. It's entertaining to say the least.

Matt and I take a seat at the edge of the pool. "How are you holding up?" he asks, sounding genuinely concerned.

I can see why he's one of Aiden's best friends. He's a really good guy.

I shrug. "I've been fine. I've mostly shut my feelings off toward the whole situation."

"Why would you want to do that?"

"It's better than being crushed by the pain."

"It's a shitty situation," he agrees. "But that doesn't mean he doesn't want to be with you, Harlow."

"He doesn't know what he wants. He's having a *baby*. I'm only here for a few more days. Even if he doesn't realize it now, he would see in a few months that we could never work."

Matt nods his head. I think he understands where I'm coming from.

"I think you should still talk to him."

"That's what everyone seems to think."

"Then why don't you?"

"There's nothing either of us could say that's going to change the circumstances we're in."

"He's my best friend, Harlow. And I know he's hurting. The only person that can fix that is you. Do you still love him?"

"No," I say without hesitation.

"I don't believe that for one second."

I playfully push him. "I don't need you to believe it," I say. "I only need to convince myself."

"He's at home right now," he says out of nowhere.

I look at him confused. "Okay?"

"I'll call you a ride. You should go see him."

I shake my head, but suddenly my mouth disagrees with my head, and I agree to his offer. Before I know it, I'm in a car heading to Aiden's house.

I walk through the front door like I have so many times before. I call for Aiden, but he doesn't answer. No one answers. His parents must be out of town again, which means Janet probably isn't here either. I walk to his room. His door is closed. I open it slowly.

"Aiden?" I say as quietly as I can.

I push the door open, and I see Aiden sitting on the bed. But he isn't alone. He's with Amanda. I can't look away. She's leaning into him, and his arms are around her.

What a picture-perfect family, I think to myself.

This isn't what I was expecting when I came. I curse under my breath for letting Matt convince me to come here. What was I thinking? Of course, he's moved on. He's having a *baby,* for crying out loud. I'll be thousands of miles away in a matter of days. Out of sight, out of mind, right? I've been out of sight for two weeks now. I've allowed Amanda to weasel her way back into his life.

All the emotions I closed myself off to take over quickly. I turn away, not even sure if he's seen me, and run back home. It's no wonder I shut off my feelings. I don't like feeling this way. Broken. Wrecked. Lost. Like I'm sinking.

I don't know if it's the alcohol, or the realization that Aiden and I are really over, but I run directly into my bathroom, almost not making it to the toilet. I don't get sick from alcohol, ever, so it must be Aiden. The heartache. The heartbreak. The loss. He promised me he wouldn't hurt me, not like this. He promised he'd never leave me, but he's already back with her. He lied. He never really loved me. I will myself to snap out of it. I need to pull myself together. I can't let this happen to me, let him affect me this way. I try so damn hard not to feel anything.

Then I'm sick again.

Chapter thirty-two

Present

Aiden is put in a medically induced coma to allow for healing after surgery. He's been in the ICU for three days. I haven't left his bedside since they allowed me back here. When I first saw him, I couldn't even recognize him. He has a tube coming out of his mouth to help him breathe. Wires stick out of him from all different angles. He looks like the hospital's puppet. Bruises cover his face and arms. The parts I can see, anyway. They washed him once at the bedside, and I saw even more coloring over his once perfect stomach. He's still beautiful to me, but it hurts to see him like this.

Jess, Max, and Matt have all been by to visit, bringing me coffee and something to eat. I haven't had much of an appetite, but if I don't at least take a couple of bites, they harp at me. I'd rather force-feed myself than be griped at.

I cancel my flight back to California. That is a no-brainer. I can't leave, not while Aiden fights for his life. The doctors talk about waking him soon, which is good news, as long as the swelling in his brain subsides.

The nurses bring me a cot to sleep on, though sometimes I crawl into Aiden's bed and lie with him. It's hard because of all the wires, but I make it work. I like to be close to him, to feel his warm skin. It's a reminder that he's still in there somewhere. I need him to be okay. He can't die not knowing how I really feel. I don't care anymore what happened that summer. It's in the past. We're living in the present now, and I don't want to go another day without him.

Doctors constantly come in and out of Aiden's room to run tests and assess his injuries. After a week, the bruises turn a yellowish brown. The swelling has gone down in his face, and he's starting to look more like himself. They're feeding him through an IV. It's supposed to help keep him strong and fighting, but I can feel him weakening when I touch him.

Aiden would hate this, feeling so helpless. I hope for his sake that they can wake him soon. The most recent scans of his brain showed that the swelling has decreased, but they don't feel comfortable taking him out of his coma yet. They're hopeful it will only be a few more days until they can bring him out of it. Then it will be up to Aiden to wake fully.

Amanda hasn't visited once. I still don't know what happened between them after that summer, not that I care much anymore. I know Aiden doesn't have a child, or at least no one has ever mentioned to me that he has a mini-me running around somewhere. That kind of news would have had to make its way back to me at some point. Over the years, I have reached my own conclusions. Either the baby wasn't really his, or Amanda lost it. For both their sakes, I hope it was the former. Miscarriage is a sad and disheartening thing.

I haven't seen Amanda once since I've been back. I don't even know if she still lives in Portlet. Jess has never posted pictures with her on social media either. If Aiden and Amanda were together again at any point, surely Jess would have hung out with them, and Amanda would be in some group pictures at the very least.

I called my dad from the hospital the day after his wedding to explain to him what happened and why he wouldn't be taking me to the airport. He seemed really taken aback. I could swear I heard him choke on his words at some point. He and Aiden must have been closer than I realized. My dad has called every day since looking for updates. He's on his honeymoon right now with Tammie in Europe, after having said he would cancel the trip. But I insisted they still go. His persistence on the matter surprised me, but there wasn't anything he could do to help Aiden had he stayed home.

Max informed me that Janet still works for Aiden, which doesn't surprise me in the least. I could tell how much she appreciated him back then. And after what happened to his parents, she was all Aiden had left. Janet takes care of things at home for Aiden, ensuring he comes back to a clean house once he's released. She's also taken care of everything that needed to be handled, such as letting Aiden's business know about the accident.

When Aiden's parents died, he took over the family business. He's the CEO of Walton Enterprises, designing and developing stainless steel appliances, a multimillion-dollar company that Aiden never had any intention of being a part of, but he was thrown into it when his father was no longer there. I can't imagine how hard that must have been for him. Losing his parents, his girlfriend, and suddenly being handed a future he never wanted. Aiden's been through a lot, and I hate that it's taken a tragedy for me to finally realize it. To realize that I abandoned him when he needed me the most.

Dr. Ignacio is the neurologist that's been keeping up with Aiden's case. He took Aiden about an hour ago for more scans of his brain. I use this as an opportunity to get some fresh air. His scans should take a little over an hour, so I walk across the street to the coffee shop and order a tea to kill time. Jolene calls me almost every hour on the hour. It's been nice to talk with her, especially when I'm alone. She knew something bad must have happened when I didn't get on my flight back home.

The clock strikes noon, and my phone buzzes in my purse. On time as always.

"Hey, Joey."

"How is he?" she asks.

"Since you asked an hour ago, he's the same. They took him for more tests. I'll know more when they get the results."

"How are you holding up?"

"The same."

"Do you want me to fly out there to be with you?"

She offers every time she calls.

"I appreciate it, but no. That's okay. Your phone calls help."

I can practically see her smile on the other end of the line. "Good."

"I'm walking back to the hospital now. He should be back soon."

"Okay, Harley," she says. "I'll talk to you in another hour."

I laugh a little. "Talk to you then."

Aiden would love Jolene. He never met her, which was very unfortunate for both of them. I make a mental note to introduce Aiden to Jolene as soon as he recovers. I've been making many plans for the things we'll do once he can go home. It makes this all more bearable, imagining what life will be like when he's out. We can finally be together, if he'll forgive me. I'll sell my house if I have to and move back to Indiana. I don't care where I'm at, but I won't spend another second away from Aiden if I can help it.

I do want to bring him to the West Coast at some point to show him around. Maybe I can keep my house as a place for us to stay occasionally, maybe a winter home. Indiana's winters are brutal, and I could do without the snow. I don't know how it would work with his business, but that's something we can discuss. Maybe he can run it remotely or open a headquarters in LA.

I also have to tell him what happened all those years ago, though I know that won't be an easy conversation for us. It was hard going through something like that alone, and I know he will feel guilty for not being there for me, but it's not like he had any way of knowing. It wasn't his fault.

When I get back to the hospital room, Aiden still isn't back. I take a seat on the nearly plastic couch intended to make family members comfortable. It's anything *but* comfortable. It's stiff, and I'm pretty sure if I sit on it too long, they'll need to rotate me to prevent bed sores.

The nurses eventually bring Aiden back. They inform me that Dr. Ignacio will begin tapering him off the anesthesia, and he should wake within a matter of hours or days. This news excites me because that means the swelling in his brain has gone down and the bleeding has subsided. They see the hopefulness on my face, and the nurse reminds me that he's not out of the woods yet, that there is still a long road to recovery. But all I can focus on is that Aiden could be waking up at any moment.

Chapter thirty-three

One week later

It's been one week since they took him off anesthesia. He still hasn't woken up.

Chapter thirty-four

Two weeks later

His body lies there, relaxed as ever. I will his eyes to open, but still, they don't.

Chapter thirty-five

Three weeks later

Nothing has happened. Nothing.

Chapter thirty-six

One month later

Aiden still hasn't woken up.

Chapter thirty-seven

Past

Aiden never tries to contact me after I saw him with Amanda, and I am too sick to even try to confront him. After about a week, I block his number. I am tired of checking my phone, a small part of me hoping that what I saw isn't real, that Aiden will fight for us. But I can't get the image of them out of my head. I am mad. Furious. And I have other things to focus on. The nausea continues. Every morning, I wake up and rush to the bathroom. Anytime I smell bacon or coffee, it makes me sick.

The day before I leave Portlet, I hear the news of Aiden's parents. They were taking a charter plane home from the Bahamas during a pretty bad thunderstorm. The small plane struggled to gain altitude after takeoff and crashed into an open field. It is all over the news. I can't imagine the loss Aiden must feel. At one point, I start to walk over to his house to check on him, but I can see people inside. He already has company, and the house is filled with several bodies. Besides, he has *Amanda* to comfort him now.

His parents' funeral is a few days later, after I am already back on the West Coast, and coincidently the same day as the Lumineers concert that I don't attend. I order an arrangement of flowers for the funeral. I don't sign my name, so he has no way of knowing it is from me. It is more for my own selfish reasons that I sent them. I know I'm a bitch, but his parents just died, and although I can't see him in person, it is a small gesture that makes me feel a little bit better about not being there. My parents tell me they went, my dad taking a special interest in making sure Aiden is okay. I don't ask how he is. I'm sure he is sad. How else does someone react to the sudden loss of their parents?

Jolene and I move onto campus. Three weeks later, the nausea still hasn't subsided. Jolene suggests I take a pregnancy test, though I quickly turn it down. There's no way I'm pregnant. There's no way Aiden could have impregnant two girls this year. I can't be pregnant. I just can't be. Can I?

"Harley, it's not normal for someone to be sick for this long," she says. "Is there *any* chance you might be pregnant?"

I think about it for a moment. I take my birth control religiously, but Aiden and I never used condoms. He also never pulled out, so I guess there is a chance I could be.

"I guess."

"That's it. Get in the car. We're going to buy a test."

An hour later, we return with three different types of pregnancy tests. Two of them show two dark lines indicating I'm pregnant, and the third one literally spells it out for me: *Pregnant*.

"Shit," I mumble. "Shit. Shit. *Shit.*"

"It's okay. We'll figure this out."

"How am I going to raise a child *and* go to school?"

"We can hire a babysitter during class. We'll rent an apartment next semester and get out of the dorms. It's okay, Harley. I'm going to be with you every step of the way."

Jolene is such a good friend to me, and right now, I have no idea what I would do without her.

"Do you think you should call Aiden?" she asks.

"No," I answer immediately. "Amanda's already pregnant with his baby. The last thing he needs is *two* baby mamas after his parents just died."

She nods. "You'll have to tell him eventually, though," she says. "The baby didn't do anything to not deserve a father."

"I know. Just not right now. Maybe in a few months or after the baby is born. Right now, all I need is you, and for this morning sickness to go away."

Jolene hugs me tight. "I'm going to be the best auntie."

A small smile escapes my lips. I'm by no means ready to be a mother, but is anyone ever truly ready?

For the next few weeks, we attend doctor's appointments, and I start taking prenatal vitamins. Jolene is the overprotective parent and makes sure I do everything the doctor says. I haven't told my parents yet. I'll tackle that once I tell Aiden, but I'm a world away right now, and this is something I can handle on my own. With the help of Jolene, of course.

I'm nearly twelve weeks pregnant when I wake up in the middle of the night with sharp abdominal pain. I feel something wet on the sheets. When I switch on the lamp, all I see is red. It only takes me a second to realize it's blood. *A lot* of blood.

"Joey!" I scream.

She rushes into my room, and her eyes immediately fall to my sheets. She doesn't hesitate when she gets me dressed and rushes me into the car. She speeds to the closest hospital, stopping frantically at the entrance to the ER.

Out the window, Jolene yells, "She's pregnant!"

When the nurses see the blood, they scoop me into a wheelchair and take me away. They tell me right away that I'm having a miscarriage. They do what they need to prevent me from hemorrhaging or developing an infection. The doctor does a quick procedure, and I am discharged just over twenty-four hours later. I am prescribed medication and left to deal with the traumatic loss on my own.

Jolene tries for weeks to get me to talk about it, but I can't. Maybe a small part of me thought I could win Aiden back with his child, much like Amanda did. It's almost like my last chance was ripped away. But not only do I feel like I lost Aiden again, I lost a piece of him, the piece that had grown inside of me. I had grown to love my baby. I grew a human in my stomach for nearly three months, and suddenly, my baby is gone. I'll never know them. I don't even know if I was having a boy or a girl.

Jolene eventually suggests that I seek counseling. I speak with the counselor on campus, and they refer me to a therapist. I now have one, sometimes two, sessions a week. We talk about the baby I'll never know, about love, and about loss, but we mostly talk about Aiden. Therapy has helped, but as I learn to accept the grief, it brings back all the emotions I tried to avoid.

It never gets easier being without Aiden. If anything, each day gets harder and harder. I have no way of contacting him directly after blocking him literally and figuratively out of my life. I don't want to unblock him and succumb to the temptation. Sometimes I think about calling him from Jolene's phone, but what good would come of that? I've accepted my fate, and as my therapist says, I need to learn to live with the heartache and find my own ways to overcome it. Find happiness within myself instead of in someone else.

I throw myself into my schoolwork, finishing the semester with straight A's. I don't visit my parents over Christmas break. I don't visit them ever again. My parents get a divorce. My mom moves to LA. My dad visits occasionally. I sleep with men to fill a void that can never be filled. This is my life now. This is my very sad, lonely life. I try to find happiness within myself, but it hasn't worked yet. The days aren't as hard as they used to be, but I still feel alone. At least I have Jolene.

Chapter thirty-eight

Present

It's a beautiful August morning. The sun shines, and the trees outside the window have white blooms. I can see moms pushing their children in strollers on the sidewalk. I've gotten to know these moms, not personally, but in my head. There's a mom who walks by almost every day at nine-thirty in the morning with her headphones in, pushing a stroller in front of her. She wears big sunglasses, the kind that make you look like a bug. I call her Dorothy. Her child looks to be about three years old, and I call him Toto. Yes, it's my own take on the *Wizard of Oz*. Dorothy and Toto have become part of my morning routine.

I wake up on the cot each morning and check on Aiden. He's breathing on his own now, but he hasn't opened his eyes. Usually, I walk across the street to grab a coffee or tea after the nurse's morning rounds. On this particular day, I chose the latter. When I get back to Aiden's room, it's almost nine-thirty, and I wait for Dorothy and Toto to take their daily stroll. Some days, I see Cinderella and Belle walking their dogs, this blonde and brunette best friend duo. My sudden Disney fascination worries me. Maybe I've gone mad.

It's been forty-five days since my father's wedding, which means it's been forty-five days since Aiden was in the accident. The doctors stopped the anesthesia over a month ago, and he still hasn't woken up. They tell me that everyone reacts differently to being in a coma. His vitals are great, and they're hopeful with his prognosis. The bruising has long since disappeared, and he looks like the Aiden I love. A much older version than the one I fell in love with, but still extremely handsome.

The doctor told me that Aiden is sleeping still and, although he can't answer me, he might hear me. Sometimes I play our favorite Lumineers song for him so there's something he can listen to. But most of the time, I talk to him. I tell him about the last eight years and everything I've been through. Maybe he'll remember, or maybe I'll have to tell him again when he wakes up. I'm okay with either, I just hope he wakes up soon.

My old therapist had suggested I give my baby a name to cope with the loss. I might mourn a person better if I can identify them, she said. I imagined that I would have had a boy. He would have had Aiden's ocean-colored eyes and his perfectly messy hair, but he would have had my nose and mouth. I named him Hayden, a perfect mix of the two of us. I tell Aiden all about Hayden and what I think he would be like right now. That maybe he would be cocky like his dad, but in the best way. Maybe he would play football with Aiden as the coach. I would happily cheer on both of my boys from the sidelines. It could have been a beautiful life, one I still hope to have one day.

I hold his hand as I talk about Hayden. Every day, I come up with another fact about him. Today, I tell him that maybe Hayden's favorite food would be minestrone, and that I would have made it for him every day that he asked. As I tell Aiden about the secret ingredient that makes my soup stand out from the rest, I feel his thumb brush over my knuckles. At first, I don't think anything of it. Then it hits me. He hasn't moved a single body part in forty-five days. His *thumb* just *moved. His thumb just moved!*

"Aiden?" I say, hopeful. I don't know if I'm imagining things.

His thumb moves again. This time, I know it's real. This is really happening. I stand up, never letting go of his hand.

"Nurse!" I yell. "Nurse! He just moved his thumb!"

Dr. Ignacio and his team of nurses run in in a matter of seconds. They're assessing Aiden's vitals and shining a bright light into his pupils.

"He's responding to light," one nurse says.

"Vitals look good," says another.

He squeezes my hand ever so lightly, almost too gentle to notice, but I feel it.

"He just squeezed my hand!" I shout as my eyes fill with tears.

They assess his reflexes. As they're doing something to his feet, I see his eyes flutter open.

"He's awake." It comes out as a whisper because I think I'm in a state of shock.

I've been waiting for this. For this exact moment. I don't know how he's going to react to me being here. I don't even know if he's going to remember who I am. They warned me that he may have memory loss or other loss of function from the accident that they couldn't assess until he is awake.

The worry I feel that something might be wrong with him when he wakes up quickly vanishes when he looks at me. He immediately smiles. He's happy to see me. He's happy I'm here. He knows who I am!

I cry hysterically. I ignore the nurses who are still doing their evaluations, and I fall on top of him. I hug him and cry into his neck. The nurses give me a minute. A minute I deserve after the forty-five days I've waited for the love of my life to wake up. Aiden slowly lifts his arms until they're wrapped around my back.

It takes everything in me to pull away from him, but I can hear other doctors approaching. They'll need to examine him and run more tests. As they take notes and ask Aiden questions, he never stops looking at me. I haven't stopped crying, but he never looks away.

After several hours, when doctors and nurses have finally left the room, Aiden motions for me to join him on his hospital bed. I happily oblige and climb into the spot that I've found myself comfortable in every day since he's arrived. I don't know if he has truly comprehended what's happened yet, but the doctors told him how long it's been and the details of the accident. He didn't have the reaction I expected. Instead, his eyes stayed glued to mine as he nodded to them in understanding.

"How long have you been here?" he whispers into my ear.

"Since the day of your accident."

"I was on my way home from the gym. That's the last thing I remember."

I start to cry again, but I try to wipe away the tears so as not to soak his hospital gown. "I thought you changed your mind about going to the wedding."

"Were you disappointed?" he asks. "When you noticed that I wasn't there?"

I nod.

He smirks. "Good."

"I didn't know I was your emergency contact," I admit softly, thinking back to that day. To the missed calls I had. To the moment I realized that I was all Aiden had left.

"I figured if anything ever happened to me, you were the only person I cared to tell. You're the only one who ever truly mattered."

"I'm so sorry, Aiden."

"What do you have to be sorry for?"

"I wasn't there for you. You found out you were going to be a dad, and I left you. I assumed you chose her over me, especially after I walked in on the two of you. And who knows, maybe you did, but that's okay. It doesn't excuse the fact that I wasn't there when your parents died. I should have been there, Aiden."

He takes a moment to let that soak in. "I didn't choose her, Harlow. And what you walked in on was her telling me she lost the baby. I was trying to comfort her, and I'd be lying if I said I didn't need someone to comfort me back. But I was never going to be with her, even if she was the mother of my child." He takes a second before he continues. "It doesn't matter now, but I found out a few months later that she faked the whole thing. She was never even pregnant."

My eyes grow big. "She lied about being *pregnant*? What kind of sick human would do that?"

"It didn't even faze me. I had more important things to worry about back then. I was busy learning the ins and outs of Walton Enterprises, mourning the loss of my parents, and I didn't want anything to do with her. She wasn't worth my time or my frustration."

"That must have been hard on you."

"It was hard going through all of that without you," he admits.

I figure right now is as good a time as any to tell him about what happened. "Hey, Aiden?"

"Yeah?"

"I was pregnant."

His body tenses. I don't know what he's feeling, but by this reaction alone, I would assume that he hadn't heard anything I was telling him when he was in a coma.

"*Was*?" he asks hesitantly.

"I had a miscarriage. A real one."

He squeezes me tightly, and his voice cracks when he asks, "When?"

"Eight years ago. I found out a few weeks after I left."

I can feel his chest move as he inhales deeply. I imagine this is a lot for him to take in, especially after finding out he's been asleep for forty-five days.

"Are you okay? Were you okay?" he asks.

"No," I answer honestly. "I was never okay. I had to see a therapist. I still can't be around kids without it hurting. It was really hard."

Aiden wipes away a tear as it falls down my cheek. "I'm so sorry, Harlow. I didn't know."

"I was going to tell you. I wouldn't keep your son away from you, but then that happened, and there wasn't anything to tell you anymore."

"Son?"

"I never found out if I was having a boy or a girl, but I liked to imagine he was a boy. My therapist told me that would help me cope. I named him Hayden."

He smiles. "That's a great name."

"I know."

"I flew to California to see you," he admits.

I turn my head so I can look at him to see if he's being serious. He is.

"What? When?"

"About a year after you left. Once I had things figured out at work, I booked a one-way ticket. I didn't know how long I would be there, but I wanted to tell you everything. That Amanda lied. That there was no baby. That I still loved you."

"You never found me?" I ask.

"I found you," he says. "I saw you walking with one of your friends. I figured it was Jolene just from the way you had described her. You looked happy, Harlow. I almost approached you, but then I saw a guy walk up and put his arm around you. I thought maybe he was your boyfriend. Either way, dating someone halfway across the country while you were in school didn't seem fair. I couldn't leave Indiana, and I didn't want to put you in that position. Besides, you probably still hated me."

"I never hated you," I say. Not for lack of trying.

"Was he your boyfriend?"

I shrug. "You know I don't do boyfriends."

He chuckles. "Was he another one of the surfers?"

"I retired surfers," I joke. "I was interested in other hobbies by then."

Aiden cringes a little. "I never should have let you walk away."

"I never would have let you convince me not to. I'm too stubborn for my own good."

"A rock."

"Exactly."

Aiden kisses the top of my head. It's the first time his lips have touched me in so long. It sends a tingle down my spine. I hold onto him tightly.

"Please don't ever scare me like that again," I whisper.

"I'll do my best."

"So, where do we go from here?" I ask a little while later.

Aiden's just eaten a Jell-O cup, though it's still hard for him to swallow.

"Where do you want to go, Harlow?"

My phone rings. I look at the clock. It must be Jolene. I haven't been answering her calls the last few hours because so much has been happening. When Aiden sees her name, he urges me to answer it. I put her on speaker phone.

"Harley?"

"Yes, hi," I say.

"How is he? What the hell is going on! I've been worried. You stopped taking my calls."

I can't keep the giant grin off my face. "Big changes from the last time we talked."

"What kind of changes?" she asks, excited.

I hold the phone closer to Aiden so he can speak.

"Hi, Jolene," he says.

Jolene screams. I have to move the phone away from us because it's a high-pitched scream sure to burst the eardrums of anyone unfortunate enough to be nearby. But it's also the best scream I've ever heard. It's the *he's okay* scream.

"Aiden!" she says. "Harley, he's okay! Oh, my God, this is so great! Aiden, do you know what you've put her through? Holy hell."

Aiden looks to me with a mischievous grin. "Harley?" he mouths.

I roll my eyes. "I'll call you back later, okay?"

"Of course. Bye! Bye, Aiden!"

I hang up.

"Harley," Aiden repeats. "I love it."

"Only she calls me that," I say.

"And now me, too." He winks. "Now, where were we? Where do you want to go from here, *Harley*?"

I lay my head onto his chest, smiling. "I don't care," I say. "But wherever I go, I want to go there with you."

Epilogue

Aiden's road to recovery is long. Once he is released from the hospital, I stay with him at his house in Portlet, and I quit my job at the firm. Aiden and I need to figure out a lot of things, but money isn't one of them. We stay in Indiana until the following year and celebrate Christmas with my dad, Tammie, and Ernie. It is one of my favorite Christmases.

We stay at my house in California for the remainder of the winter, spending a lot of our time at the beach, loving on one another every chance we have, making up for lost time. The rest of the winter turns into the rest of the year. Neither of us is ready to let go of our beach life. The following year, we return to Portlet because Aiden is selling his family home. It is a bittersweet goodbye, but he is ready. Luckily, he can run Walton Enterprises remotely, meaning we now have the freedom to live wherever we want.

Aiden and I plan to road trip back to California now that the house has sold and summer has begun.

On the first night, we pull up to a quaint cabin backed onto a lake. It isn't his family's lake house like I had expected, but rather the cabin he brought me to the night of graduation. It's been exactly ten years since we've been here, and I immediately know why he's brought me back. We both run with excitement to the tree marked with our initials inside a heart.

"See," I say. "It's a good thing I marked which tree! There are dozens now."

Aiden laughs and begins to dig. He pulls out the small familiar chest and takes out the artifacts we left behind. First, he takes out the Lumineers CD.

"I stopped listening to them for a long time," I admit, eyeing the decade-old CD. "I can't remember the last time I even held a CD in my hand, now that everything has gone digital."

"Me too."

We continue looking at the artifacts one by one, talking about the memories and how far we've come since that day. I don't know if I ever truly believed we would return to this place, especially after eight years apart.

Aiden's looking into the chest again. "It looks like there's one more thing."

Confused, I try glancing over his shoulder and into the chest. "What? We only put four artifacts in there. What is it?"

Aiden distracts me with the empty chest as he pulls out a small jewelry box from his pocket. The moment he gets down on one knee, I throw my arms around him and cry into his neck.

"I haven't even asked you yet, babe," he says, laughing.

Dammit. I'm ruining the moment. I try to wipe away the tears, but I'm already so emotional. My mascara is probably running down my face at this point, and it's hard to catch my breath.

"I'm sorry," I manage.

Aiden's grabs my hands, and we stand up together.

"My Black Sheep," he begins. "I have loved you every single second of every single day since the moment I first saw you at that café. Your beauty took my breath away then, and it continues to do that to this very day. I have never met anyone quite like you. I knew you deserved better than what you had in the past, and I could not imagine you being with anyone, so I did my best to be better for you. I'm *doing* my best. I have felt every emotion that someone could feel with you, and I would do it all over again just to get to this moment. To be loved by you, Harlow Brooks, is the greatest privilege of my life."

He gets back down on one knee and opens the box. I'm in shock. I can't believe this man loves me. I can't believe what he's about to do. "Will you please do me the honor of being Harlow Walton and becoming my wife?"

"Yes!" I say right before I jump into his arms. "Yes, yes, yes."

Now we're both crying, and hugging, and he's spinning me in circles. I still haven't seen the ring, but I don't even care. Aiden will be my husband, and I'm going to be his wife. I'm the lucky woman who gets to be loved by this man. Who knew after all this time that this moment would ever truly come? After everything that's happened, I get to call Aiden Walton mine forever.

He sets me down, takes the ring out of the box, and slides it onto my finger. I get to look at it for the first time, and it's easily the most stunning ring I've ever seen in my life. I'm mesmerized by it.

"Wow," I say astounded.

"A beautiful ring for a beautiful woman."

I smile. "I love you so much, Aiden."

"I love you, baby."

He kisses me, our first kiss as an engaged couple, and it feels different than the rest. It feels stronger.

"There's one more thing," he says.

"What?" I ask, curious.

"This cabin," he says. "It's ours."

"What!" I yell.

"Now we can visit whenever we want."

I take a moment, eyeing the land around us, the sand, the water, the beauty. "I don't want to just visit," I say. "Let's live here. Let's raise our family here."

Aiden caresses my cheek, smiling. "That's a wonderful idea."

The End

Acknowledgments

I can't believe it, but here we are again. Thank you to everyone, once again, who made this book possible. To everyone who read my first novel, *See You Never*, and encouraged me to keep writing, and to everyone who liked, shared, commented, and wrote reviews in support of *See You Never*, thank you. I would never be able to continue writing if it wasn't for all the people willing to take a chance on me, willing to give a new author this opportunity.

I wrote *Rocky Love* shortly after I finished writing the rough draft of *See You Never*. I remember thinking this book was totally different than my first, more my speed. It's filled with love and heartbreak, and it hits me right in the feels even to this day. Harlow's character is absolutely nothing like me, and I think that's why I love her so much. She allows us as readers to watch her grow, to go through life with her, and ultimately witness her walls get knocked down. And Aiden. Sweet, sweet Aiden. Ladies, if you ever find yourself an Aiden, make sure you never let him go.

I had one special Beta Reader for *Rocky Love* that I would like to thank. Kirsten Iversen, you read my book in its roughest form. From laughing at my errors to getting the book ready for my editing team. Thank you for all the time you've put into both *See You Never* and *Rocky Love*. You're a true friend.

I want to thank my family for supporting me with this unexpected dream. However you guys can help, you've been ready and willing. We are all navigating this industry together, and I'm so thankful to have you by my side. Especially you, Mom.

I want to thank Rare Apparel/Fuse Salon and Spa in Frankfort, Illinois for being the first brick and mortar store to stock their shelves with my book. You've allowed me to expand my readers in a way I couldn't do alone. Thank you from the bottom of my heart.

I also want to thank Sundog Books in Seaside, Florida for being the first bookstore to sell a copy of my book. Neighborhood bookstores are quickly becoming my favorite spots to visit, and it is a dream to have my novels on their shelves.

Thank you once again to everyone at The Pro Book Editor. Debra L Hartmann has continued to guide me through the publishing process and is teaching me how to be grammatically correct along the way. My books wouldn't be what they are without her.

For anyone who likes books like *See You Never* and *Rocky Love*, or anyone who just likes to read romance novels in general, I've created a book club on Instagram where I share all my favorite authors and books. Check out @ladybookers for all the book recs!

Readers, thank you once again. One published book has now turned to two, and I have even more stories to share in the future. You can look out for *Give Her the World* next, and *See You Soon*, the highly anticipated sequel to *See You Never*.

About the author

Delaney Lynn is a Public Health Nutritionist and avid romance reader/writer. She started the Lady Bookers Book Club via Instagram in 2019, frequently sharing her favorite authors and novels. We invite you to follow Delaney's book club @ladybookers on Instagram and connect with the author @laneyylynn on Instagram.

GIVE HER THE WORLD SNEAK PEEK
Chapter One

Hayes

"Another round!" my teammate shouts from the other end of the bar.

It's the first day of syllabus week, the first week back to school when teachers assign no homework and we spend approximately fifty minutes in each class simply reading the syllabus. It's pointless really. It's not like we don't have access to our syllabus through the campus portal. There's no reason to even go to class this week, and most students don't. Unfortunately for myself and the rest of the East Valley baseball team, if our coach caught wind of us skipping class, even on syllabus week, we'd have extra sprints to run after practice.

"Murphy!"

I turn to find my best friend Jason holding up another shot of Jameson for me. I pull back the shot, and a collective cheer sounds throughout the bar as we finish our ninth shot of the night. It's tradition every year for the senior class baseball players to take one shot for each championship East Valley has taken home—our own tribute to all the great players who have made it to the big leagues. Only seven more shots to go. Thanks to our undefeated season last year, East Valley has officially won sixteen championships.

"Fuck, dude. We shouldn't have pre-gamed before this," Jason says.

"You," I correct. "*You* shouldn't have pre-gamed. I feel great." I give him a teasing nudge.

"How many more?" he asks.

"Seven. Come on, next rounds on me."

I walk to the bar to order a shot of Jameson for each of the eight seniors participating in this year's championship shots. "Eight shots of Jameson, please," I ask the blonde bartender, grinning.

Even in the dark lighting of the sports bar, I can see her cheeks blush. She's cute—cute enough that I can hopefully flirt my way to a few of those shots being free, seeing as I don't have much extra cash to spare. I'm here on a full-ride scholarship, which was the only way I was ever going to be able to attend college. We're not supposed to work during the season, though I've kept my job since freshmen year and coach hasn't said a thing. As long as it doesn't interfere with my stats, he doesn't mind me pocketing a few extra bucks a week. My parents especially don't mind. In fact, it was their idea.

The cute bartender returns with a tray full of Jamo. Looks like my charm worked. I count ten shots, so that's two free. Jason and I will be ahead by one round, and he'll be one shot closer to finding his head buried in the toilet.

After the guys each grab their respective shots, Jason and I look at the four remaining.

"Ready, man?" I ask as he eyes the liquid like it's poison.

The bar is packed, but the bartender is staying close by, making eyes at me like she wants to strike up a conversation.

I bite. "Hey," I call out to her. "Think you can take one of these for my friend here? Just don't tell the guys. He won't hear the end of it."

She smiles as she leans against the bar, pushing her perky tits on full display. Jason's gaze moves from the shots to her chest, but her eyes stay on me. "Sure," she says.

I pick up two of the shots, Jason and the bartender each taking one for themselves.

"And what is the name of my savior?" Jason asks, still eyeing her chest.

Her eyes flicker to Jason for a moment before looking back to me, her focus on my lips. "Natalie."

"Natalie, it is a pleasure to meet you," Jason says as he downs his shot.

Natalie holds up her shot glass to mine in cheers.

I oblige and down the first one, followed by the second.

Natalie is making it a point to blatantly check me out, and I know if I want to get laid tonight, this would be a sure thing. I mean, who the hell am I kidding? Of course I want to get laid. But even still, I know nothing is going to happen between us. I pass her a wink and walk away to the other side of the bar where the rest of the baseball team has pulled together a few tables.

Another round of shots has already been brought to the table. Damn, am I going to be fucked up tonight.

"Shut the hell up, everyone! I'm going to make a toast!" shouts our catcher, a short and thin guy named Tony, but we all call him Bony. It doesn't matter how many calories the guy eats or how hard coach works him in the gym, he doesn't beef up. But he's one of the fastest guys on the team and can throw one hell of a baseball. He's also a damn good catcher.

"Atta boy, Bony. Let's hear it!" shouts Kevin, Jason and I's roommate and our second baseman.

"This one's for you, Hayes Murphy, for leading us to another East Valley victory and the reason we're all getting extra fucked up this year! You're the best god damn pitcher I've ever had the privilege of catching for. Let's do it again, brother."

I hold up the shot someone passed me and give Bony a head nod. I don't need to get sentimental with him right now in the middle of this bar, but he's the best catcher I've ever had. After I down my twelfth shot of the night, I find Bony and give him a one-armed hug. Jason's arm falls to my shoulder from behind, quickly pulling me back from Bony.

"You gonna hit that?" Jason asks, nudging toward the bar.

"Who?"

"The bartender. She's been making eyes at you. You gonna hit that?"

I shrug. "I don't know. Night's still young."

Jason rolls his eyes. "Come on, dude. I've known you your whole life. Why do you always do this?"

"Do what?" I play dumb.

"Let the easy ones go. Don't you want to get laid?"

"No shit, I want to get laid."

"Then why are you letting Natalie go to waste? Not that I mind. I happily take the rejected women off your hands each time. But look at her. She's hot as fuck."

I shake my head and laugh. "She's all yours," I say, though I might regret that later when I'm rubbing one off in the shower.

"Dude, come on. You haven't brought a girl home in months."

"Are you keeping track of my sex life now?" I chuckle.

He rolls his eyes. "Fine, man. Fuck you. I tried to help. I apologize in advance when you hear Natalie screaming my name through the walls later." He winks before he walks away, straight to Natalie who still has her eyes on me.

It's never been my thing to sleep with the girls who practically throw themselves at me. Having been the star player on my baseball team since before I could properly fuck, I have no shortage of women who are willing to sleep with me. Problem is, most of them just want to be able to say they slept with Hayes Murphy, East Valley's star pitcher and soon to be MLB rookie of the year. No one doubts I'm going to get drafted this year and likely head right for the big leagues because my stats are better than most of the guys in the minor league. In high school, the attention was cool, but I got bored of it quickly. Once I realized I would be playing pro one day, I gave myself some standards. It's not like I would be taking advantage of these girls. Like I said, they willingly throw themselves at me. I know that they want to sleep with me, but I find it way more attractive when a girl could give two shits about who I am.

Two hours later, I finally take my last championship shot. Jason sat at the bar talking to Natalie up until twenty minutes ago when her shift ended and he walked her out to her car. He got inside, no doubt having her take them back to our place. She eyed me yet again on her way out, but I looked away, pretending I hadn't seen. Frankly, I'm just not interested in Natalie. I am, however, interested in the bombshell who just walked into the bar alone. Her hair is pulled back in a long ponytail, her brown hair swaying when she walks. Her bright blue eyes noticeable from across the bar, they are the perfect contrast to her dark hair and tan. She's petite, with grabbable hips and the perfect size breasts. Her lips have to be my favorite thing on her though, plump and naturally pouty, causing my dick to stir in my jeans. I'd put her in her mid-twenties, probably only a year or two older than me, though you'd never guess with my six-foot-three build and lean muscle from years of playing ball.

She doesn't so much as glance my way when she walks in, clueing me in that she has no idea who I am. Anyone from around here knows the East Valley baseball team, doesn't matter their age. They like to acknowledge our winning records and congratulate us on the most recent championship. We're well-known in this small town, especially me as the pitcher. This chick though, I already know she doesn't have the slightest clue who the rowdy bunch in the corner is.

I eye her as she takes a seat at the bar, another bartender appearing quickly to take her drink order. She glances around the bar, taking in her surroundings and completely missing my eyes on her.

Damn. She doesn't even notice me. And I love it.

I slam the rest of my beer and set the empty glass down. Sixteen shots and a couple beers deep, I'm in no way feeling shy. Not that I'm ever shy. I slide into the bar stool beside her, careful not to show my interest too soon. The bartender drops off her drink before switching her gaze to me. Her eyes widen as she notices who I am, though I have no desire for her to let this mystery woman know. For tonight, I just want to be a random guy at the bar who can hopefully get the beautiful woman sitting beside him to notice him.

"What're you havin'?" the bartender drawls, her southern twang a noticeable change to the midwestern accents that are prominent here in Timbers, Michigan.

I nudge my head toward the drink she just set down. "I'll have what she's having."

The bartender walks away, and I instantly feel the woman's eyes on me like heat in a fire. Her gaze is burning through my skin as she slowly scans over my body.

"What if you don't like what I ordered?" she asks.

I tilt my head to face her, locking gazes with her blue eyes for the first time. I have never seen eyes like hers. I'm not even sure that they're blue anymore. I can see flecks of dark blues and greens, giving her eyes the most rare tint of turquoise. Damn, are they beautiful.

"You look like you have good taste. I'm not worried," I quip.

"Hmm. So, you'd be alright with a tequila-vodka mix on the rocks?"

My eyebrows arch. "You've gotta be shitting me. You ordered a tequila and vodka? Who does that?"

Her face remains serious for one…two…three seconds before she bursts out laughing and dammit if she doesn't have a beautiful laugh too. "I kind of wish I did order that. But no. It's tequila and sprite." She holds up her glass and takes a sip through those plump, kissable lips.

Is everything on this woman perfect?

The bartender reappears with my tequila-sprite. "Wanna start a tab or are ya'll together?" she asks with a sinister look.

"Yeah, just put them both on my tab." I hand the bartender my card, and she takes it with a disappointed sigh.

"You don't have to pay for my drink."

"It's no big deal." Though I already spent way too much on booze tonight and my bank account is going to be hurting until my next paycheck, something tells me a few drinks with this woman will be worth it. "So, you're not from around here, are you?" I ask.

"How can you tell?"

I smile. "I just can."

"No," she admits. "Just moved to Timbers a few days ago. I start my new job tomorrow and couldn't sleep. Figured this might calm my nerves a bit. How about you? What brings you to…" She eyes the drink menu with the sports bar's name spread across the top. "Off-Base this time of night?"

I can't tell her that its tradition for the baseball team to come here every year to celebrate our championships, because that would give away who I am. She doesn't seem like the kind of girl who would chase a guy based on his future status as an MLB player, but they often never do.

So, I lie. "Met up with a few buddies. No reason other than to throw back a few."

She looks around the bar, stopping at the table in the corner that houses the last remaining seniors of the night. She might have seen me come from that way, though I hope none of them give away who we are.

Her eyes meet mine again. "Well, thanks for the drink." She takes another sip, and I follow suit.

"Where'd you move from?" I ask, eager to learn more about her and keep the conversation flowing.

"Chicago. It wasn't cold enough for me in the winter, so I figured I'd move up north," she jokes.

"Ah, not a fan of the snow? You've definitely been living in the wrong part of the country then."

"No kidding. Luckily, we have a few months still before the hibernation begins."

"Cheers to that." I raise my glass. "How about another?" I ask, eyeing her near empty glass.

She looks to her drink for a moment, contemplating before her turquoise gaze meets mine. "Sure, let's have another."

"Normally I at least find out a woman's name before I buy them their second drink," I joke.

She laughs, that beautiful fucking laugh that I could listen to for hours and never grow tired of. Fuck. That must be the alcohol talking. I'm not usually this much of a sap, though her laugh is enthralling.

She holds out her dainty hand to mine. "Rayna."

Even her name is beautiful. I don't stand a chance with this woman. I smile, shaking her tiny hand in my callused pitching one. "Hayes."

I call the bartender back over, ordering two more of Rayna's drink of choice. Truth is, I should probably stick to beer. The mix of tequila, beer, and Jameson isn't going to feel so great in the morning.

"Here ya'll are. Let me know if I can get ya'll anything else. Last calls in about twenty or so," the bartender says, setting down our drinks.

Rayna looks at her watch. "Shit. I didn't realize how late it was."

"Bar closes early during the week. Don't worry, still plenty of time to get a full eight hours in before the big day tomorrow."

She smiles, and my eyes drop to her lips. I can't help it. They move delicately over the straw as she takes a sip of her new drink. I'd give anything to trade places with that straw right now.

She gives me a knowing smirk. "I live down the street, if you want to continue this at my place. I make a mean tequila and vodka. You shouldn't knock it till you try it."

Damn. A woman not afraid to get right to the point. She's checking off all my boxes tonight. I definitely won't be walking away from Rayna anytime soon.

My gaze moves to her chest briefly, where her swollen breasts are being held beneath her fitted shirt. I take the new drink and down it in a few gulps before leaving the empty glass on the bar and waving over the bartender to close out my tab. Rayna laughs, sipping casually on her drink. The glimmer in her eyes is telling. We both know where tonight's going to lead. She needs a distraction, nervous to start at this new job of hers. Me? I just need someone who doesn't know who the fuck I am. It's almost no use trying to get laid unless I'm on the road traveling somewhere. Luckily, Rayna is from Chicago, she just moved here, and she's the hottest chick I've ever laid eyes on. I think my night is going to end just fine.

Once the tab is paid, I lead Rayna out to the parking lot, my hand grazing the small of her back. If she minds, she doesn't let on.

"I parked over here," she says. "Wanna just ride with me?"

"Sure." Not that I had another choice. My car is back at my place since I got a ride over with Kevin. It's not like I could even drive right now, given the night I've already had and I have no desire to fuck up my future.

Rayna stops beside a 2001 red Toyota Camry. "It's not much, but it gets me around," she says.

"Looks just fine to me." I drive my dad's 1992 Dodge pickup. It probably has twice as many miles than her little car has, but also gets me around just fine. These kinds of cars only last if they're well taken care of. When I get inside, I can tell that she takes care of it. It may not be a new car, but you wouldn't be able to tell with the all-black leather interior in pristine condition.

There's a unique smell in the car, and I quickly familiarize that scent with her. "Your car smells like vanilla and cucumbers."

Rayna's eyebrows raise. "Impressive." She opens the glove box in front of me and pulls out a bottle of hand lotion that pictures a vanilla bean and cucumber on the front. "Quite the sniffer you got there," she teases, laughing as she tosses the lotion back into the glove box and starts the engine.

Five minutes later, we're pulling into an elegant housing complex lined with storefronts on the first level and five stories of condos above, which comes as a surprise after seeing the kind of car she drives. She has to be rich to live here.

Rayna parks in the enclosed parking lot before shutting off the engine and looking at me. "We're here," she says softly, seeming nervous.

I didn't know this about myself before, but suddenly this shy and innocent version of Rayna seems even sexier than the one who got straight to the point, asking me to her place. *Just keep ticking off those boxes, Rayna.*

She gets out of the car slowly. I follow her lead as she shuts and locks her doors. Her car looks odd in this complex. I could tell by the engine knocking as we drove here that her bearings are beginning to wear out. She may take care of the car the best she can, but there's nothing she can do to prevent the engine from getting old. She'll have to take it in soon.

Rayna doesn't speak as we enter the complex through a side door. I follow her to the elevator and wait with her quietly until the elevator dings its arrival. She hits the number three as the elevator doors close. The tension in the air is thick. We both know what I'm doing here. She must be attracted to me if she invited a stranger back to her place after only two drinks. There's no doubt in my mind that I'm downright attracted to her. If the strain in my jeans isn't giving it away, then the dirty thoughts about her lips on my body sure are.

My thoughts are interrupted as the elevator jolts to a stop. The doors glide open, and Rayna quietly walks to a door labeled 32 C. She scans her keycard and walks in.

"It's all rather extravagant for my taste, but my brother insisted if I was going to be living alone that I find the safest place in Timbers. And well, this place was deemed the safest." She hangs her keys on a hook near the door. "But a little over the top, in my opinion."

I glance around. She's right, it's fancy as hell. The all-white marble counter tops, white cabinetry, white trim, and cement flooring all scream money. So, she's rich. But she drives an old Camry.

"Show me around?" I ask, hoping to calm her nerves.

"Right," she says. "Well, this space is pretty self-explanatory. Kitchen, living area. There's a bathroom through that door." She points to a door near the far end of the living room before she walks toward the hallway. "There's an extra bedroom I converted into a study, so my desk is in there, and then the bedroom is right there." She swallows, her voice sticking at the last few words. She's still nervous.

I get the feeling she doesn't do this often. With my pickiness, I guess I don't either. It's been a few months since I've been with a girl. And I've never been with a girl like Rayna. Frankly, I think she's out of my league.

"Can I make you a drink, Rayna?" I ask, backing away from the bedroom and toward the kitchen. I'm in no rush for this night to end, and I'd like to make her comfortable before I take all her clothes off.

She laughs to herself. "I'm sorry, I should have offered. I don't do this sort of thing."

I reach for her hand, squeezing it gently in mine. "Neither do I."

I can see her shoulders relax ever so slightly, her turquoise eyes studying my face before they lock on my lips. I can't help but pull her in closer to me, desperate to calm her nerves by making her comfortable with me. Her body is tense as I wrap my arms around her slender body. I tower over her petite frame, but she somehow melts into me perfectly. I can feel her body relax as I gently stroke her back. I settle my head on top of hers and get a whiff of that vanilla cucumber scent again.

"Your hair smells like your lotion," I mumble.

Her laugh vibrates against my chest. "I like the scent. I use the same brand for my shampoo, conditioner, body wash, and that lotion in the car."

I take a deep inhale. "I like it too."

She smiles as she looks up to me. Her eyes have softened, and I can tell she's warming up to me. To the thought of me.

I brush a loose strand of hair away from her face and tuck it behind her ear. She has long, soft hair. Even with her hair pulled back, it falls well below her mid back. I move my hand until it's cupping her cheek. Her skin is silky smooth, not a blemish in sight. She is the most beautiful woman I've ever seen, and I can't believe I have the pleasure of sharing a night with her.

Her breath hitches as I gently brush my thumb over her cheek, my gaze fixed on her eyes while hers are on my lips.

"Rayna," I whisper and her eyes flicker to mine. "Is it okay if I kiss you now?"

All the alcohol from the night hardly phases me as I'm about to lean in and kiss the softest lips I've ever seen. I sure as hell wasn't sober when Rayna walked into the bar, but over the hour or so I've been with her, I've sobered up greatly, despite her drink of choice. I'm more alert to her every sound, to the rapid beat of her pulse, to her breathing, to her tense and relaxed stature. I've studied this girl more tonight than I've studied the last three years of college.

Her head nods only slightly, and if I wasn't paying attention, I'd probably have missed it. My lips fall slowly to hers, almost timid in their decent to finally feel those pouty lips on mine. The moment they touch, their softness brushing against mine, I already know this night is going to be better than I ever imagined.

She opens for me quickly, allowing my tongue to explore hers with a deeper kiss. I pull her body closer to mine, one hand settled at her waist, the other reaching up to her long, silky hair. As our kiss grows deeper, Rayna becomes more comfortable. Her arms reach around me until they're gripping my back, trying with all their little might to pull me even closer to her.

I lead Rayna backward until her back is against the wall. I lift her as her legs automatically wrap around my waist and invite the bulge in my pants to press firmly against her. Her hands find my hair and grasp at it with desperation. I keep one palm firmly gripping her tight ass as I hold her up, the other pressed against the wall. We're going to have to make our way to the bed soon because I'm not sure how much more of this woman's soft moans I can take before I'm desperate to be inside of her. I still haven't seen her bedroom, though I know which door it's behind, thanks to her little tour.

I take my hand off the wall and hold onto her so she doesn't fall, then carry her to the door she claimed as her room, our lips locked the entire way. She reaches behind me for a light switch as I enter the threshold. Bright lights capture us as I get my first glimpse into her bedroom with the unfortunate loss of her lips on mine.

I eye the bed, a giant king-sized bed with dark orange bedding that is a stark difference to the bright whites of her living space. The rusty orange color might be that rare touch of Rayna in this place, leaving me to appreciate the color contrast all the more. I gently place her on the bed, kneeling in front of her so that we're at eye level.

"Is this okay?" I ask. The last thing I want to do is pressure her into something she doesn't want, though by the way she was kissing me, I'd guess she wants this just as much as I do.

"Yes, Hayes," she answers softly.

I stand up, lifting my shirt over my head and exposing my muscular figure, thanks to nearly nineteen years of baseball. Her eyes drop over my chest before they fall even lower, eyeing the V that disappears beneath my pants where a noticeable bulge urges to break free. Her eyes quickly flicker up to mine, perhaps embarrassed that I caught her staring at my junk. I can't help but chuckle.

Right now, I'm thanking my lucky stars I didn't settle for that bartender earlier tonight. Jason can have her. All I want right now is Rayna and her turquoise eyes; her pouty lips; her soft, silky skin; and that long, dark brown hair. I don't need to see her naked to know her body's going to be a homerun. Those grabbable hips have been easily on display in her tight jeans, the ones she's unbuttoning right now. She shimmies out, clad only in a skimpy pair of underwear and a formfitting tee. I'm dying to see her breasts.

I cup my dick over my jeans in anticipation. The damn thing hurts with how hard it's straining against the fabric. Just the thought of her nearly naked, sitting in front of me, is enough to do me in. But I hold it, eyes focused intently on her breasts as she slowly removes her top.

And fuck if I didn't think she was perfect before, her flawlessly, petite yet curvy frame is on display for me. Her breasts are the perfect size, perky and just waiting for my touch. Her matching bra and panties combo is so sexy, yet also an unwelcomed barrier to the real treasures that lay beneath.

"Fuck, Rayna."

I quickly remove my jeans in my haste to start touching her, to explore her body and her perfect curves. There's nothing graceful about the way I slip out of my pants, my dick still hidden behind my boxer briefs, though there's much more give in the elastic material. I quickly dive for her, my mouth finding her perfect lips for another deep kiss. My hands roam over her breasts, down to her waist, until they find that sensitive spot between her legs. She's so wet for me already, my fingers stroking above the soft cotton material as I continue to kiss her.

Her bra and panties fall to the floor, eventually followed by my briefs. I don't know where tonight will lead, I don't know how tonight will end, but one thing's for certain, I can't get enough of Rayna, no matter how hard I try.

TAKE A LOOK INSIDE *SEE YOU NEVER*

Prologue

Ember

I can still remember the day I met Sawyer Christensen at our high school's homecoming parade freshman year. I was invisible, the shy new girl who had to break out of her shell before anyone could really get to know her. My mom's job had caused us to relocate and start over for the first time since my dad died. Not the most ideal situation for someone with an introverted personality.

Sawyer was on the varsity football team, but he wasn't your typical star quarterback who smooth talked his way through the entire cheerleading team. He played the sport because he enjoyed it. He wasn't anything special when it came to his football talents. He wasn't even a quarterback. And although he didn't make it a point to sleep with every cheerleader (per se), he *did* know how to say all the right things. As most would agree, a guy who knew how to make a lady swoon didn't have a hard time getting her into bed.

My mom and I had moved from Milwaukee to Haven Springs, a small town in the suburbs of Chicago where everybody knew everybody. I, however, hardly knew anyone, outside of the few people I met in my neighborhood. But being the new girl in town, I hadn't gone unnoticed.

I remember being so full of nerves on that first day of school. There were so many new possibilities as I was practically handed a new life. I had no idea what to expect, and though it scared the hell out of me as I walked through those double doors that led to my new future, I couldn't help but feel a little thrilled.

A fiery redhead sat beside me in first period. I recognized her from the bus ride to school. Something about her over-the-top personality drew me to her, though I knew I was the complete opposite. She didn't hesitate to introduce herself when she first sat down.

"Hey, new girl, I'm Taylor."

"Ember," I said shyly.

"Do you have any friends here?" she asked.

I shook my head.

"Well, consider me your first. You'll need one to survive high school."

I smiled.

I first noticed Sawyer in the hallway between second and third period. When he passed by my locker, our eyes somehow found one another. I had no idea who he was then, but I couldn't ignore the fluttering in my core that appeared when our eyes locked. If I had to pinpoint the exact moment I fell in love with him, it might have been then. How could a stranger give me butterflies before we even spoke a word to each other? I never believed in love at first sight until I saw him.

Sawyer was tall, though not quite as tall as most of the other athletes at our school. His T-shirt clung to him in all the right places, leaving little to the imagination. Undeniably fit, he had dark brown—almost black—hair that slightly hung over his eyes.

Wow, his eyes. Dark brown like chocolate, and when they gazed into mine, it felt like he looked right through me. Those chocolate eyes instantly melted me as I stood, unable to move as they stared back at me. I couldn't help but wonder if he felt what I was feeling.

I had always considered myself an average girl. Not too pretty, but not ugly either. I was shorter and more petite than most girls in our grade. My thick and wavy hair, a mixture of blonde and brown, hung loosely over my shoulders. My most prominent feature has always been my eyes, which had a unique emerald hue to them. My mom always said my eyes were rare, that only two percent of the world's population has green eyes.

Sawyer and I continued with our frequent hallway glances for nearly two months. He never made it a point to talk to me, and I sure as hell never built up enough courage to talk to him. We didn't have any classes together either, so I often found myself detouring to my locker between every passing period hoping to steal a peek of him again.

The first time we spoke was the day of the homecoming parade. I sat on the curb outside of the school with Taylor and a few of her friends, waiting for the parade to kick off. I saw Sawyer in the distance talking to some of his football buddies. My eyes remained glued to him. He wore his football uniform with those spandex pants that clung to his ass, showing every curve of muscle his legs had to offer. He was *so* attractive.

He turned his head and I snapped my gaze in the other direction, but it was too late. He had already caught me staring. A minute later, he walked toward us with a couple of his teammates, his chocolate eyes fixed on me. I stood as he approached, my legs wobbling, praying they wouldn't give out on me in front of him.

"Hey, Ember," he said.

He knows my name?

"Hey," I said, trying to remain calm.

I picked at my nails, my pesky nervous habit. The way he said my name, so calm and smooth, nearly made me collapse. I didn't know another person could make my heart drop to the floor with just the sound of their voice. I could hardly handle what his stare did to me, but now, he spoke directly to me.

I tried to ignore the intense fluttering in my stomach, but the feeling became more overwhelming as he inched closer to me, merely a step away. If he walked any closer, our bodies would collide. The thought made my heart skip a few beats. I tried to remain calm and focus on my breathing. Sawyer was an all-encompassing being, and when his attention directed toward you, you poured every ounce of yourself into it. I savored that moment and tried my damn best not to buckle under pressure.

Everyone else faded into the background as I concentrated on Sawyer and those mesmerizing eyes staring directly through me. I heard nothing else. I saw only him, so close I felt his breath as it swept across my forehead. I tilted my head back to meet his gaze, but not before I glanced at his lips. They looked soft and plump, the perfect shade of pink. I instantly wondered what it would feel like to kiss him. He smirked as though he knew what I was thinking.

His voice came out raspy. "You're the new girl, right?"

I let out a squeaky "Yes."

He made me so nervous, I could hardly form words. But he didn't seem to care. His smile remained.

"I haven't been able to take my eyes off you, Ember."

What am I supposed to say to that? "Oh," was all I managed.

He chuckled. "How come I haven't seen you outside of school?"

I shrugged. I hardly knew anyone. The only real friend I had made was Taylor, but we hadn't hung out outside of school yet.

"I don't know many people. I just moved here a few months ago."

"Well, we should change that," he said as he showed off his perfectly white teeth.

I blushed.

"We should hang out sometime," he continued. "I want to get to know you, and that's hardly possible to do in passing. It's not nearly enough time to get to know my future wife." He winked.

Wife?

Did he just say *future wife?*

He left me speechless. I had never been speechless before. Only Sawyer Christensen could do that to me.

Sawyer and I dated for six years. We were high school sweethearts and eventually attended the same college. Those six years consisted of a lot of ups and downs. Sawyer became known for cheating on me at parties, and I became known as the girl who always took him back. I didn't want to lose Sawyer. He wasn't someone that you let go of. When we were together, our relationship was unlike anything else. We were inseparable. We were so in love. I figured having him in some capacity was better than not having him at all. Ultimately, I realized the heartbreak was inevitable.

I understand now how ridiculous that is. After six years of breakups, makeups, and heartaches, I can finally see that I deserve better. I realized that today—this morning, actually.

Sawyer and I always schedule our classes on the same days so we can drive to campus together. We had even been able to register for a few of the same courses this semester. He'd texted me early this morning, letting me know that he is skipping class today because he isn't feeling well. I reply right away.

Me: Sorry you don't feel good. Do you want me to stop over and grab your assignment?

No answer.
I wait a few minutes before I text him again.

Me: I'll stop by and grab it. Hope you feel better. Let me know if you want me to bring you soup or something after class. Love you.

Sawyer and I have been together for so long that I don't hesitate when I walk into his house uninvited. I've done it so many times before that his home is basically my second and vice-versa. Sometimes it already feels like we're married. We talk about moving in together, somewhere closer to campus, and had begun apartment hunting a few weeks back. It's a big step for us, but it only makes sense. We practically live together anyway, and it will shorten our commute.

I pull into his driveway, quickly punch in the garage code, and walk in. I head straight for the stairs that lead to Sawyer's bedroom.

"Hey, it's me. I'm grabbing your assign—"

I look around his room when I realize I'm talking to nobody. Sawyer isn't in his bed. The perfectly arranged bed set gave away that it hadn't been slept in last night. Sawyer *never* makes his bed.

Where is he?

I grab his assignment off the desk, shove it into my backpack, and amble down the hall to see if he is sick in the bathroom, but it's empty.

Maybe he isn't home, but where else would he be?

I walk downstairs and back toward the door I entered, prepared to call his cell, and that's when I see it. That's when I see *her*.

I stop dead in my tracks. She throws herself off him so fast it's almost comical. After a few dreadful moments of trying to catch her footing while also making a valiant effort to cover herself, she eventually wraps a blanket around her bare chest and rushes toward the door. I stand still, undeniably in shock. I catch a glimpse of her long bleached blonde hair as she runs out.

Of course, she's blonde. I look back to where she came from and see him shuffling on the couch. *Found him.*

"Sawyer?"

He stares at me with those big chocolate brown eyes, straight through me, as he always has. He knows what I'm thinking. He always knows what I'm thinking

Of all the times Sawyer Christensen has cheated on me, I have never seen it with my own two eyes. It is exactly what I need to finally meet the truth. I have been blind to it for a long time, but I know now. I don't care how great he is, or how beautiful his eyes are, or the overwhelming feeling that takes over when I'm in his presence. I don't care anymore. I don't deserve this, and he sure as hell doesn't deserve me.

He sits up on the couch, hastily throwing a shirt on over his head.

Realization hits. *Did I just catch them having sex?*

As if he can read my mind he says, "Ember, it's not what you think. We only kissed."

I gawk at him for a few moments. *Did I really just witness that?* Quickly, rage takes over, forcing words out of my mouth. "Are you even *sick*?"

He says nothing. He doesn't have to. I already know the answer. How can he have a girl over this early in the morning and expect me to believe they only kissed? She was half naked, for crying out loud.

Relationships can't exist without trust, and I can finally admit that I stopped trusting this person a long ass time ago. After all that time, after all that hurt, it's finally my turn. I'll show him what it feels like to be the one left with a broken heart.

"Sawyer, I'm done."

He rushes over to me, nearly tripping on the pillows that spew across the floor. I can see the fear and regret in his eyes. He fears losing me, and rightfully so. But does he really regret it? He'd never thought I would be the one to leave him. Why would he? I love him with all my heart. Or rather, I *had* loved him with all my heart.

"Baby, no. *Please.* We only kissed. I promise. It was so stupid, and I regretted it the second it happened. I was going to tell you. Baby, *please*. I love you so much, you know I can't live without you. I need you, Ember. She doesn't mean anything to me. You have to believe me."

"Fuck you, Sawyer."

I don't give him time to respond. Or maybe he says something else, but I'm no longer listening. I'm done this time. *Really* done. It's as if suddenly all the negative aspects of our relationship aren't being hidden from me anymore: every breakup, every night I'd stayed up crying, every girl he'd cheated on me with. Why had I stayed in this relationship as long as I had?

He follows me outside onto his driveway. I get in my car and slam the door shut. His mouth continues to move as I disregard whatever he's saying. His face is full of sorrow, and I already know he's begging me not to leave. I throw his assignment out the window, continue to ignore him, and drive away.

I drive around aimlessly for fifteen minutes waiting for the tears to come, but they don't. They never do. Why don't I feel sad? I feel…relieved? Is it over? It is over. It is *finally over.*

Made in the USA
Middletown, DE
11 October 2021